Life Lost, Life Found

by

Jill St. Anne

Grosvenor House
Publishing Limited

This book is published by
Grosvenor House Publishing Ltd
28-30 High Street, Guildford, Surrey, GU1 3EL.
www.grosvenorhousepublishing.co.uk

A CIP record for this book
is available from the British Library

ISBN 978-1-78148-366-4

Book One:
Life Lost

One

Kate leaned against the tiled vanity for support and forced herself to take deep, calming breaths. She had turned pale in the mirror, even paler than usual, and she had broken out in a clammy sweat. But she would not faint. She'd get herself together and figure this out. She had to figure this out.

Cindy knocked on the other side of the door. "Hey, let me in. What does it say?"

Kate rechecked the test window on the white plastic wand. Still blue. But if she could trust anyone with this information, it would be Cindy, her best friend since grade school. She unlocked the door and sank down onto the toilet seat. "It says I'm in big trouble."

She handed Cindy the wand and waited for her reaction.

Cindy looked out from under a thick blonde fringe with concerned eyes. Her hair had a light green tint. As with most of Kate's teammates on the high school varsity swim team, the chlorine never seemed to fully rinse out. "Maybe it's wrong—"

Kate shook her head. "How could I have let this happen? What am I going to do?"

Cindy lowered herself to the floor and hugged her knees, encased in baggy denim overalls. "I guess you should tell Stuart."

"No way. He would die. A baby would ruin his life. And his parents would kill him."

"He loves you. You have to tell him."

"I can't." She hadn't planned to cry, had specifically decided that she wouldn't, but her eyes filled with tears all the same. "I have to get an abortion."

"You always told me you wanted a lot of children. Maybe this is an early start."

"Cindy! At seventeen?"

"You could talk to your Aunt Mary."

"Are you kidding? She was so happy when I got accepted into Berkeley. She'd never forgive me. Besides, would you tell your mom?"

"I guess not. But, you can't just go to our local doctor and ask for an abortion, can you?"

Kate felt the sinking feeling of defeat. "I didn't think about that."

"Maybe there's a doctor in Chicago who'll do it."

"And how do I find one? Flip through the Yellow Pages?"

"I'll ask my sister. She's been through this. She won't ask any questions."

"No! I don't want anyone to know. I mean it, Cindy."

"Can you think of a better idea? You don't have much time, do you?"

Kate shook her head. It had all been so romantic. Prom night. The way Stuart had taken her hand and had led her down to the beach, where the full moon fell in a quivering, silvery path across the water. The soft sand, cool under her feet—but not half as soft as Stuart's lips on her neck, on her chest, and then on her belly. He apologized for not bringing a blanket, but she didn't care. Then he pulled out a rumpled, old-looking condom packet. At the time, it had seemed insurance enough.

But Cindy was right. She didn't have many options. It had already been more than three months since prom night.

"Do you really think your sister would know someone?" More than anything, Kate wanted to go home and lock herself in her bedroom. "And you promise you won't tell her it's me?"

Cindy got up and then held out a hand and pulled Kate to her feet as well. "Not even if she tortured me. Let's just hope it's not too late."

* * *

Kate lay on her bed and stared at the ceiling, too limp to move, and all cried out. Stuart Carson had been her boyfriend since the spring of her sophomore year, and she still couldn't believe her good fortune. As the most popular and handsome boy in school, he could have had his pick of the most beautiful cheerleaders or pom-pom girls in her school. Instead, he had chosen her.

Mister Big Man on Campus. Mr. Tall Dark and Handsome lettered in all three sports—football, basketball and baseball—the junior who drove the totally cool black Jeep Wrangler. Almost every day she saw him enter the locker room after his baseball practice just as she walked to the girls' locker room, pale and dripping wet after swim practice.

The ritual around five o'clock each afternoon was for the baseball players to hang out for a few minutes after practice and watch the pom-pom girls kick up their legs and shake what they had under their tight sweaters.

When the girls finished their routines, the guys hit the showers.

One afternoon, just as the stampede started and Kate dashed from the pool toward the locker room, she slipped on the gymnasium floor and landed directly in front of Stuart Carson. Because he was looking the other way at one of the cheerleaders, he fell head-over-heels on top of her, a misstep that caused four other boys to also fall in a small heap of bodies, with Kate at the bottom. The boys wasted no time pushing themselves up, but when Kate tried to remove herself from the slippery floor, she fell again, the wood as slick as black ice.

One of the boys said, loud enough for her to hear, "What a klutz. I'm glad that Mack Truck wasn't on top."

But Stuart didn't laugh. He helped her up, a concerned look on his face. "Are you okay?"

She mumbled a quick thank you and ran into the locker room. The guy was right, she was a klutz, and she hoped to never see any of them again.

But the following day, as she struggled with the combination on her hall locker, she felt a tap on the shoulder. Stuart Carson. All six feet two inches of him. His hair, wavy and dark brown, hadn't dried from his morning shower, and he stood so close that she could guess at the brand of soap he used.

"So, do you have any broken bones?"

She felt her face heat up. "I didn't notice any."

"Glad you're okay." A small crooked smile formed on his lips as he extended his hand. "I'm Stuart."

She shook his warm hand, but fixated on his thick black eyelashes and a small scar above the right side of his lip. "Kate Kryowski." Her aunt always called her Katherine or Katie, but she preferred Kate.

"Cry . . ."

"Cry-OW-ski. It's Polish."

Since that auspicious first meeting, they had seen each other every day, and whenever she had a swim meet, Stuart woke at dawn to watch her. He saw her wet almost as often as he saw her dry, and his eyes never failed to light up at the sight of her. She wasn't about to kill that feeling with the burden of pregnancy.

Nor could she enlist her aunt's help, though as a former nurse, she might have a few ideas. When Kate's parents died, her Aunt Mary gave up her nursing career in Chicago and moved back to the family farm in central Illinois, so Kate could stay in familiar surroundings. For eleven years, Mary had treated Kate like the daughter she had never had. And last month, when Kate had received notice of a full swimming scholarship at UC Berkeley, her Aunt Mary had shrieked at the news.

"Katherine, my girl, you've earned this. I'm so proud of you."

"I can major in Nutritional Sciences there, and Stuart will be there. Boalt Hall is one of the best law schools in the country."

"Ah, yes, Stuart." Mary sighed and patted her heart. "How could I forget?"

No way would Kate follow the good news of her scholarship by telling her aunt that she was pregnant. Nor would she set aside her plans to become a biologist. Kate's father had built a thriving medical practice before he died, and until recently Kate had imagined that she would one day follow his example and become a surgeon. But two summers as a hospital volunteer had taught her that she wasn't cut out for surgery. The hospital protected young volunteers from anything too disturbing, but even minor accidents had made her queasy. Blood in a test tube was the most she could handle.

And she would handle this, too. But however certain she had sounded with Cindy, an actual abortion was something else altogether. They'd had the debates in English class—was it a fetus or a child? Was abortion right or wrong? She leaned toward the fetus argument: that it was no more wrong to abort a fetus than to spontaneously abort through miscarriage, but she'd never really made up her mind. And abortion was a choice; miscarriage was not.

She considered telling Aunt Mary that she wanted a year off between high school and college. If she was very secretive, maybe she could go away, have the baby, and give it up for adoption somewhere. She might even enlist the help of her aunt's friend Claire. Busy, bustling Claire, her face almost as red as her hair. Claire's whole life revolved around that adoption agency where she worked. But then one more person would know, or several, and going away would cost even more than an abortion. And if she turned down the scholarship, who knew if they'd offer it again? She could never afford the fees on her own.

She closed her eyes and tried to come up with something else, but too many thoughts collided, none of them connecting in any useful way. Her only hope was Cindy's sister.

* * *

Kate went at Cindy's house, and fortunately both of Cindy's parents were out for the day.

"You didn't tell her it was me, did you?"

"I said I wouldn't and I didn't. You don't have to keep worrying."

"I keep imagining what Aunt Mary would say if she found out. I don't know which would hurt her more, the pregnancy or the abortion."

"She doesn't need to know. Are you going to call?" Cindy passed the telephone receiver to Kate.

"And they definitely won't need a parent's consent?"

"No, they said they wouldn't."

Kate stared at the number scrawled on a yellow Post-It. She pressed her finger to the first key, got as far as the area code and the next three digits before she disconnected.

"I can't call from here. What if your parents see the number when they get their long distance bill? They might check. We need to go to a pay phone."

"Good thinking. Unless I have a long distance card." Cindy fumbled around in her purse until she found her wallet and then searched through it. "Ta-da! Let's just hope I have some minutes left."

Kate took the card, squinted at the tiny numbers on the back, and pressed the keypad. This time a voice directed her to put in the code, followed by the number she wished to call. "*You have thirty minutes remaining for this call.*" She mimicked the voice and then braced herself as she reached the clinic and the number rang.

A brusque female voice answered on the third ring. Kate explained that she needed to talk to someone about an abortion. Her vocal cords had tightened, and her voice came out small and thin. At the other end of the bed, Cindy bit her bottom lip.

"Now they've put me on hold." The "queasy listening" music, meant to calm callers, contributed to her restlessness almost as much as the impending conversation. After nearly a minute she held up a hand as a chirpy voice replaced the music. Her name was Susan, the woman said, and she needed to ask Kate a series of questions, starting with her full name.

Kate's mouth had gone dry, yet her hands felt clammy and cold. "Mary Jackson." If they could help her, she reasoned, she'd give her real name when she arrived in person.

"Address and zip?"

Kate made one up.

"Telephone number?"

Another fabrication.

"Birth date? And when was the last date of your period?"

Kate answered truthfully. In the silence that followed, she could almost feel the difference between this pause and all the others.

"Oh dear," Susan said, "you're thirteen weeks pregnant. That means you're already into your second trimester."

"What does that mean?"

"It means we can't legally perform the operation."

Kate's stomach turned to lead. "Pardon me?"

Cindy moved closer. She mouthed the word *what* but Kate only shook her head and waved her off.

"I'm sorry, dear; we won't be able to help you."

"Are you sure? What am I supposed to do? There must be someone. Or someplace else?"

The nurse didn't say anything for several seconds and then her voice changed slightly, sounding almost confidential. "There is one other option. But it's risky."

"I don't care. What is it?"

"There's a doctor in Champaign, near The University of Illinois, who performs late term abortions."

"May I have his name?"

"All I know is that he works out of The Life Institute."

* * *

"So we'll call there," Cindy said, when Kate relayed the gist of the conversation. She took the telephone and called directory assistance. She scribbled the new number on the same yellow Post-It and then went through the routine with the card again before she passed the phone back to Kate. "You've still got twenty minutes."

"It's ringing," Kate said, followed quickly by "Hello?"

The Life Institute would see her on Saturday morning. Kate would fill out all the forms then, have the consultation and examination, and if all went well, they'd do the procedure the same day.

"I'll drive you," Cindy said. "We can tell our parents we're going to Champaign to do some shopping."

"What about the name? The Life Institute?"

"It makes no sense to me," Cindy said. "But I heard you ask how much it would cost. What did they say?"

"They'll discuss fees on Saturday. But as long as they don't demand everything up front, I'll think of a way to work it out. I only hope they can do it."

Two

The sun rose just as Cindy pulled up to Kate's farmhouse, a large, white Queen Anne home complete with turrets and fish scales. Kate slumped down in the passenger seat and strapped on her seat belt. She no longer got sick every morning, but her belly protruded more than ever. Lately she'd had to wear clothes that hid the swelling—baby dolls and bulky sweaters—so that neither her aunt nor Stuart would notice anything different. But that wouldn't fool them much longer, if the doctor refused to help. She closed her eyes and pressed up against the headrest. Deceiving Stuart hurt the most.

If she had told him, he would be driving her to Champaign right now. No one understood her the way he did. The first time he had driven her home after school, he'd asked that question she normally dreaded—why did she live with her aunt and not her parents? But telling him had been different, and natural.

She didn't remember much about them, she had said. They had died in a boating accident when she was four. She still had a newspaper clipping, and it looked horrible—just one big fireball in the water.

It still made her sick to look at that clipping, and maybe Stuart sensed the subject made her uncomfortable.

He slowed his Jeep and looked over at her, his face softer, as if even the idea of such a loss shocked him.

"I'm very sorry to hear this," he said with none of the squeamish discomfort or pity most people oozed, only genuine feeling. "Do you have any brothers and sisters?"

"Nope," she had said, "just me and my aunt."

And how many guys would get up at dawn to attend all of her swim meets, and cheer until they were hoarse? After each of her races, Stuart came down to the deck and gave Kate an affectionate slap on the shoulder. "Wow, another great swim! You always make it looks so easy. I can't believe how smooth your stroke is."

"Everyone on the team calls her 'La Machine,'" Cindy had said once.

Stuart had hugged her close, wet swimsuit and all. "La Machine. I like that. It fits you perfectly."

He had never been anything but supportive and caring, and they never had ridiculous arguments about trivial things, like so many of her friends and their boyfriends. He might have seen the impossibility of having the baby. They could have talked it over and managed this together. But what about the 50/50 chance that he stood on the other side of the abortion debate? She had heard about young couples that tried to make everything work too early. They rarely stayed together.

Better that Stuart not know at all than risk losing him. From that day forward, she would ensure that he never heard a word about the abortion. Ever.

"You're so quiet," Cindy said. "Are you having second thoughts?"

Kate opened her eyes and flicked her gaze toward Cindy. She shrugged, unable to explain her conflicted thoughts. Then she saw the institute for the first time. "Look. I think that's it."

A sign welcomed them to an impressive, two-storey Georgian structure situated in a park-like setting. Cindy pulled into the circular driveway. "Not exactly what I was expecting."

Kate looked up at the white brick and forced a smile. "Me neither." Whatever she had expected—dingy cinder blocks, pre-fab construction—it hadn't been this.

A tall flagpole stood in the middle of a neatly trimmed lawn, the American flag limp in the still morning air. Cindy rolled her vehicle to a stop at the front door. A woman in a white uniform walked out of the building and greeted them at the car. She instructed Cindy to park behind the building, and then opened the car door for Kate and extended her hand.

"Good morning," she said, her voice pleasant. "My name is Hilda. We've been expecting you."

Hilda led Kate through an oversized door, framed by two white pillars, and into the foyer of the building. The waiting room was furnished with Persian carpets and English antiques. Again, not what Kate had expected. Hilda asked her to sit for a moment, and then brought forms for her to fill in and left again. By the time Kate completed them, Cindy had joined her.

They sat in silence until Hilda returned and said she would escort Kate to the doctor's office.

"Can Cindy come with me?" Kate asked.

"Only until the doctor arrives, but when you're taken into the operating room, she'll have to return to the waiting area."

Cindy held Kate's hand as they waited, and they both visibly appeared startled when the door opened and a man in a white coat entered. He had a full head of untidy, graying hair. To Kate, he looked like a combination of a mad scientist and a dishevelled English professor.

"Which of you is Kate?" he asked.

"I am." Kate raised her hand.

"I'm Doctor Franke. How are you feeling?"

"Nervous."

He sat behind his desk. "I'll take some time to explain the operation. It's uncomplicated, but we'll need to administer a general anesthesia. Do you know what that means, Kate?"

"You'll put me to sleep?"

"It's nothing to be frightened of. All it means is that you won't feel anything during the operation. You'll wake up groggy but should snap out of it in a few hours." Dr. Franke looked down at some papers on his desk. "Now, as far as the actual procedure is concerned, the first thing we need to do—"

Kate held up her hand. "I don't want to know the details. I just want to get this over with."

"Very well." He rose from behind his desk. "Let's get started."

Cindy gave Kate a hug. "Don't worry. This will all be over in less than an hour. I'll wait for you right here."

The last thing Kate remembered before falling into a deep sleep was counting backwards, starting from twenty.

Three

Kate opened her eyes. "Where am I?"

"McDonald's," Cindy said. "Almost home. I listened to music on the drive back, and you slept the whole way. How're you feeling? Dr. Franke said you'd be hungry from fasting since last night."

"Not hungry, but I have a headache."

"He said there'd be a lot of bleeding today and tomorrow, so he gave me these pads." Cindy reached around to the back seat and handed Kate a box of sanitary napkins. "You'll need to change them every few hours. He also said to read this." She handed Kate a sheet of post-op instructions. "They highlighted 'no intercourse for three weeks.'"

Kate unbuckled her seatbelt fast and put her hand to her mouth. "I need to use the bathroom. I think I'm going to be sick."

"Go. I'll get you some Ginger ale or Seven Up. It might help to settle your stomach."

In the ladies room, Kate braced herself over the sink until her queasiness subsided. She splashed water on her face and pushed her hair back. Her hands shook, and she felt weak in the knees. She was so glad her Aunt Mary could not see her like this.

Cindy was already sitting at a table with a tray of food when she returned. Kate sat across from her, on a plastic seat. She reached across and touched Cindy's hand. "Thanks for everything."

"You're welcome. I just hope we never have to deal with this again. What did they say about payment?"

"They said because I'm still a student, it's covered under insurance."

"Insurance? For an abortion?"

"Hey—I wasn't about to question it."

* * *

Kate entered the farmhouse and eased the door closed behind her. She felt physically and emotionally ill. Not only had she lied to Stuart, but she had also been lying to her aunt, and both of them deserved better. She tried to sneak up the stairs, but Aunt Mary had heard her come in.

"Is something wrong, Katie?"

"I'm fine. It's just been a long day."

Mary untied her apron and approached Kate. "It's not just today. You haven't been yourself for weeks now."

Kate felt her face heating up. "I've had a bad cold and it's really got me down. I'll be better in a few days."

Mary touched her forehead. "You don't feel hot. Maybe the best thing is to take a nap and skip your morning practice tomorrow."

"Good idea." Kate started up the stairs. She wished this day had never happened.

"I'll wake you in a few hours for dinner."

Kate turned and forced a smile. Her hands felt clammy and she had begun to shiver. The last thing she wanted to do was eat. "Thanks, Aunt Mary."

She clung to the banister, her feet heavy as she climbed the stairs that seemed endless. The fact that she was no longer pregnant didn't fix everything. Stuart would be flying out to California next week to start college. She'd join him there next year, but how would she get through this year without him? What if he met someone prettier than her at school? What if he wanted to break up with her before he left? She tried to think of something else as she crawled under the bed covers and had almost drifted off to sleep when the phone rang. Then her aunt shouted up the stairs.

"Katie—Stuart's on the phone."

Kate groaned inwardly and dragged herself to the doorway of her bedroom. How could she talk to Stuart like nothing had happened? She called down the stairs. "Will you tell him I'm still sleeping?"

She stood on the top landing and listened to her aunt speak to Stuart on the kitchen phone. "I'll have her call you before we sit down to dinner."

Kate waited through a pause. "Yes, I agree, she hasn't been herself lately. I've never seen her like this." Another pause. "I don't think that's a good idea, Stuart. She's very tired. She'll call you in an hour."

Kate went back to bed, aware that she had only bought herself a few hours. This wasn't a nightmare from which she would awaken after a short nap. This was reality. She dozed until she heard tires crunching on the gravel drive outside her window. Judging by the darkness, she must have slept for at least three hours. She got up from her bed and looked out the window in time to see Stuart step out of his Jeep. If ever she had needed to put on a good act, it was now.

She opened the window. "Stuart! What are you doing here?"

"I was worried about you. Is everything okay? We were going to Al's and then Mirror Lake tonight."

Shoot. She had totally forgotten.

"Hang on," Kate said. "I'll be right down." When she ran a brush through her hair, it looked limp and unwashed, so she twisted it up and fastened it with a clip.

She kissed him at the door and prayed he couldn't read her mind. "Sorry, Stuart. I overslept. Let's have some dinner and then we'll drive over there."

"Do you think your aunt will let you camp overnight?"

"I doubt it. I feel like I really pushed her the night of your prom."

He pulled her close for another kiss and touched the tiny rectangular birthmark at the nape of her neck, a spot he often kissed and caressed when he saw it exposed. "At least we had that night together."

Kate's stomach lurched every time she thought of the consequences of 'that night.' They had made love every weekend since then, and now she had to abstain for three weeks. The timing could not have been worse. At Berkeley, hundreds of girls would be throwing themselves at him. But deep down she knew they were a good couple, and if he really loved her he'd wait.

Four

By the time Kate reached her senior year at Berkeley, Stuart had finished his undergrad studies and was in his first year of law school. Their time at Berkeley had flown by. In her junior year, Kate had studied under one of the most recognized scholars in nutritional science, and the thrill of learning how various herbs, spices and foods could alter metabolism and health had left her more excited than ever. She could help people improve their health through dietary choices, and through research could contribute to the body of knowledge that already existed.

As an added bonus, she swam in a beautiful outdoor pool every day—much better than the indoor one back in Illinois, which had reeked of chlorine. And despite Stuart's new, demanding timetable, they still met for dinner most nights and spent weekends riding mountain bikes, exploring San Francisco, or venturing up to the wine country. When their schedules allowed, they met in the afternoon for lunch and picnicked on the lawn around the Clock Tower in the quad.

Stuart's spring break did not coincide with hers, so Kate planned a solo trip to Hawaii. Her senior studies at Berkeley focused on her thesis: *The effects of Hawaiian botanical life on metabolic regulation.* In Hawaii, she could study numerous plants she could only read about on the mainland.

Early on a Saturday morning, Stuart drove Kate to San Francisco's International Airport for her 8 a.m. flight.

In the parked car, Stuart picked up her hand and touched the class ring he had given her before he went away to college. "If I had the money, Kate, this would be an engagement ring. We're meant to be together forever."

* * *

An hour later, Kate lumbered through the narrow airplane aisle under the weight of her cumbersome backpack, which knocked against several passengers as she passed. She quietly apologized as she made her way to the back of the plane. Relieved to see no one seated in her row, she heaved the backpack into the overhead compartment and settled into the window seat.

From her handbag, she pulled out a guidebook of the Hawaiian Islands. Although the purpose of her trip was to study, she looked forward to making time to body surf and explore remote parts of the islands. She had just started to skim through the guide when a clean-cut man in his late twenties dropped a bag that looked like an overstuffed briefcase on the seat next to her.

Lanky and tall, he wore an eager expression. "Hi," he said, with a strong Southern accent. "Guess we're flying to Hawaii together."

"Guess so," she said, with a nod and slight smile. With luck, he would not talk for the entire six-hour flight.

The man shoved his other piece of luggage into the overhead compartment and sat in the aisle seat. "First time to Hawaii?"

Kate nodded. She didn't speak, but held up her guidebook for him to see.

"I go every year at this time," he said. "It's perfect, not too many tourists."

Kate pretended to read her book, not comprehending much, as her seatmate continued to jabber on about a flight school in Oklahoma. His white tee shirt had the logo of a red airplane, and under it were the words: *Tulsa Flying Club.*

He quieted as the flight attendants recited the safety announcement, but as soon as they finished, he turned to Kate again. "I'm Win. Short for Winston." He extended his hand.

"I'm Kate." His hand felt calloused and rough in hers, but he had a firm grip. "Nice to meet you."

"I always feel that we fellow passengers should introduce ourselves. You never know what could happen up here in these wild blue skies of ours. Plus," he gave her a little wink, "we're stuck with each other for the next six hours."

She looked again at his tee shirt. "Are you a pilot?"

"Sure am." He patted his chest. "A Certified Flight Instructor for the past seven years."

She closed her book, giving up any idea of reading.

"What island do you plan to visit?" he asked.

"I want to study the plant life, so after a few days on the beach in Oahu, I'll go over to Kauai."

"You'll love it," he said, his face animated. "It's lush and green, with waterfalls all over the place."

"Sounds beautiful."

"How will you get there?" he asked.

"Probably take a ferry."

"I have a better idea. I'm renting a plane. I'll fly you."

* * *

On the tarmac in Honolulu, Kate and Winston each accepted a fragrant necklace of orchids: the traditional Hawaiian lei. The air was hot and humid, but not uncomfortable. Kate set her backpack on the ground while Winston called a local airport to arrange a plane. She had never flown in a small plane before, but Winston seemed like a good guy, and he was a flight instructor. A little adventure would be fun.

She watched all the people with their dark tans and colorful Hawaiian shirts. She could hardly wait to put on her new bikini, lie on a beach and get an honest-to-goodness, beach-vacation tan. From all her years as a competitive swimmer, she had a permanently white belly and white crossover marks on her back. When her stomach tanned, she might even consider a belly ring.

"We're good to go," Winston said. He hailed a cab and instructed the driver to take them to the private airfield.

While he dealt with the paperwork, Kate made a quick call to Stuart from the payphone. The ring went to voice mail: "I miss you already," she said. "I wish you were here."

She mentioned that she had met someone on the plane who was giving her a tour of the Islands by air. "I'll call you tonight," she said. "Or tomorrow at the latest."

Winston spent nearly twenty minutes doing his pre-flight inspection on the little two-seater, single engine Cessna, and then motioned her to get in.

He climbed aboard and joined her in the small, hot space. "Open the door until you're buckled in," he said. "It'll keep the air flowing."

Kate buckled her seatbelt and then shut the door and listened through her headphones as Winston and someone in the tower mumbled as if in a foreign language. The engine revved up and then back down and then slowly the plane taxied onto the runway.

She heard "clear for take-off," and then Winston pulled back on the yoke and pushed the throttle forward. Within seconds they were airborne. At about 500 feet, Winston banked sharply to the left and Kate felt her heart lurch, and then settle again as the plane leveled off. As they soared over the blue-green ocean, she spotted a pod of dolphins swimming underwater and watched as they arced over the surface and dove back into the sea.

From 1000 feet Kate saw much more than she would have imagined. Off in the distance she thought she saw a whale spouting, so she pointed it out to Winston. He flew over, and sure enough, the massive, black body of a whale swam alongside that of a much smaller one. How spectacular she thought, to see mother and baby, swimming in the big ocean together.

They flew over Molokai, then Lanai and Maui before approaching the big island of Hawaii. Kate looked for sandy beaches and saw only black rocks surrounding the Island.

"Ancient lava rock," Winston explained.

In the distance, she saw a plume of gray and pointed. They flew closer, so she could see Kilauea, an active volcano, still spewing steam from recent activity. Occasionally, Kate glimpsed a sandy beach, most beaches the property of resorts or private residences, she had read. The guidebook had also reported that in some cases owners had sand shipped in from Saudi Arabia. She could hardly wait to lie on any sand; she didn't care where it came from. Only *after* sunbathing and playing in the waves would she begin her research. First she would sip a few tropical drinks and enjoy her vacation.

For almost an hour they enjoyed a smooth flight, and then a loud sputtering sound came from the engine. Kate turned to look at Winston; he appeared to have everything under control, but speaking to him through the headphones, she asked about the noise.

"Some minor engine trouble. Maybe a spot of dirty fuel. It'll pass in a minute or two."

But it didn't.

Through the headphones she heard him breathing. "What's wrong?"

"I don't know. I'll try a few more maneuvers to see if I can clear the engine."

The plane dropped a few hundred feet and Kate felt her stomach drop along with it. "Winston, tell me what's happening!"

"I don't know—try to stay calm. We may have to ditch the plane."

"We're flying over the ocean! Where would you put it down?"

"There's only one place," he shouted. "And it's going to be rough. Brace yourself for the impact."

Then the engine cut out altogether. A look of fear was chiseled onto Winston's face. "May Day! May Day!

November; three niner three; Bravo Alpha! May Day! May Day!"

Kate heard those last words as the small Cessna slammed into the water, as if into concrete. Her forehead smashed into the windshield, and the plane flipped over once, then twice. Each time the plane hit the water a different part of her body hit the inside of the fuselage. When the movement finally subsided, Kate couldn't believe that she was still alive.

She looked over at Winston and saw his face covered in blood. She undid her seatbelt and reached over to him. Her entire body ached, but she could still move. Winston remained motionless.

"Winston!"

No response.

His head hung down toward his right shoulder in a manner Kate would not have thought possible. She picked up his wrist and felt for a pulse. Nothing. She tried his neck. Again she felt nothing. Her hand was sticky with blood as she pulled it away from his neck.

The plane was sinking.

Water pressure against the partially submerged door made it impossible to budge. Thinking fast, she positioned herself on the seat, faced the window and kicked with both feet as hard as she could. On the second try, the window broke loose.

The open wound on Kate's forehead stung fiercely as she plunged into the salty, ocean waters. The plane sank fast. She pushed off and swam free of it, and then treaded water long enough to spot land. She calculated the distance from the accident to the shore as less than a mile. Under normal swimming conditions in a clear pool this would be nothing, but fighting the strong currents and three-foot swells wouldn't be easy. She took a deep breath of humid air, gathered every ounce of strength in her traumatized body, and took her first stroke. Forcing all fear and doubt from her mind, she pulled against the water and swam to save her life.

As Kate fought each wave, she kept her eyes focused on the stretch of white sandy shore in front of her. She knew to avoid the vast black mass that bordered the beach, as lava rock was famous for ripping boats to shreds. She pushed aside thoughts of the sharks that swam in these rough waters and focused on making it to shore safely. She swam hard for ten minutes and then turned over and floated on her back, thankful for the warm, buoyant water, to rest her aching body. She turned her head and squinted at the horizon, searching for the plane, but all she saw was the tip of its wing. The fuselage had completely submerged.

Kate continued to float on her back, feeling like a loose piece of wreckage, bobbing up and down with each wave. She closed her eyes and tried to regain her strength, but when she opened her eyes, she saw a major storm brewing above. If she was to make it to shore before the waves grew larger and more dangerous she couldn't waste time floating like a child, pretending to be a starfish. She rolled back onto her stomach and started the second race of her life against Mother Nature, the greatest opponent she had encountered in all her years of competitive swimming.

The powerful current became increasingly difficult to fight, and the white strip of sand slipped away from her as she drifted off-course toward the black lava field. Less than 100 yards away from land, she still ferociously fought the crashing waves, but as she drew closer, the strength of the ocean threw her body into a violent spin. She held her breath as she spun out of control underneath the swirling whirlpool.

When the wave finally ebbed back into the sea, Kate found an opportunity to resurface and gasp for air. She gulped a precious mouthful of oxygen and tried to ease into the shore, letting the momentum of the waves push her to safety; but the force of the water was too powerful. Another wall of water built behind her. This wave overtook her and again caught her in a crashing spiral of salt water. Her head slammed into the rugged rocks and she felt a piercing, sharp pain as everything faded to black.

Five

The massive estate of Dr. Roland Schmidt encompassed 10 lush acres along the oceanfront of the Kona Coast. Kainu, a young Hawaiian groundskeeper, hunched over the grassy border along the lava rocks and clipped small sections of grass as instructed by the head gardener. Off in the distance he heard a small plane overhead, and then the sound faded. Close by, water heaved and slapped against the rocks. Beyond the rocks, Dr. Schmidt's private, white-sand beach stretched out to the ocean.

A bright flash of light caught the corner of Kainu's eye. He stood and shaded his eyes with his hand and scanned the blue ocean in front of him. The sun caught the reflection of something on the water in the distance, possibly a fishing boat. He crouched back down and continued weeding. The light continued to flash in the distance, so Kainu looked again out at the ocean. He saw something white bobbing in the water, but then it disappeared as the object vanished into the ocean. He continued working and had nearly finished clipping the grass when he noticed a large pale object lying against the black lava rocks, just outside the boundaries of the sandy beach. He walked closer, and saw that it was a body, and then ran across the rocks, his feet not bothered as they were hard and calloused after a lifetime of walking on crusty rock and sharp coral.

From a distance, he couldn't discern whether the body was that of a man or a woman, but he knew from the alabaster skin that the person was not Hawaiian. As he neared, he recognized the listless body of a woman. She looked young, probably no more than 20 years old. He knelt down and pressed his dark fingers against her neck and felt a faint pulse. Blood oozed from the side of her face, so he took off his tshirt and pressed it against her skin. He knew not to move the body himself, so he ran as fast as he could back to the house.

* * *

By all accounts Dr. Roland Schmidt was a recluse, and he had built his compound with security and privacy in mind. Once a celebrated cardiologist, he became the head of his department at Queen's Hospital in Honolulu in his late thirties. In his forties he started a company that invented a synthetic heart valve, which revolutionized heart surgery. Then, when an international conglomerate bought the company, Dr. Schmidt retired from practicing medicine and moved with his new wife to the Kona Coast of Hawaii, where he started Stemgenetics, a company that built its reputation on stem cell research.

Kainu found Dr. Schmidt in his study, wireless reading glasses perched on the end of his nose. The doctor swiftly removed his glasses when he saw Kainu rushing toward him. The gardeners never entered the house; something must be wrong. Dr. Schmidt rose up from behind his desk.

LIFE LOST, LIFE FOUND

"What's the matter, boy?" Aside from the house manager, his chief of security and the head chef, Dr. Schmidt did not know the names of his domestic help.

"There's a girl out on the lava rocks," Kainu gasped. "Hurry!"

Dr. Schmidt followed Kainu out to the ocean. As soon as he spotted the body, he took off at a run.

"Go back," he ordered Kainu. "Call 911. Now!"

As a physician he was trained to look, listen and feel. He rubbed her sternum vigorously to determine if she would respond to deep stimuli. He brought his ear down to her mouth to listen for any sign of breathing. He heard nothing. He placed his middle three fingers on her carotid artery hoping to feel a pulse. Still nothing. He bent over her to perform CPR: two quick breaths into her mouth, followed by rapid chest compressions. After several rounds of this procedure, he heard the wail of a siren in the distance.

He continued with the CPR as the fire truck drove across his lawn and screeched to a halt at the foot of the lava field. Two paramedics, one male, one female, charged out of the truck. The female paramedic ran toward the lava field, clutching a wooden spine board about the length of a surfboard. The man carried a large backpack of medical equipment.

"She's not responding to CPR," Dr. Schmidt said.

The paramedics stabilized her neck with a plastic C-collar and intubated her to get oxygen into her lungs as soon as possible. The female paramedic inserted a clear, plastic tube down the victim's mouth and into her trachea. The male firefighter pumped the clear plastic bag connected to the tube, while the female placed the EKG electrodes on the victim's chest. The EKG rhythm looked like a chaotic wave, her heart literally beating all at once. The paramedic shouted: "She's in V-Fib. We need to shock her!" She charged the defibrillator and yelled, "Clear!"

They shocked her once with 200 joules, and then felt for a pulse. Feeling nothing, they recharged the defibrillator and gave her another jolt at 300 joules. This time they got a pulse, but still she was not breathing spontaneously.

The paramedics' hand-held, two-way radio crackled with instructions from the base station. "We'll airlift the patient by helicopter to the ICU at Queen's Hospital in Honolulu."

"Roger that," the male said.

Twenty minutes later, a MediVac chopper landed on Dr. Schmidt's lawn. The pilot and flight nurse jumped out of the helicopter and loaded the patient into the back of the air-ambulance.

Dr. Schmidt bullied his way onto the helicopter, saying, "I'm a close personal friend of the victim."

After a short flight, they landed on the rooftop helipad at Queen's hospital. The ICU team, shielded their eyes from the intense wind created by the spinning blades, and ran out with a gurney to meet them. They loaded their patient onto the gurney and rolled her directly to radiology where she was immediately placed on a table and into a CAT scanner to look for bleeding.

The CAT scan showed no cervical spine injury; she was not paralyzed, but the scan did reveal a large left frontal lobe subdural hematoma. In layman's terms, her brain was being squished by its own bleeding and would kill her if she didn't go to neurosurgery immediately. The hospital staff rushed her to the operating room, where she was prepped in minutes.

The surgeon drilled a hole in the area of the skull over the top of the blood clot and placed a catheter into the hole to let the blood escape and relieve the pressure on her brain.

When they wheeled her back to the ICU, nobody knew if she would recover from surgery—the anoxic period during the near drowning might have been too long. A neurologist hooked her up to an EEG to monitor her brain activity, which was minimal. They could only wait.

Six

The shrill ringing of the phone in Stuart's apartment awakened him out of the dead sleep he had fallen into while studying. His undergrad studies had been difficult, but law school left him in an interminable fog, disoriented, buried under books and papers, certain of only one thing—that nothing was ever certain. He picked up the phone on the fourth ring, just before it went to message.

"Stuart." Mary's voice was nearly unrecognizable. She sounded as if she couldn't breathe. "There's been a terrible accident . . ."

"What do you mean?" The fear in Mary's voice made the hair on the back of his neck stand up. "Did something happen to Kate?"

He could hear Mary sobbing, but she didn't speak. "Mary! Please tell me!"

"A plane crash . . . in Hawaii . . ."

Stuart grabbed the television remote and switched on the local news. A major airline crash would be a big story on the ten o'clock news. The weatherman stood in front of a map of California and pointed to a swirl of clouds near Alaska. Fear numbed Stuart's senses. He fumbled with the remote and almost dropped the phone before he spoke quietly into it. "Mary. Breathe. Tell me what happened."

He heard her take a deep breath.

"A small plane crashed off the island of Hawaii." Her voice trembled. "Kate's purse was found in the wreckage."

"My God . . ." Stuart fell into his chair near the TV and the phone dropped from his hand. He picked it up and attempted to stay calm. "I'll leave for Hawaii as soon as I can get a flight. I need to be with Kate."

A chill went through him as Mary broke into deep gasping sobs. "What? Mary?" Now he couldn't breathe. He felt stuck in a moment of time, unable to breathe, unable to hear, his entire body trembling.

At last she spoke: "Stuart, I'm so sorry. They haven't found her body. They don't think they will—"

"No." He clasped his forehead and squeezed hard. He shook his head. "No. That can't be true."

"The body of the pilot was found in the wreckage, but not Kate's—"

"Oh my God. Mary, this can't be happening."

"The coastguard searched all last evening before notifying me. There are sharks." Again, she broke down.

"I can't accept that! I need to see Kate." He tried to stand and fell back down into his chair. "We had plans to get married."

"Please come home, Stuart. I need you here. We have to think about a funeral."

Seven

"Listen, Conrad," Dr. Schmidt pointed his index finger at the chest of ICU doctor Richard Conrad. "She's my niece. She stays on life support until *I* make arrangements for her to be moved to my estate."

The hospital loud speaker cackled incessantly throughout the corridor of ICU, but their voices rose above it.

"Roland, with all due respect, she's on record as a Jane Doe. Unless you can bring in her ID, we're pulling her off life support. A case like this costs the hospital nearly $10,000 a day."

"I don't care what it costs!" Schmidt yelled. "She stays on!"

Two doctors in green scrubs brushed past, pushing an accident victim on a gurney. They exchanged a look and kept moving.

Dr. Conrad lowered his voice: "You have no right ordering me around, Roland. You're no longer a practicing physician here."

"That may be, but I still hold a seat on this hospital's board. And let's not forget, if it weren't for my heart valve and the renown that came with it, this place would just be another sleepy island hospital."

"This is and always has been a respectable hospital." Now Dr. Conrad pointed his finger at Dr. Schmidt. "And if I remember correctly, it was Dr. Reynolds who invented the heart valve, not you."

"That's bullshit and you know it," Dr. Schmidt said. "It was my idea and he took it from me."

"Listen Roland," Dr. Conrad put his hand on Dr. Schmidt's shoulder to calm him. "I'm sure your new company will bring you the fame you deserve. But the fact remains that our patient has no identification and the paramedics said you didn't seem to know who she was at first. Find us her family or bring in the ID, and then we'll talk."

Dr. Schmidt took a deep breath and exhaled. "Imagine how I felt to see her there this afternoon. I couldn't think. I'll be in tomorrow to take full responsibility. Put her in my custodial care."

"Once we have the documentation."

"Just do it, Conrad, or I'm affiliating Stemgenetics, along with all the research and grant money it generates, with another hospital."

Dr. Conrad swung around and walked down the hall toward the nurse's station. Under his breath he uttered, "Jackass."

* * *

The following morning the coastguard notified all hospitals to be on the lookout for a Jane Doe who may have been pulled from the ocean and brought into one of the local ERs. The nurse on duty at Queen's Hospital pulled their Jane Doe's file and saw Dr. Roland Schmidt, retired head of Cardiology, listed as her custodial doctor. The form indicated that she was his niece, not a Jane Doe after all. With great relief, she picked up the phone and notified the coastguard that their patient had been identified and was in capable hands.

* * *

A thick cloud of cigar smoke hung in the air of Dr. Schmidt's study as he read the front-page headline of the Honolulu Star Bulletin. **Small Plane Crashes Into Ocean: Pilot Killed and Passenger Presumed Dead.** He took off his reading glasses and tapped them on his desk as he slowly drew on his cigar. After a few more puffs, he folded the newspaper and placed it into a manila folder, which he locked in his file drawer.

Then he made a call. "Do you have it? Good," he said, his voice terse, "Bring it here ASAP. And get me everything you can find on the passenger of that plane. And then I need a passport – and I need it yesterday!"

Within the day, Dr. Schmidt produced a passport of his supposed niece. Later that week, he moved her to his private estate where a team of ICU nurses provided around-the-clock care.

"She's lucky to have you as a family member," the nurse said, as she typed the details of the assignment into her computer. "Name?" she asked.

"Luana." He had named her after the white and purple flowers that grew in abundance on his estate.

Eight

Rain streamed down the airplane window as Stuart landed at Chicago's O'Hare airport.

Mary greeted him at the gate. She looked as if she had aged ten years since he last saw her. Her previously brown hair had turned mostly gray and the skin on her cheeks and jaw sagged loosely. They gave each other a warm hug and then Mary led Stuart to her station wagon.

Stuart broke the silence first. "Did you talk to Kate once she reached Hawaii?"

"I wish I had," Mary said. "She called me the day before she left. She was so excited." Mary pressed her hand on Stuart's knee. "She did say, though, that she would really miss you and that she wished you could go with her."

"I feel horrible about not being with her."

"Our poor dear. Her first adventure on her own and look what happened." Her tears came so quickly and heavily that she had to pull over to wipe them away.

"Change places with me," Stuart instructed. "I'll drive."

When they had changed places and Stuart was behind the wheel, he said, "You need to rest. This is going to be a rough week."

Nine

onth after month slipped by without Kate showing any signs of recovery. Dr. Schmidt focused almost entirely on her recuperation. For the moment he was the only man in her life, and that was how he intended to keep it once she recovered. He visited her daily, talking to her like he had known her all his life, holding her hand and stroking her hair.

Spring rolled into summer. The onset of summer winds went unnoticed in Luana's perfectly controlled environment. During the afternoons, when otherwise dormant volcanoes spewed gray volcanic ash into the air, the general population suffered headaches, watery eyes, and breathing difficulties, but Dr. Schmidt made sure the temperature and humidity in Luana's room remained at a constant level. Sheer curtains were drawn to diffuse the bright sun, and at night a small lamp glowed in the corner of her room. The day nurses, Nora and Sheila, urged the doctor to open the windows for fresh air and to allow Luana to hear the hypnotic sounds of the ocean, the sea gulls and the birds in the aviary. He permitted this as long as the temperature remained constant, and he mandated that they close the windows if they sensed the presence of *vog*, the volcanic fog. Dr. Schmidt maintained his daily visits, not only to check on Luana but also to make sure that the nurses read to her and played classical music in the background.

Then one afternoon Nora noticed that Luana had partially bit the tube in her mouth, and she alerted Dr. Schmidt.

He excused himself from a business meeting and hurried to Luana's room to see for himself. When he arrived, Luana remained motionless. He stroked her hair and squeezed her hand. "You'll be just fine my darling. You have me now to protect you. Everything will be just fine."

He sent his helicopter to pick up the neurologist, and upon his arrival, Dr. Landis rubbed Luana's chest above her sternum to see if she responded to stimuli. She didn't move at all. With his index finger he pulled up her eyelid and shone a flashlight onto her pupil. Her pupils remained still and showed no sign of recognizing the light.

"Roland, I'm sorry. She's still comatose."

"But she bit the tube!" He looked at Nora for support. "Didn't she? You saw her, right?"

"I did, doctor. It was the first sign of any movement in over four months. I alerted you immediately, as instructed."

Dr. Landis turned to Roland. "There's nothing we can do right now. But of course, call me again if there are any other signs of recovery."

"I'll walk you back to the helicopter."

When the two doctors left the room, Nora stood over Luana and adjusted the tube the neurologist had disturbed. To Sheila, she said, "I'm worried about this girl. If and when she wakes up she'll be indebted to him."

"I heard someone say he doesn't even know her."

"That's how most patients enter a doctor's life. They don't know them before they need care. Let's just hope this one's strong enough to make the break." Then Nora laughed. "I see nothing, I know nothing. But she does remind me of Alana. Whatever happened to her?"

"His wife? I'm not sure anyone knows," Sheila said.

* * *

The following week, while Nora was drawing blood, Luana flinched. Nora wiggled the needle, and Luana moaned. Something was most definitely happening. Nora called Dr. Schmidt, who once again sent the helicopter for Dr. Landis. This time Dr. Landis brought an EEG monitor with him and performed a battery of neurological tests. Her brain wave activity showed signs of cognitive alertness.

"It's time to take her off the ventilator," he said.

* * *

When Luana finally opened her eyes, three strangers stared down at her. She focused on the middle-aged gentleman with wireless glasses and thinning gray hair. Her mouth felt dry and her throat sore. "Where am I?" she whispered.

"You're safe with me, dear." He took her hand in his.

"Who are you?"

"My name is Dr. Schmidt. I'm a close family friend. This is Nora, and this is Sheila." He smiled. "Do you know your name?"

Luana stared at him. As hard as she tried, no name came to mind. Her heart sped up and her tongue felt thick and dry. "May I have a glass of water, please?"

"Take your time," Dr. Schmidt said. "Do you have any idea how you got here?"

Tears welled up in Luana's eyes. "I don't know my name." She took the glass of water Sheila offered, and drank it in three gulps. "You said you're a friend of my family, but where is my family? Why am I here?"

Dr. Schmidt turned to Nora and Sheila. "I'd like some privacy with my patient. You're excused until I call for you."

When the women left, Luana looked at the doctor. "You said 'my patient.' Are you a doctor?"

"I am. My name is Dr. Roland Schmidt. And you're currently under my care."

"My family. Where are they? Why can't I remember my name?"

"Your name is Luana Kramer and you were in a terrible accident. You and your parents had just arrived here in Hawaii, to stay on my estate as my guests. One afternoon, about six months ago, your parents took my boat out to sea for a short pleasure cruise. A huge explosion killed your parents, but miraculously, you swam to shore, though the sea got the best of you. You were found nearly dead, lying on the lava field adjacent to my beach."

"I've been here six months? And my parents are dead?" Luana broke down.

Dr. Schmidt handed Luana a box of tissues. He tugged one out and gently wiped away her tears. "You'll be fine. I'll take care of everything."

"What has happened in the last six months? Don't I have any other family?"

"You were in a coma, Luana," Dr. Schmidt comforted her. "You're an only child, and it appears that you lost some of your memory, but I'm here to help you as you regain it."

"Thank you, but I should go home now." She began to sob again. "Where do I live?"

"Home is here for now. You've suffered a terrible trauma and you'll need expert care and observation. For the past six months, I've provided around-the-clock care for you, and I'll continue to do so until you're well. Your memory needs to return naturally, in its own time. Forcing it could cause real psychological damage. I know it would have been your parents' wish to have me provide for you."

"Thank you." She did her best to hold her tears back. "How can I ever repay you?"

Dr. Schmidt smiled. "Don't worry about that. Everything will work itself out."

Ten

With Sheila's help, and a regimen of basic but arduous physical therapy, Luana gradually regained her strength and a bit of her former muscle tone. She started walking, supported by the parallel bars: first, one step, then two and finally three in a row. Her balance and coordination felt off, but by the end of the week, she barely held the bars.

She drew a picture of a clock when the neurologist asked her to and was able to tell the nurses the time. Simple mathematical equations didn't faze her, but faces and events from her past eluded her. Her sense of smell and taste remained intact, but she had no memory of her life before the accident.

As her strength and coordination developed, she rode the stationary bike for ten minutes, then twenty and finally thirty.

While in the coma, Luana had lost thirty pounds and was no longer the solidly built, muscular woman who had washed ashore six months ago, but a woman who could have passed for a fashion model. Slim hips and broad shoulders framed her tall, athletic body. Her nose, broken during the accident, had been surgically repaired during her first week in the hospital, and her round face had become angular, with high cheekbones and a square jaw.

In addition to weight training, and as part of her therapy, Luana swam in Dr. Schmidt's Olympic-sized swimming pool overlooking the ocean. The golden brown tan she developed suited her lean body and turned her drab hair to sun-kissed blonde.

Sheila calculated that Luana swam several miles each day in the therapeutic sunshine. "If I didn't know better," she said, "I'd guess that you were headed for the Olympics."

Although her memory about certain things was non-existent, she did recall some aspects of her past. She asked Dr. Schmidt's chef, Joseph, to buy her some avocados and papayas so she could put them on her hair as a natural conditioner. Unsure how she knew to do that, she nevertheless loved the result as her hair grew thick, down to the middle of her back in length. Dr. Schmidt couldn't take his eyes off her.

They had dinner together each evening in the small dining area off the kitchen. Luana would have preferred to eat outside, but as a guest, she didn't press the issue. And while she accepted the glass of chilled white wine Dr. Schmidt had Joseph pour her at dinner, she usually only drank a few sips, and preferred instead sparkling water with lemon wedges.

When she grew impatient waiting for the natural recall of her memory, as Dr. Schmidt had insisted upon, she broached the subject most often on her mind. "Roland, I must have some extended family. I want to know who they are and regain contact with them."

He shook his head. "I strongly advise against that. If the people who killed your parents know you're alive, they'll come after you too."

"Are you telling me the explosion wasn't an accident?" Her mouth gaped open at the thought. "What are you saying?"

He watched her closely. "It was murder, Luana. Your father discovered that MP Pharmaceuticals had used orphaned Rwandan refugees for their phase one human trials. He planned to blow the whistle, but he didn't get a chance."

Luana covered her mouth with her hand, and stared at Dr. Schmidt. Then she put her hands in her lap and straightened her spine. "You need to tell me more. Did my father work for MP Pharmaceuticals? And if so, who are they?"

"He was a scientist in research and development. The company's most recent wonder drug is an anti-obesity pill. Your father and I were very close. He came here for support and to discuss his approach with me before he went to the press. He knew the drug would mean billions to the company, and they had already threatened him."

"I suppose they would, if they were the sort of people to use starving children to test a diet pill. Who else did my father tell?"

"Outside of the company, only me, as far as I know, and for your safety, I kept that and your survival a secret. I had a visit from someone from the company, who impressed on me the importance of keeping the incident out of the press, given the 'sensitive timing.' He showed me gruesome photos of my boat and the explosion, and said the company would take care of everything, if I would 'allow them that freedom.' I'm sure they had no idea that I knew more, so I agreed. The wreckage disappeared, and the story disappeared with it, nothing in the news at all, all the locals paid off.

"As far as the staff know, you arrived alone, and they've been instructed to ask you nothing, tell you nothing, for your psychological health. I'm only telling you enough to keep you from putting your life in danger. They're ruthless, Luana. They killed your parents and they wouldn't think twice about killing you to keep you from learning more. Nothing can be done to bring your parents back or help the children they hurt, so stay out of it."

Eleven

*L*uana slept little that night and rose early the next morning. To take her mind off her troubled thoughts, she swam nearly twice as many lengths as she usually did. Then, showered and dressed, she headed for the kitchen, where she had already spent many hours with Joseph, Dr. Schmidt's fulltime chef, helping him prepare Dr. Schmidt's formal lunches with business associates, and her private dinners with him.

In his early fifties, gray hair pulled back in a ponytail, Joseph had an air of calm that often dissolved whatever tension Luana felt when she entered the kitchen. Perhaps sensing her mood, he now presented her with a large bowl of fruit to cut for a salad.

Luana pitted and cored and chopped quietly for several minutes, and then without preamble, asked: "Did you see my parents before their accident?"

Joseph stopped in mid movement as he pulled a pan from the oven. "Now there's a subject that could send me packing." He set the pan on the stovetop and leaned against the counter to face her. "Dr. Schmidt wants you to ask him questions like that. We're under strict orders to not discuss your past with you. Your recovery is unpredictable, I'm told, and I'm not to jeopardize it." His voice was warm and sympathetic, but firm. "I'm not saying I agree, but that's the way it is. *Comprende?*"

She turned away from him to hide her disappointment. "Yes. *Comprende*."

"So how's that salad coming?"

"It's coming." She gave the mixture a more vigorous toss than was necessary and pushed it across the surface of the kitchen island. She saw no harm in asking a few simple questions of others, but she didn't want to get Joseph in trouble, either. He had exercised such patience with her and had encouraged her interest in cooking, allowing her to make the salad each evening, and then work her way up to cooking the entire meal. The least she could do to repay the doctor for his kindness was to cook him dinner occasionally. And the least she could do for Joseph was respect the boundaries he set. So she forced a smile, and changed the subject.

"You know what I'd love to make tonight, Joseph?"

"What's that, kiddo?"

"Chocolate chip cookies."

"Really? You don't strike me as a cookie girl. Where did this craving come from?"

"Not sure, but I can't stop thinking about warm gooey chocolate chip cookies."

"I have flour, eggs and sugar, but no chocolate chips," he said, as if their previous conversation had never occurred. "We'll need to go into town for those."

"Now?"

Joseph looked up at the kitchen clock. "I can't right now. Roland has guests coming for lunch. I need to prepare everything and have it ready by noon. Maybe you should ask him if you could borrow a car."

"Before I go, I'll set the table for you to save you some time."

"Now there's a thought. I'm a bit under the gun."

Luana found Roland in his office, reading the paper. "Good morning," she said. "Do you mind if I borrow a car to do some grocery shopping?"

Dr. Schmidt set the paper down. "Absolutely not. Only Joseph is allowed to use the cars. Besides, you'd get lost. And after the shock you had last night, anything could happen. Wait until he's finished serving lunch and then the two of you can go."

"Whatever you say . . ." Despite his rigidity, he was right about one thing. She had never left the estate and would have no idea where to go.

*　*　*

When Joseph learned of Dr. Schmidt's response, he offered to take Luana to a produce market only a few minutes drive from the compound. As he searched for parking at the market, she peered out the window at the swarms of people jostling each other in front of the stalls.

With Joseph, she had planned colorful, tasty, healthy meals, and had written her recipes, all of which required fresh vegetables, fruit, and herbs, in a notebook she kept in the kitchen. She had enjoyed trying new ingredients and hoped to find plenty more here. If she ate healthier for her own benefit, it would help the doctor's health as well. Dr. Schmidt favored heavier foods, such as steaks, ribs and pork chops, and the vegetable each night consisted of potatoes and more potatoes. She never knew potatoes could be prepared so many different ways: fried, mashed, smothered in cheese sauce and even made into pancakes and dumplings. She and Joseph made tantalizing green salads, but Dr. Schmidt never touched them.

In addition to his poor eating habits, he didn't exercise much and after dinner only retired to his study to smoke a cigar, drink some Scotch and read the paper. Just the smell of whisky made Luana cringe, so she didn't join him but often walked on the beach instead, and then returned to the solitude of her suite to read and write in her journal. From her upstairs window at Dr. Schmidt's estate, she had a view of the white, sandy beach and sapphire blue Pacific Ocean. Yet, despite her easy life in an idyllic setting, she often ached with loneliness. Aside from Sheila and Joseph, she had no friends. She had so many questions about her past, and she wondered if she would ever have answers. Each night at dinner she questioned Dr. Schmidt about her previous life, but still the past eluded her. She needed to learn more, and to do so, she'd have to expand her world.

After parking the car, Luana walked close to Joseph but stopped on the fringe of the market. "I don't know about this, Joseph. I'm feeling claustrophobic. I'm not used to all these crowds."

"Of course you aren't used to this. You haven't left the estate in over six months and it's been almost a year since you were out in the world." He patted her on the back for encouragement. "C'mon, kiddo. You can do this."

Once in the marketplace, the abundance of brightly colored fruits and vegetables melted her fears away. She moved from stall to stall, examining the vast array of fish arranged on benches of ice and picking up different fruit and veggies. She brought them close to her nose and inhaled the scent of ripe peaches and apricots. Fruit she had never seen before, such as guavas and java plums, attracted her. She tasted whatever anyone offered— sliced up fruit, sips of mango/coconut smoothies, olives, bits of bread dipped into olive oil, caramelized nuts and pieces of home-made pies and cakes. Then she sampled everything macadamia: ice cream, butter, cookies and bread. Gluttonous, she wanted to try everything, get everything and eat whatever she could. She also embraced the spirit of the market and within minutes was bartering with stallholders as she filled up her basket. She chose shrimp as big as tiny lobsters, red chili peppers, yellow onions, a braid of garlic and cilantro leaves that smelled as if they had been picked minutes before. They found a stall that sold spices of every color possible. The bright yellow saffron caught her eye, and a red paprika mix. She had lost her ability to name them, but she loved the colors and smells of both. With a metal scoop she dug out two healthy portions of each and placed them into two small plastic bags.

"What do you plan on cooking with all this, Luana?" Joseph asked.

"I'm not sure yet."

"That yellow spice you chose is saffron, and it's quite rare. That scoop will probably cost a couple hundred dollars."

"What? You must be kidding!" Her face grew hot with embarrassment. "I'd better put it back."

"Not all of it, but certainly most. You only need a small amount to enhance a dish."

Luana handed the stallholder the bag. "Sorry," she said, "I was overly enthusiastic."

The woman smiled at her and graciously poured out most of the contents of the bag.

"Thanks for catching that," she said to Joseph. "I'm sure Roland wouldn't have been thrilled to know I spent a fortune on a small bag of yellow spice." She placed her new purchases into her basket along with the vegetables and took inventory. "Okay, we have the fish, the veggies and the spice. Maybe I could make a stir-fry or something. Should I get chicken too?"

He looked over to the next stall at a display of sausages in a row. "I'd say forget the chicken and go for the chorizo. Nice and hot! And with paprika, they'll be perfect."

Luana walked to the next stall and asked for a half-dozen sausages. "What about rice? Do we have enough at home?"

"Just basic white rice. You could choose a more delicate grain."

They located a stall that sold every type of rice imaginable: red, brown, white and wild. There must have been at least twenty small barrels full of different types of rice. She chose a white, Indian basmati, with a slight floral scent. The stallholder thanked her and scooped a pound of it into a burlap bag.

Luana could hardly wait to get back to the kitchen and start cooking. First she'd sauté the onions . . .

* * *

Usually, Joseph set the table in the dining room for Luana and Dr. Schmidt, but tonight Luana wanted to break that habit. She had never understood why

Dr. Schmidt would want to eat inside when his terrace commanded the most spectacular view of the ocean.

"Joseph," Luana called from the butler's pantry. "Will you please show me where the china, the crystal and proper linen napkins are stored? I'd like to eat outside tonight. I'll go ahead and set the table."

"That may not be the best idea, Luana."

"Don't be silly."

"Dr. Schmidt doesn't take well to other people altering his routine."

"Well, I say it's time for a change!"

She picked orchids from the garden and floated them in a shallow glass bowl. She sliced lemons picked from his tree and placed them in crystal glasses that she filled with sparkling water.

In the midst of this setup, Dr Schmidt poked his head outside. "What's going on out here? You know I prefer to eat indoors."

Luana looked up from her masterpiece. "It's a warm, lovely night. Why in the world shouldn't we eat outdoors?"

"It's something I don't like doing."

Luana followed him. "Roland, c'mon. I spent a lot of time on the table and cooking the dinner. Please do this as a favor to me."

"Once," he said, with little expression. "I'll see you at seven."

After the first course Dr. Schmidt loosened up a bit and uncharacteristically raised his glass to Luana. "If this meal ends as up tasting as good as it has started, I may have to fire our chef."

Luana laughed at his compliment. "It was fun, Roland. I enjoyed it and it's the least I can do. But you'll definitely need to keep Joseph on—especially to cook for all your business guests."

"I'm not sure I agree," he said, when he tasted the main dish. "This is expertly done."

"Thank you," she said, glowing with her success.

Dr. Schmidt ate a healthy portion of everything offered, and then wiped his mouth with his napkin and sat back. He sipped some water and said, "So, what's for dinner tomorrow?"

"I'll have to see what's fresh at the market. Joseph and I got there late today and a lot was picked over. I'll go first thing tomorrow morning."

"That's not possible. Joseph doesn't start until ten."

"I know how to get there, now. It's easy. I'm sure I won't get lost."

"I can't permit that. Wait until Joseph arrives, then he'll drive you." He abruptly got up from the table. "If you'll excuse me. I have work to do."

Luana took a sip of cold white wine and looked out across the Pacific Ocean at the pink and purple hues painted on the evening sky. How had such a pleasant evening ended on such a down note? She finished her glass of wine and watched the orange sun disappear into the dark, blue sea. From the silver ice bucket she poured herself another glass of wine and took a few sips. A warm breeze brushed her cheeks. She finished her glass and set it down, a bit lightheaded. She hadn't drunk this much since recovering from her coma.

What had she said that had made him so upset? Rather than take her usual walk along the beach, she knocked on the door to Roland's study. "May I come in?" She waited for him to answer but didn't hear anything for several seconds.

After nearly a minute, he spoke: "Come in. What is it?"

A cigar smoldered in a brass ashtray on his mahogany coffee table, and he lounged on his leather couch with the windows closed, reading a medical journal and drinking scotch from a crystal glass. He didn't look up from his magazine when she entered the room.

The stench of his cigar made her feel sick and want to leave, but she stayed and waited for him to greet her. When he didn't, she spoke first: "I'm sorry if I said something to offend you, Roland."

He looked up from his magazine. "Please sit down, Luana." He patted the leather couch with his palm.

The cigar smoke, combined with a bit too much alcohol, left her increasingly nauseous. She sat on the opposite end of the sofa, as far from Roland as she could. He motioned her to sit closer to him. She moved reluctantly, her sixth sense sending signals of caution.

He set the magazine on his lap. "Luana, do you understand how much I've done for you?"

"I do, Roland, and I'm very grateful. I'd like to continue cooking for you. It's nothing compared to what you've done for me, but at least I feel that I'm giving something back."

He took another swig of scotch. "I'd like that. I just don't want you going shopping by yourself. It's not safe for you to be alone."

"Then I'll wait for Joseph."

He moved closer to her and put his hand on her leg. "Luana." He set his glass on the table and whispered, "Can't you see? I don't want to share you with anyone."

She inched away from him, but he reached his hand around the back of her neck and pulled her face toward his.

She resisted and pulled back until he let go.

"You have a life any woman would dream of. Everything you want is right here—a private chef, a personal trainer, a beautiful home, a successful man to take care of you. Many women struggle their whole life to achieve far, far less."

Luana didn't speak. Of course, he was right. What sane woman wouldn't want what she had? But she wanted autonomy, too.

He again pulled her closer and tried to kiss her. Instinctively she pulled away, but he forced his mouth over hers. The smell of cigar and whiskey made her want to retch, but when she leaned back, he only pushed harder. The magazine fell to the floor as he forced her to lie on the couch. His lips were on hers, but she felt only abhorrence. Whatever a legitimate, loving kiss felt like, she hoped it wasn't this.

Twelve

*T*he next morning she awoke feeling sick from drinking too much and even sicker when she thought about her encounter with Roland. To avoid him, she snuck into the kitchen, ate some leftover fruit salad with yogurt for breakfast, and then immediately dove into the pool. She finished her workout, and then hopped on a bike and rode to the market in defiance of Roland's orders. What harm could there be in going to the market alone?

Except that she didn't have any money. At her favorite produce stand, the merchant said that Joseph always charged everything to the house account.

"This one time, you can do the same," he said.

In case she encountered a problem with Roland, she bought produce for the entire week, but only enough fish for the evening meal. Joseph wouldn't mind running to the market to buy fish for the rest of the week.

When she arrived back at the compound, around 10:30 a.m., Joseph was already in the kitchen preparing lunch for Dr. Schmidt and his business associates. Luana had almost finished unloading the bags from the market when Dr. Schmidt walked into the kitchen.

"Good morning, Luana. I see that you already did some shopping."

She smiled, hoping to disarm him. "I bought enough fresh produce to feed an army."

He lowered his voice: "I trust Joseph drove you?"

"I did, sir. The merchants are getting to know her quite well. I'd like to put her on the account, if you don't mind."

"I do mind, and I won't authorize it." Without explanation, he turned to leave the kitchen.

Luana sat on one of the kitchen stools and looked at Joseph. "Thanks for bailing me out, Joseph, but what's going on around here? Why is it such a big deal to shop for food by myself?"

He poured himself a strong cup of coffee and sat down on the stool next to Luana. "You'd have to know Roland's first wife Alana. I only met her when they married and she moved to the estate, so I don't know anything about their history, but after the marriage, Roland wouldn't allow Alana to see any of her friends off the estate. She had been working as a human resources manager, but he made her quit. She didn't have keys to any of the cars, and she had no check writing privileges. The staff did all the shopping."

"I'm seeing a pattern emerge."

Joseph nodded. "I've struggled with how much to tell you, but I think you should know. When Alana needed something, Roland allowed her to use his car and driver. If she wanted to see her friends, she could invite them over for lunch, a swim and tennis, but she couldn't leave. He drilled it into her that she was one of the few women in the world who could live in such luxury. She should be thankful that she had a full staff to cater to her every need. But what she needed most, of course, was her freedom and independence."

The doctor suffocated her, Joseph said, and Alana grew to resent him until life on the compound became hell in paradise. When she wanted to end the marriage, he threatened to kill her. She told him she felt dead already, but he said that she had no idea how painful death could be. At that point she panicked and realized that she would have to escape, though she had no idea where Dr. Schmidt kept the keys to the cars and knew that she couldn't evade the doctor's driver on one of her shopping furloughs. The driver followed her every step, and at home, Dr. Schmidt instructed the guards at the gatehouse to not let her leave unless accompanied by himself or his driver.

Alana knew that she only had one chance. Every year, the doctor invited the board of directors over to his estate for his company's annual meeting. The men drove their own cars to the estate and that the valet service parked them along the side of the driveway, usually with the keys left in each car in case the vehicles needed to be rearranged.

Alana greeted all the guests and offered them an afternoon drink, and then she excused herself to the kitchen to help prepare the lunch. With the men ensconced in the library, she put on a navy blue blazer, a white shirt, and a yellow tie. She pulled her hair up under a ball cap and wore sunglasses. The security cameras recorded everything, and all hell broke loose later, but with her disguise in place, she slipped out the service entrance in the back of the kitchen and took the car parked closest to the entrance.

At the gatehouse, she waved to the guard she had seen every day for the last five years of her life, and without hesitation, he opened the gate. She sped off to the airport, where she left the car in the parking lot, and boarded a 747 to the mainland. No one heard from her again.

"Now I'm beginning to understand," Luana said. "And I suppose he and Alana ate on the terrace often?"

Joseph nodded.

"I see."

"Be careful, Luana."

She nodded. At dinner she would avoid any potentially controversial subject. She desperately wanted to clear the air about what had happened the previous night, but with Roland's volatile temper, she'd need to tread carefully. At some point, she also needed to tell him that she wanted to move off the compound. She wanted her independence. Her *freedom*. But first, she had better look for a job that would provide the financial means to make moving possible.

* * *

For dinner that night, she cooked a fish entrée topped with mango chutney. The dish was tasty and light, yet satisfying. She kept the conversation innocuous and trivial. With luck, perhaps Roland had been too drunk to remember his actions.

When Joseph tried to pour her a glass of wine, she placed her hand over the glass and politely declined. She needed to keep her wits about her tonight.

"Luana," Roland said, "I insist you have a celebratory sip of wine."

"What are we celebrating?"

"Our relationship, of course."

Luana's stomach tightened and she felt the blood drain from her cheeks. *What was he thinking?* And even worse, what was she supposed to say to him?

"I'm not certain what you mean."

"I want you to be my wife," he said without emotion.

She dabbed a white linen napkin to the corner of her mouth and chose her words carefully. "I think that's a little premature, don't you?"

"Not after everything we've been through."

"You're a wonderful, generous man, Roland. And of course, I'm beyond grateful for everything you've done for me, but I need some time to think about this."

"As you wish. I'll give you some time, but I know you'll come around soon."

"I'm sure you're right." She forced a smile and then folded her napkin and placed it next to her plate. "In fact, I think I'll take my walk now and do some of that thinking."

"Meet me in my study after your walk. We'll talk more."

"Good, I'll see you in an hour." *As if.* She wouldn't be going back there any time soon.

"Lovely dinner, Luana," he said to her as she got up from the table.

Unable to respond, she left the house, and on the beach, she walked longer than usual, plotting how to avoid another encounter. If she stayed out too long, he might come looking for her, so she needed to get back. But instead of dropping by his study, she would go directly to her room and figure the rest out from there.

She made it to her room and locked the door. Then she brushed her teeth, washed her face, and turned the light off, praying that he wouldn't stop by. She had only just settled when the sound of footsteps thumping up the stairway confirmed her fears. He tried the doorknob, and then pounded on the door.

"Luana, open up," he yelled. "Why are you locking me out? This is my house, for God's sake!"

Too scared to speak, she wanted to jump out the window and run, but she knew that would anger him more. Instead, she ran to the bathroom, pulled off her tee shirt and threw on a terry-cloth bathrobe.

She feigned calmness and opened the door. "What's all the commotion about? I was just in the shower."

"Why did you lock the door?"

"I always lock it. Just force of habit I guess."

"If you're going to be my wife, Luana, we need to see if we're physically compatible." Before she could stop him, he pulled her robe open and threw her down on her bed.

He was too strong to resist. "Roland, I'm not ready for this." She began to cry. "I'm sorry; I just can't do this right now." He held her wrists and pinned her down on the bed with the full weight of his body. She couldn't move from beneath his grip. Fearing the worst, she rolled to the side enough to lift her leg. With no other recourse, she kneed him in the groin.

With a curse and a deep howl, he released his grip, and in a voice laden with vitriol, he said, "That was a big mistake, Luana." He eased up from the bed and stumbled out of the room.

Luana couldn't stop crying. She gathered the strength to walk to the bathroom and took a long hot shower, futilely hoping that the water would wash her fear away.

Thirteen

*J*oseph looked up from the kitchen sink where he was scrubbing potatoes, despite the late hour. "You look horrible, Luana. What happened?" He turned the water off and stopped what he was doing. "You're shaking. What's wrong?" He pulled out a bar stool for her and poured her a cup of coffee. "Sit down."

She accepted the warm coffee and took several sips. "I need help, Joseph. I have to move as soon as possible. And I need a job."

"What's the rush?" he asked. "Why don't you look for a job first and after you find something, then move?"

"That's what I had planned to do, but I need to move today."

Joseph set his coffee cup down. "You're not telling me everything. I want to help you. I hope you know that you can confide in me."

"You'll just have to trust me. I need to leave."

"Is it Roland?"

"I'd really prefer not to go into it."

Joseph looked at her, and Luana could sense that he knew. He sat down next to her at the counter. "Alana was physically and possibly sexually abused. I'm afraid you're in the same situation. Am I right?"

Luana nodded.

Joseph shook his head. "I worried this might happen."

"I know. That's why you told me about Alana, but now you see why I have to leave today."

"Let me make some calls."

He walked to the wall phone and punched in some numbers. "Kirsten Mayou, please," he said into the receiver. "Kirsty—hello. Joseph here." Joseph smiled at Luana who still sat shivering on the stool. "Yes— everything's fine at Dr. Schmidt's. I have no complaints. But listen, Kirsty, I need a serious favor. My apprentice here for several months Luana, is ready to do some cooking on her own. Any chance the Kea Lani could use a hard-working line chef?"

Luana had never heard of the Kea Lani, and she tensed up when Joseph did not speak for several seconds. *What was Kirsty saying?*

"That could work." He gave Luana a thumbs-up and a big wink. "Thanks, Kirsty. I owe you one. And you won't be disappointed."

Joseph hung up the phone and walked over to Luana. "Okay, kiddo. You've got yourself an interview!"

Luana jumped off the stool and gave him a big hug. "Thank you so much! Now, where is the Kea Lani, and who's Kirsty?"

"Kirsty Mayou and I started out in the restaurant business nearly thirty years ago. She now manages the five restaurants at the Kea Lani resort, one of Hawaii's finest. But she won't be there tomorrow. The assistant manager, Kali, will interview you."

"I don't care if I have to scrub toilets, I just need a job."

"Well you may just get one. And if it all works out they'll provide you with onsite housing. The rooms are small, and you'll have to share a bathroom with several other women, but it will get you started."

"Oh, Joseph, thank you so much!" She kissed him on the cheek. "I won't let you down. I'll be the best toilet scrubber, waitress or whatever!"

He patted her back. "I know you will. Now let's figure out how to get you out of here."

Fourteen

Before dawn, Luana snuck out of the house and waited by the service entrance to the kitchen. She shivered in the cool morning air. Although it was still dark, she spotted Joseph, in silhouette, walking toward her.

He put his hand on her shoulder. "Okay, kiddo. Did you get any sleep?"

"No, I'm too eager to get out of here. Let's go!"

Joseph's car, a 50s model station wagon, looked like a hearse, painted white.

"Is this what I think it is?"

Joseph patted the dashboard. "Sure is. Picked it up when the local funeral home closed down."

"I thought if any business was recession proof it would be that one."

"The kids didn't want to take over what their dad had started. They're running a surf shop."

* * *

The luxury at Kea Lani resort became evident the minute she and Joseph stepped onto the property. Waterfalls tumbled every few hundred feet and tropical plants with bright flowers and intoxicating scents grew everywhere. Even though Luana had never been to

France, she imagined that this is what a Parisian *parfumerie* should smell like. Manicured walkways meandered through lush green grounds. Silent golf carts, driven by the housekeeping staff, were the only reminder that they hadn't been transported to a deserted island.

Kali Hale, a lady in her late fifties with smooth brown skin met Joseph and Luana on the walkway and extended her hand to each of them in a professional manner. "Welcome to the Kea Lani, Luana."

"I can't tell you how happy I am to be here."

"Why don't we go into Kirsty's office so we can take care of some paperwork?"

Luana turned to Joseph with tears in her eyes. "Thank you for everything." She gave him a big bear hug. "I'll miss you. Please don't be a stranger."

"Don't worry, kiddo," he said, his own eyes misty. "We'll stay in touch. But don't call me. When Roland finds out that you split, he'll have the phone tapped for sure. I'll call you tomorrow after you get settled in."

Her smile faded. "What will you tell him?"

"Haven't given it much thought. I'll think of something." Joseph put his hand in his pocket and pulled out a few bills. "Here, it's only fifty bucks, but it should tide you over until you get your first paycheck."

"You don't have to do this, Joseph. I'll be fine."

"Please. It's nothing."

Luana hugged him again. "Thank you so much." She watched him turn away and walk down the pathway, his gray ponytail lifting in the warm breeze. She would miss him.

Stepping into Kirsty's office was like entering a Robinson Crusoe playhouse. Kali sat behind a large Koa wood desk, neat and relatively clear of papers. She indicated that Luana should sit in a bamboo chair covered with heavy white linen. She pulled an application from a filing cabinet and handed it to Luana.

"Why don't you fill this out; we'll talk after it's completed. It should only take a few minutes."

"Thank you."

Pen in hand, Luana couldn't wait to get started. She stared at the typed page for a few seconds before it dawned on her that she knew almost nothing about herself. Previous work experience? Address? Personal references? What about the one that said 'social security number?' Her hand trembled as she gripped the pen and wrote her name on the first line. Under personal and work references she wrote Joseph's name.

"Is something wrong?" Kali asked.

Luana set the pen and paper down on the desk. "I'm afraid this is all that I can answer."

"I'm not sure I understand. What are you having trouble with?"

"There's a lot about myself that I don't know. Especially my social security number."

"Why's that?"

"I was in a terrible accident nearly a year ago. I almost died, and was in a coma for six months, but that left me an amnesiac."

Kali considered her with skepticism. "Oh really?"

"But please, Kali—you have to hire me. I desperately need this job."

"Sorry to break it to you, but there are a lot of people who desperately need a job." She held up Luana's nearly blank application. "And from the looks of your application, they're a lot more qualified than you."

"Kirsty knows my situation. Can you call her?"

"Kirsty's out all week." Kali sat up straighter and put her elbows on the desk. "I'm in charge and I'm making the decisions."

"Is it possible I could volunteer?"

"I'm sorry. There's nothing I can do."

Fifteen

Roland stormed into the kitchen. "Where the hell is she? It's nearly seven-thirty and she knows we always eat at seven!"

Joseph mopped his forehead with his chef's towel. "I'm sorry sir; she just called and told me she's in San Diego."

"What are you talking about? How did she get there?"

"I didn't ask, but she said she's visiting a cousin who's sick."

"How could you believe that bullshit? She doesn't have a cousin. She doesn't have anyone! I'm the only person in her life." Roland pointed his finger at Joseph and pressed it into his shoulder. "And you're on thin ice here! I should've fired you the minute you started getting friendly with her."

Roland stormed back to his office and slammed inside. Through the closed door, Joseph heard him shouting: "I want her found and I don't care how much it costs! And don't screw up like last time!"

Sixteen

*L*uana left the office discouraged, but not broken. Maybe she could get a job as a gardener or maid somewhere. She found a pay phone and called Joseph. The kitchen phone rang, but then she remembered what Joseph had told her about Roland tracing calls, and she hung up after one ring. For the first time since her accident she was alone, and felt like a cub leaving the comfort and protection of the lion's den for the first time.

She started back toward the main road with no idea where she was, other than that she remembered seeing a convenience store about a mile back on their drive into the resort that morning. The sun already beat down on the asphalt, softening it, but she had no choice but to walk in her flip-flops, the heat scorching through the thin soles. In her hurry to leave, she hadn't eaten breakfast. She wished she at least had a bottle of water.

About a half-hour later, she reached the store, thirsty and already tired. Inside, the air-conditioning cooled her hot skin, and she grabbed a large bottle of water from the cooler. She drank it while waiting in line to purchase it and a granola bar.

"May I speak to your manager," she asked the cashier, as she paid.

The girl pointed. "She's in the back. The last door on the right."

Luana walked through the aisles of junk food, paper goods and cleaning supplies to the back of the store where she saw a filthy white door. She knocked on it, and when no one answered, she pushed it open.

Behind metal shelves stuffed with boxes a Hawaiian woman worked at a desk. She looked up from her papers. "What can I do you for?"

"My name is Luana. I'm looking for a job."

The woman laughed. "Isn't everyone?"

"I'm just wondering if you have any positions available."

The manager reached over to the side of her desk and held up a stack of papers. "See these? These are all applications for no positions available."

"What about you? Do you need a cleaner at home, or a cook?"

"Ha!" she laughed and pointed to herself. "You are looking at the cleaner and cook in my house."

"May I fill out an application anyway?" Luana asked.

The woman opened a drawer and handed a piece of paper to her. "Sure, what the hell."

Luana stared at the application, aware once again that she had nothing to offer, not even a telephone number.

The manager stopped her. "Ya know what? My cousin down the street owns a gas station. He could use a cute girl like you working the till."

Luana brightened. "Really? What's his name?"

"Rick. The place is called Rick's Gas Café. I'll call him and tell him you're on your way. What's your name again?"

"Luana. Luana Kramer."

The woman gave Luana directions. "Shouldn't take you too long to walk. Good luck."

"Thank you," Luana said. "Thank you very much."

Before she went back out in the blazing heat, she bought another bottle of water and left her empty behind. After another twenty minutes of walking, her skin burned in the late morning sun, but in the distance she saw a building and hoped it was a gas station. Ten minutes later, which seemed like thirty, she arrived. The sign that hung from a tall white pole was a replica of the one in *Casablanca*, a favorite of numerous classics she had watched with Joseph.

She entered the gas station and asked the attendant for Rick.

"He's upstairs. Eating breakfast."

Luana walked up the outside stairs to the second floor and knocked on the screen door. The owner appeared to be in his mid-thirties and offered a welcoming smile when he saw Luana.

"You must be Luana. My cousin told me you'd be coming by."

She extended her hand. "And you must be Rick. I see we share an interest in Humphrey Bogart movies."

He grinned. "Well ain't that a coincidence? I've seen every one. At least ten times each."

Luana smiled back at him. He seemed much nicer and more positive than his cranky cousin from the convenience store.

"Where are my manners?" he said. "Please, please come in."

Luana stepped into what appeared to be his home, a neat and tidy space decorated with light wood floors, and modern, if slightly worn, furniture. Sunlight flooded in, but a ceiling fan kept the apartment cool. She had expected an apartment above a gas station to look a lot worse.

Rick indicated a tan-colored leather sofa. "Please, sit down."

Luana sat, and said, "I guess your cousin told you that I'm looking for a job. She said you might want someone to work downstairs."

"Well, not really. I need some help, but you may not be up for what I have to offer. Our nanny Clarisa, just took off for vacation. We—my wife and I—have twin boys, and let me tell you, they're a handful."

"How old are they?"

"Nine months. They're sleeping now."

Luana thought that she could easily handle two little boys who slept most of the day. "So you mostly need me to help your wife, or does she work?"

Rick roared with laughter. "Don't let her hear you talking like that. If you ask her, she'll tell you she works 24/7. She works downstairs in the little shop and café, and honestly doesn't have the energy for the boys full-time. So yes, you'd be helping her with both jobs: the boys and the shop. And cleaning. By the end of the week you'll feel like a slave and I guarantee you'll never want to get married and have children—ever. My wife is ready to pull her hair out and run for the hills."

"After that pep talk all I can say is: When can I start?"

"Not so fast. I'll need some references."

Luana's face fell. Of course they would need references. She knew Joseph would give her a glowing reference but she couldn't call him, or even send a letter.

"Listen Rick, I'll be honest with you. I just left an abusive relationship with nothing except the clothes on my back. If you take a chance with me, even for one week, I promise you won't be disappointed. If you're not happy I won't ask for any wages."

Rick's animated face became expressionless, while Luana's heart raced.

Then he said, "I'll do you one better. I'll pay you up front so you can buy yourself some clothes—from our shop of course. We sell mostly beachwear but what else do you need on this island? Free room and board too. The room's nothing great but it's comfortable."

Luana jumped up from the couch and shook Rick's hand. "Thank you. I won't let you down. So when do those boys wake up?"

"Probably not for another 45 minutes. But there's a lot to do before then. You can start by cleaning the kitchen."

Luana found the cleaning supplies under the sink and got busy washing and drying the dishes. They had a dishwasher, but it was already in use.

Then a sickly-looking woman emerged from the back of the apartment. All bones beneath a worn terry cloth bathrobe, she looked exhausted. Her hair was a mess and plump purple bags under her eyes looked as if they had weights attached.

Elbow deep in soapsuds, Luana dried off. "Hello," she said, extending her hand. "I'm Luana."

"I'm Janie. And you must be an angel here doing my dishes." She managed a smile and shook Luana's hand. "I can't believe Rick finally hired a cleaner. I've been pleading with him for weeks. Especially with Clarisa gone, there's no way I can stay on top of the housework, the shop and the boys."

"When does she come back from her holiday?" asked Luana.

"You mean *if* she comes back."

Before Luana could ask what that meant, a loud wail came from the back room. And within seconds, like an earthquake, the house shook with screaming and crying.

Janie threw her hands up in the air. "Guess the boys are awake. There goes my shower. I haven't had one in days . . ."

Luana followed Janie. The boys' room was decorated like a rain forest with murals of trees, monkeys, waterfalls and exotic birds painted on the walls. The boys, sitting up in their snug blue sleep suits were clenching their fists and screaming. A siren would sound muted compared to the noise coming out of their little mouths.

Janie picked one baby up with one arm and the second with the other.

"This is Roger and this is Richard," she said as she loosened her robe and attached Roger to her right nipple and Richard to her left.

"That was pretty fierce," Luana said, when the crying stopped. "Do they always scream like that?"

Janie nodded. "When they're hungry they do. And they're *always* hungry."

"I obviously can't breast feed them, so what should I do if you're downstairs and they start crying?"

"You'll need to give them some formula in a bottle— and quick. But they prefer their mama, so best to find me right away. My life as a woman has changed from loving wife and business owner to an around-the-clock milk bar."

When the babies finished feeding, Janie put them down on the carpet and let them crawl around. "You'll need to watch them like a hawk. They get into everything and they want to put whatever they find on the floor into their mouths."

"I'll be fine. Why don't you hop into the shower while I watch them?"

Janie smiled. "That's the best offer I've had all week."

*   *   *

It was nearly four o'clock before Luana realized that the afternoon had slipped away without her having eaten or even having used the washroom. The boys flew around the apartment on their hands and knees like battery-charged sweepers and Luana never sat down for fear they would get into something. When she turned her head for less than a minute to pull something out of Richard's mouth, Roger knocked over a plant. After she righted the plant, Richard pulled the electrical cord on a clock radio and it fell on his head. The chase was non-stop.

Janie had emerged from the shower only to pass out on the sofa. Luana didn't have the heart to wake her, so the sink-load of dirty plates and glasses remained. She was only four hours into the job and thought she might to collapse.

*   *   *

As the days passed, the job only became more difficult. With Luana living in the apartment, Rick and Janie asked her to wake up in the night to give the boys the bottle so Janie could finally catch up on her sleep. Luana had to remind herself that she had begged Rick for a job, and at least she had a place to live. Every penny she earned she saved. She didn't have time to go the bank, but she also didn't need to buy food, as she ate with the family. She had wanted to do the shopping for Janie so that she could buy fresh fish, fruit and vegetables—and perhaps run into Joseph at the produce market—but Janie insisted that she pick up groceries at Rick's cousin's place down the road. They certainly did not eat as she had on the Schmidt estate, but eating food out of a can was better than living with a monster. And a gilded cage was still a cage.

About three weeks into her job, Luana sat in the living room holding both boys in her arms. They each sucked on an afternoon bottle and were for once quiet. She looked out the window and saw Joseph's white hearse downstairs next to one of the gas pumps. Her heart skipped when she saw him and she jostled the boys as she tried to find a way to stand. She wanted to run down and talk to him, but she had her hands full. She banged on the window with her elbow, but not before Joseph had already closed his car door. Still holding the boys, she watched him get into his car.

When the boys finally fell asleep, Luana put them in their crib. She wrote a quick note to Joseph explaining her circumstances, and then she walked downstairs and gave it to Chuck, the attendant. "Next time you see the man who just drove away, will you please give him this note?"

"Sure, but this is the first time I've seen him. He's not one of the regulars."

"It's important that I contact him, so if you see him again I'd appreciate it. Even better, tell him I work here and live upstairs."

"No problem," Chuck said. He pushed his graying hair back with one hand. "Can I just say, Luana, you look awful. How are you doing up there?"

"It's only been three weeks but it feels like a year."

"What do you do on your day off?"

"I only have Sunday off so I try to sleep, but most of the time I end up working."

"You need to get out of dodge, girl. Head to the ocean. It's only a mile away. Use one of Rick's old bikes. Tires probably need pumping but they should be good to go."

"I'd like that."

He winked at her. "I'll have one of 'em ready for you by this Sunday."

Sunday arrived with the same beautiful weather, but all Luana wanted was to close the curtains in her room and try to get some sleep. She felt as if she were morphing into Janie, a once vibrant woman whose life had spiraled downwards into a dark abyss of diapers, dirty laundry and days of despair. Janie loved those adorable little boys, but Luana worried that she may be suffering from severe post-partum depression. Even Luana was beginning to feel depressed. Not sleeping, and eating poorly without exercise and fresh air would take its toll on anyone, but already she had a soft spot for those two little munchkins. Her heart melted when they gave her that gummy smile and fell asleep like two little snuggle bears in her arms, however, she couldn't go on like this much longer. She needed to get in touch with Joseph, or better, get over to the Kea Lani, where Kirsty would be back to work. With that thought, she fell asleep and didn't wake until she heard a loud crash and then a bone-chilling scream.

Seventeen

Within seconds of the scream, both boys wailed. Luana jumped out of bed. The scream had come from the master bedroom, not the boys' room, so she knocked on the closed door. "Are you alright?"

Rick yelled from beyond the door. "Janie—Oh my God! Call 911."

She made the call and left the boys crying to rush back to the master bedroom. She knocked again and entered to find Rick bent over Janie, who lay unconscious on the tile floor, wrapped in a towel, her hair wet from the shower. Rick had blood on his hands, and Luana saw streaks of blood on the floor.

"Can I do anything?" she asked.

"Just the boys. Did you call the ambulance? She must have slipped, but I'm afraid to move her."

"They're coming."

By the time the ambulance arrived, ten minutes later, she had the boys playing with squeaky toys.

"I'll go to the hospital with her. You'll need to stay here with Richard and Roger."

"Of course."

She watched the paramedics leave with Janie and Rick, and by then the boys were screaming again. She pulled them from their crib and tried to calm them, but they were inconsolable. Certain that her head would soon explode from all the noise, she returned them to the crib to look for bottles.

She found none prepared but spotted two dirty bottles in the sink. She washed those while the boys continued their ear-piercing screams. On her workdays, she kept a pitcher of formula in the fridge, but today she had to make a fresh batch. With every minute spent washing the bottles and preparing the formula the wails from the bedroom escalated.

Finally, with bottles washed and formula prepared, she sprinted back to the bedroom and gave the boys the only thing known to keep them quiet. As soon as they started sucking and blissful silence had set in, Luana began to cry. This job and the stress that went along with it were too much.

For selfish reasons, she prayed that Janie would be okay and have only a minor cut, but being knocked unconscious wasn't good. She could never manage the boys and the messy house on her own. She needed to get out of this chaos—and fast! The first minute she had free she vowed she would hop on the bike and ride to the Kea Lani.

To escape the apartment, she waited until the boys finished feeding, and then she changed them and carried them downstairs and put them into their buggy. A break from the monotony of feeding and changing would do them all good. No parks existed around the gas station, so they walked along the barren main road in the heat. Sizzling hot blacktop and gas fumes were a far cry from the Hawaii she had become accustomed to. She longed for the luxury of the Schmidt estate, especially her swims, the beach and the gourmet meals. And of course Joseph.

Chuck waved her into the shop when she pushed the buggy back toward the gas station.

"Any word from Rick?" she asked.

"They're gonna spend the night in the hospital. Janie has a concussion. She's conscious but they need to monitor her."

"I'm glad she'll be okay," Luana said, her thoughts already on how she would get through another all-nighter.

* * *

The following morning at dawn Rick returned. Luana had not slept more than an hour or two. She felt completely drained, but she could see Rick was just as wrecked as she was.

"How's Janie?"

"They're keeping her an extra day just to make sure."

"If you want to take a shower and catch a few hours of sleep, I can manage for a bit longer."

"You're a life saver. I know you've been working overtime lately, and you're doing a great job. I'll give you a couple hundred bucks as a bonus."

"Thank you," she said, unable to tell him that all she really wanted was a week off.

As soon as Rick woke, Luana hopped on a bike and rode over to the Kea Lani before anyone could disrupt her plans. When she rode through the gate, she felt as if she had entered a different world. Living above the gas station for three weeks, even the fragrant fresh scent of Hawaii had been lost from memory and replaced with diesel fuel. The salty ocean, sweet flowers and moist breeze—all this only a mile away—had vanished into the hot air hovering above the highway.

Within seconds, she felt like she had come home, and she vowed to do anything to get back here. She propped her bike against a palm tree and walked to Kirsty's office. In her shorts, flip-flops and tee shirt, she wasn't dressed appropriately for an interview, but she didn't care. Outside Kirsty's office she saw Kali standing by the door. She knew that Kali would do her no favors, so she turned around and walked to reception.

A young man with ultra-bright white teeth smiled at her from behind the reception counter. "May I help you, Miss?"

"Do you have a pen and piece of paper, please?"

Luana wrote a quick note to Kirsty expressing how sorry she was to have missed her the previous month and apologized for not getting in touch sooner. She briefly explained what had happened on the morning of the interview. With that, and hoping for a bit of luck, she sealed the envelope and handed it back to the concierge.

"Will you please make sure this is delivered to Kirsty Mayou?" she asked the concierge.

"Of course, Miss. I'll take care of it myself."

"Thank you," Luana said, "I hope I'll see you soon!"

"Me too, Miss. Have a nice day."

Luana was back at the station in less than an hour. She bounded up the stairs and prayed that the boys wouldn't scream when she entered, but Rick had one in each arm, each with a bottle in his mouth. He looked like the picture-perfect dad, content and calm.

"Any word from the hospital?" she asked.

"I'll pick Janie up in an hour or so." He looked down at his boys and gave them each a kiss on the head. "You know, this is the first time I've spent more than a half-hour alone with these little guys. I've really been missing out. Once Janie gets back, I'll spend more time with them. I want her to get some rest, and you can catch up on the house work."

Luana smiled. "I've never seen them so peaceful."

"And Luana," Rick said, "I haven't forgotten that you worked all day yesterday and all night. I need to leave in a few hours for the hospital but if you want to take some time off, please do."

"That would be great. I'll just finish the dishes and then go to the ocean for a bit."

The phone rang while she was in the kitchen. She looked around the corner at Rick, but both boys were asleep in his arms. He motioned her to pick it up.

"Hello, Rick's Gas Café," she answered. The voice on the other end of the line brought a smile to her face. "Thank God," she said.

Eighteen

*L*ess than an hour after she had hung up the phone, Luana bounded downstairs to where Joseph and his white hearse waited for her. She ran into his arms like a long-lost lover.

"I was worried sick about you!" Joseph said.

"I know. I should have got a message to Kirsty sooner but this job has literally been non-stop."

"I can tell. You look awful."

"Thanks."

Joseph patted her on the back. "No worries, Kirsty's looking forward to meeting you."

Kirsty Mayou looked fit and trim, but also like she had spent too much time in the sun. Her spiky blonde hair was bleached nearly white, and although Luana judged her to be in early middle-age only, already a map of wrinkles spread across her face when she smiled. But her smile was warm and extended to her bright blue eyes. She greeted them outside the same straw-covered cabana where Kali had interviewed Luana three weeks ago.

Kirsty gave Joseph a lingering hug that implied they had at one time been more than just friends, and then turned to Luana. "Welcome to the Kea Lani, Luana. I read your note, and I admire your courage."

"I can't tell you how happy I am to be here."

They entered her office, while Joseph waited in the reception area. Kirsty sat and rested her forearms on her desk. "Given your stellar recommendation from Joseph and the fact that I know you're a hard worker, I'm happy to give you a job."

Luana felt as though she had just won the lottery. "Thank you so much. I need to give notice at my other job, but I should be able to start in a week."

"We're taking a big risk with you, Luana, but I've spoken with my boss, and we'll categorize you as an immigrant. We can give you a work visa for six months, and after that you'll need to sort out your social security number and start the process of applying for legal immigration."

"That's fine. I'll get started on that right away." How, she didn't know, but she'd deal with that later. "Oh—I forgot to ask. What will I be doing?"

"The outdoor poolside café needs a waitress for its breakfast and lunch shift. It's not much, but eventually you could apply to cook."

"That sounds perfect! Thank you again."

Kirsty filed the application form in her drawer and stood up from behind her desk. She handed Luana her card with her direct line on it. "As soon as you sort out your other job, call me and we'll have you start right away."

"If I could start tomorrow I would, but I need to give the family I'm working for some notice."

Kirsty smiled. "I wouldn't expect anything else from you."

When they walked into the reception room, Luana gave Joseph the "thumbs up" signal and grinned.

He rose and hugged her. "You've been through hell, my girl. I'm glad to see that you finally got a break." He shook Kirsty's hand. "Thank you."

Kirsty nodded. "I'm sure she's everything you said she is. We're happy to have her here."

In the car, on the way back to the gas station, Luana asked Joseph something she had feared for nearly a month. "Does Roland have any idea I'm still in Hawaii?"

"He doesn't, but I'm sure he'll find out soon enough. He's hired a PI. You need to watch your back."

They pulled up to the gas station and Joseph turned off the car. "Do you need me to go upstairs with you while you give your notice?"

"No, I need to do this myself."

"You've landed on your feet before, and I know you'll do it again."

"Thanks for everything, Joseph. You've been such a good friend to me."

"My pleasure. When you're ready to start at the Kea Lani, place a call from anywhere but here, and I'll swing by to drive you over, so you can start this new life of yours."

"Sounds like a plan. I'll give you a few days notice."

When Luana saw Rick on the floor playing with the boys she broke into a huge smile.

"Great," Rick said, "you're back. I need to go get Janie."

"Before you do, I have something I need to tell you."

Rick looked up at her. "Everything okay?"

Luana took a deep breath. "Really good actually. I got offered a job at the Kea Lani."

Rick whistled. "Wow that came out of left field."

"Of course I'll stick around while you look for someone else, but I'd like to start as soon as possible. Any chance Clarisa's coming back?"

"We haven't heard from her, but I'll try to track down her cousin. As much as we drove her crazy, she really became part of the family. I'm sure she'll eventually come back. I'll call when I get home from the hospital."

"I really appreciate you taking a chance on me. The job certainly lived up to everything you warned me it would—and more. But it was an experience I won't forget."

"No, thank *you*. You came along when we desperately needed someone and you offered more than we had hoped for. I wish you the best of luck at the resort." He shook his head and whistled. "Sure is some sweet place. You're gonna love it."

Nineteen

*C*larisa returned within the week when Rick doubled her salary and promised to give her more time off. She had missed the little boys, she said, and she understood how desperately Rick and Janie needed her help.

Joseph picked Luana up the day Clarisa arrived and drove her to the Kea Lani. He gave Kirsty a quick kiss on the cheek when she met them. "Everything all settled? I don't want to leave her here like I did last time."

"I'll be okay," Luana said. "I don't want Roland to question where you've been."

Joseph looked at Kirsty. "You're going to take care of her, right?"

Kirsty smiled. "Of course. She's in good hands."

"I'll check in on you in a couple of days. And remember, don't call the house. You're not out of the woods yet."

Joseph left them in the lobby and Kirsty turned to Luana. "Okay, now. I'll walk you over to your new living quarters, but from what I've heard about the Schmidt Estate, your new room will be a major—and I mean *major* downgrade."

"Yes, but remember I've been living in a small bedroom off the laundry room in an apartment above a gas station for the past month."

"Good, it will make your transition a lot easier."

As Kirsty had forewarned, the dormitory was very different from the Schmidt Estate, but there was no highway in sight, and best of all, not a hint of gasoline fumes hung in the air. From the outside, the buildings blended in nicely with the rest of the resort. There appeared to be five residences, long, one-storey buildings with straw roofs, clustered around a lawn with a sandbox and children's playground in the middle.

Kirsty pulled a key from her pocket and opened the main door to one of the buildings. A sign above the door read: 'Sandy Cove.'

"You'll be in room 22," she said. "It's at the end of the hallway."

Luana followed Kirsty down a narrow, faintly lit hallway.

Kirsty explained that the overhead hallway lights stayed off during the day to conserve energy, but several fans lined the ceiling, which kept the building cool. She gave Luana her key and pointed to the end of the hall. "These rooms don't have private baths. You'll find two communal bathrooms and shower facilities located at either end of the hallway."

Luana fumbled a bit with her key, but when the door opened, light from the sliding glass door poured in. Although small, the room had a fresh airy feel, with light peach paint and white trim. A twin bed was pushed against one wall. Starched white linens, and a towel and washcloth were neatly folded and stacked at the end of the bed. A desk, nightstand, a dresser, and a mirror furnished the tiny room. A small bar refrigerator hummed in the corner.

"You have no idea how happy I am to move in," she said.

"There's no phone," Kirsty told her, "but the payphone's down the hall. And the hotel phone is in the hallway. Feel free to explore the grounds this afternoon if you'd like. But just so you know—the three main pools and the spa are off-limits to employees." Kirsty grinned. "But the ocean's not!"

"Perfect. I'll take a swim after I unpack."

"The employee cafeteria is in this same cluster of buildings," Kirsty added, as she prepared to leave the room. "Just walk outside and turn left. Dinner's served a six."

"I'll be there!"

"And don't forget, you'll need to show up at the beach shack tomorrow morning at five o'clock sharp."

"I wouldn't think of oversleeping. Thanks again."

Kirsty shut the door behind her, and Luana fell back onto her bed and kicked her legs in the air. She was free.

Unpacking her few belongings from her straw beach bag took a total of three seconds. Aside from some toiletries and underwear, the only other items she owned were a pair of jeans, one pair of shorts, a couple of tee shirts, a brightly-colored sarong, a bikini and a pair of flip-flops. She changed into her swimsuit, grabbed the stiff towel from the end of the bed and headed to the ocean. In the blistering hot mid-afternoon sun, she couldn't get to the water soon enough. She had missed the sensation of diving into the waves like a child misses its mother's embrace.

As at Dr. Schmidt's, the resort had a sandy beach. She kicked off her flip-flops, dropped her towel and ran across the burning sand toward the ocean. Knee-deep in the cool water, she waited for a perfect wave about to crash ashore. She had learned to love body surfing while living at Dr. Schmidt's, and with every afternoon off, she would do it here as well. She saw a mammoth wave approaching the shoreline and dove in and swam with strong strokes out to meet it. The wave looked like an enormous blue wall when she turned around and began swimming as fast as she could back to shore. She felt the force of it behind her, and as soon as she sensed that she could no longer out-swim the wave, she straightened her body like a plank and let it carry her in. She rode the wave for several minutes before she crashed onto the shore. She stood up, wiped the sand out of her eyes, and waited for the next one. As she rode wave after wave, she lost track of the time. Only hunger pangs and the setting sun made her realize that it must be close to six o'clock and time to dry off.

She took a quick shower in her room and then walked to the cafeteria, where a sea of faces looked up at her when she entered. If she weren't so famished from an afternoon of body surfing she would have returned to her room right then. Instead, she grabbed a tray and stood in line to choose between macaroni-n-cheese, lasagna, and some yucky looking meat covered in gray gravy. She would definitely pass on that one. The vegetables appeared to be soaked in butter, so she passed on those as well and piled greens, cottage cheese, and fruit onto her plate. It wasn't much, but at least it was healthy.

She navigated the room with her tray, hoping for somewhere to sit alone, but each table was partially filled with people. She took a deep breath and joined a group of Hawaiian women who introduced themselves one-by-one.

Lena, the young Hawaiian girl seated next to her was devouring a plate of mac-n-cheese.

"Tomorrow is my first day," Luana said to her. "What part of the hotel do you work in?"

"Housekeeping. How about you?"

"The Beach Shack." Luana looked at the other girls. "Do any of you work there?"

They all shook their heads *no*, but soon the awkwardness dissipated as they opened up and told Luana about their jobs.

Her first meal out of the way, Luana returned to her room, light-headed and exhausted. She set her alarm, collapsed onto her bed and fell into a deep sleep, the first in a month where she slept for eight hours without hearing a crying baby.

* * *

The Beach Shack was located adjacent to the sandy beach, next to one of the pools. Luana knew at first glance that this was the 'party pool.' No more than four feet deep, it had a waterfall at one end and a swim-in bar at the other end. Like Kirsty's office and the staff quarters, the restaurant had a straw covered roof and large ceiling fans.

When she arrived, two young Hawaiian boys were rolling up tarps that protected the inside of the restaurant during the night, exposing a long, shiny breakfast and lunch bar made from Koa. A fountain with ceramic dolphins spurted water at the entrance to the restaurant, and everywhere Luana looked, she saw plants. On the patio, several large palm trees provided shade for tables and chairs constructed from the same wood as the bar.

A young man in his late twenties approached her. He had sun-bleached blonde hair and white creases around his eyes that morphed into wrinkles when he smiled. He wore a floral shirt, navy-blue board shorts and flip-flops.

"I'm Mark," he said. "I'm the manager around here. You must be Luana."

"I am." She shook his rough hand. "Nice to meet you."

"Glad to see you're prompt. We start serving breakfast at six, but I asked you to come in early to show you how things work around here."

"Great—what do I need to know?"

Mark showed her the kitchen, told her how to write up an order, ring it up on the cash register and where to place the order so the chef would see it. He pointed out the water, condiment and beverage station and then showed her which tables she would serve. He had a casual, laid-back style, a twinkle in his eye and an ever-present smile. She could tell that he worked in the restaurant so that he could surf all afternoon.

He took her to the women's locker room and gave her a key. "You're locker number 16. You'll find your uniform in there. They're pretty much one-size-fits-all."

The 'uniform' turned out to be a grass skirt and a red-and-white flowered bikini top. When she saw them hanging from the hook in her locker, she laughed out loud. She held the grass skirt to her waist to check the fit and fastened it around her. The bikini top was small, but not distasteful. Then she noticed a small, straw wreath sitting on the top shelf in the locker.

She walked out of the locker room holding it. When Mark saw her he pointed to his head.

Luana laughed, and put the straw wreath on her head.

"You look great, Luana. You'll do just fine." He directed her to the far end of the kitchen where trays of scrambled eggs, bacon, bagels, cream cheese, fruit and yogurt lay spread out on a long metal table. "Better grab something to eat before the folks start beating down the doors."

A young man she had noticed hosing down the floors earlier was now eating a huge plate of bacon. The eggs smelled good, and her stomach grumbled, so she took a large serving spoon of scrambled eggs and several pieces of pineapple and papaya. She sat down at one of the small tables in the corner and finished her breakfast in three minutes.

Customers entered the restaurant promptly at six, mostly mainlanders on holiday with jet lag, she suspected. The first couple she served was elderly, perhaps in their early seventies, so sweet and friendly that she forgot her nervousness.

Table after table filled up without much of a break in between the groups of customers. Most diners left her cash as a tip, a handful of coins, or sometimes bills as well. Large or small, with each tip she pocketed she felt a twinge of gratitude at receiving money of her own.

While she worked, it seemed like a year had passed since she had lived on the Schmidt estate, and she rarely thought of Dr. Schmidt, but a few minutes after eleven, she glanced at the wall clock and imagined that Joseph would be in the kitchen preparing lunch.

She had just served a table of teenage boys two orders of three-egg omelets and home fries, when Mark tapped her on her shoulder and gestured that she follow him.

Her heart sank to her stomach as she wondered what she had done wrong.

She followed Mark back into his office, where he held up the phone. Her hand shook as she took the receiver. "Hello." Her voice was barely a whisper as she waited to hear who was at the other end of the line.

"It's me," Joseph said. "I know you're working and you can't talk, but call me after your shift is over to tell me about your first day. Roland's having a business lunch by the pool and I learned that he didn't tap the phone."

"I'll call as soon as I'm off. I hope I didn't get you in trouble."

"Don't worry; he still doesn't know anything."

"I'll call you in a few hours, then."

She returned the receiver to Mark, who had taken on a stern expression. "I'm sorry. I wasn't expecting that call. I don't even know the number here."

"Let's try to not have it happen again. You can see how busy this place is. But don't worry about it; Kirsty transferred the call, so I figured it must have been important." He looked at her without his customary smile. "Everything okay?"

"Everything's fine," she lied. "I better get back to work."

Exactly at 2:30 p.m. she handed over her last table to the girl taking over the afternoon and evening shift. Despite her growling stomach, she went first to the pay phone, rather than to the kitchen.

Joseph answered the phone on the first ring. "So how was your first day?" he asked.

"I really like my manager Mark. He's an easy-going guy who runs a good restaurant but doesn't take himself or the job too seriously."

"Be careful, Luana. Don't break too many hearts."

"He's not my type."

"So—what is your type?"

"Don't worry, Joseph, you'll always be my first love."

"I'll settle for that."

They spoke for a few more minutes until Joseph said, "I have to plate my braised pears before they fall apart."

"I'll call you in a couple of days," Luana said. "Maybe on your day off you could come over here for lunch?"

"Sounds like a plan. Take care, kiddo."

When she had changed out of her grass skirt and bikini top, she grabbed a turkey sandwich from the kitchen.

Mark caught up with her as she was leaving. "Where are you off to this afternoon?"

She held up her sandwich: "Body surfing, when I'm finished eating."

"I'm headed out to the ocean, too. Have you ever tried long board surfing?"

Luana shook her head and munched on a corner of a turkey sandwich.

"I'll teach you, and then I'll take you to dinner. I know this casual beach place that doesn't even require shoes."

She remembered Joseph's warning about "breaking hearts," and another about fraternizing with the boss, but she shrugged both thoughts off. "I'll be right back. I just need to run back to my room and throw on my suit."

Twenty

*L*uana met Mark at the lifeguard station. There hadn't been a lifeguard there for years, but the faded red, wood structure was a good landmark. He balanced a surfboard at least ten feet long on its end and patted it when he saw her.

"This will be your ride for the next few hours."

"It's huge," she said. "And I'm warning you, I've never surfed on a board. I have loads of practice body surfing, but that's about it."

"Where did you learn to body surf?"

Luana hedged. "Oh—just down the road a bit." She threw her hand in the direction of the coast. She didn't want to admit that she had lived with Roland, however extenuating the circumstances.

Mark glanced in the direction that Luana mentioned. Anyone who had spent any time on the island would know that the beaches down the coast were private, and situated on some of the priciest real estate in the world. He had the expression of someone who wanted to ask more but knew enough not to.

"Okay then." Mark picked up the surfboard and heaved it onto his shoulder. "Let's hit it!"

At the shoreline, Mark placed the board onto the wet sand. Small, gentle waves lapped at the board, but the stabilizing fin remained lodged in the sand.

Mark jumped on. "The first thing I'm going to teach you is to get comfortable standing in a surfing position." He planted both feet firmly on the board, crouched down and held his right hand above his knee and his left closer to his hip.

"That sounds easy enough." Luana hopped up on the board when Mark stepped off. She put her feet where he told her to, crouched down a bit and held her arms the same way Mark did. She felt steady and secure until a large wave breaking on the shoreline threatened to dislodge the board from the sand. She held firm and only lost her balance a bit.

"Looks like you're a natural, Luana," Mark said. "Now let's try it in the water."

She threw him a dubious glance, certain that she'd make a fool of herself. "If you say so."

Mark told her to lie on the board and paddle out with her hands. Luana took to the board naturally and her thin muscular arms allowed her to speed out faster than Mark could swim. When she was about fifty yards out, Mark shouted to her to stop.

He caught up and treaded water beside her to catch his breath. "Jesus, Luana, you're sure a fast swimmer. I could barely keep up with you."

Luana pushed wet hair out of her eyes and straddled the board, letting her legs dangle in the water. "Okay, what's next?"

"First let's turn the board around, so the front faces the shore."

Luana spun around, easily maneuvering the long board.

"Okay, now try standing up."

While still treading water, Mark stabilized the board with one hand while Luana attempted to stand. She moved herself from the sitting position to a kneeling one and then gripped the sides of the board and pulled her feet under her. Slowly, she released her hands and inched her way up. She wobbled a bit as she raised her body with her thigh muscles, but held her hands out to her side to keep from tipping over.

"You're up," Mark shouted. "Now try to maintain your balance when I let go."

Luana looked down at Mark. "I think I've got it. Go ahead and let go."

She held about five seconds on her own, until a small wave hit the back of the board and she toppled into the ocean. When she came up for air, Mark had grabbed the board to keep it from drifting away.

"Nice try, Luana—you almost had it. Let's do it again."

She dunked her head down in the water to slick her hair off her face, and then climbed back on. Mark helped while she hopped up with no trouble and followed the same steps as before. She steadied herself for a few seconds, and then told Mark to let go.

"Are you sure?"

"Yup—I'm ready!"

Her legs shook a bit as she stabilized the board, but she stayed up for several seconds.

"Hold it as long as you can, Luana. You're doing great!"

She was holding her own and it felt awesome, but after only a minute Mark said, "Looks like you got the feel of it. Now ease yourself back down."

"I can't believe how tired I am just from standing on the board."

"You're using all of your core muscles and your leg muscles to stabilize the board."

"That was fun," she said, "but I didn't go anywhere."

"One step at a time," Mark said. "You have to hold your own before you can ride a wave."

Luana wiped the water out of her eyes. "I'm ready now. But how do I do it?"

"Okay—lie on the board again and wait for a wave. When you see one coming behind you, paddle as fast as you can and then ease yourself up. The force of the wave will push you forward."

Luana rolled onto her belly and waited for a wave. She kept her head turned, looking behind her. She saw a wave developing in the distance, though it took a few seconds to grow. She turned to face the beach, and when she felt the force of the water, she paddled. The wall of water built behind her, gathering strength, so she brought herself to a stand, shaky but balanced. As the wave grew bigger, it propelled her forward, just as Mark had said it would.

She was actually surfing! And riding the wave was easier than standing on the board in still water. As the wave drove her toward shore, the wind felt cold and exhilarating against her wet face. She moved fast, only barely aware of the other surfers in brightly colored suits and boards of various sizes swarming around her. She focused on her board and her wave until the shore appeared out of nowhere. Mark had forgotten to tell her that part, but the wave broke and the board slowed and became unstable. Rather than let the board slam her into the beach, she jumped off and fell to the sand.

She looked around for Mark but didn't see him, so she grabbed her board and dragged it ashore. Within seconds Mark swam in to meet her.

"Wow, girl, you were awesome! You're really meant for this! Ready to do it again?"

"You bet!" Luana grinned.

Mark borrowed a buddy's board and they surfed together for another hour. She had several spills, but nothing that prevented her from hopping up again and riding the next wave.

The sun had dipped low when they called it a day.

"I can't believe how much fun that was." Luana grinned as she dried her hair with a sandy towel. "I had such a great time."

Mark shook the water out of his hair and ears and then toweled himself off. "We'll do it again. But first let's grab some dinner."

She wrapped a towel around her waist and snatched up her flip-flops.

Mark put the surfboard on his shoulder and they both treaded through warm sand back to the resort. "When you're ready, look for a beat up, old Land Rover," he said.

* * *

Luana took a quick shower and met Mark at the employee parking lot. Sure enough, there he stood, outside an army-green truck, their two surfboards sticking out the back of it. The Rover had no top, nor doors, only a cracked windshield.

Mark smiled when he saw her approaching. "Hey, girl," he said. "You ready for a few drinks and dinner?"

"As long as you get me back here by ten." She winked. "I have to be at work early tomorrow morning."

"No problem—me too!"

She hopped into the Rover and strapped on a thick, black shoulder harness. The metal buckle burnt her skin.

Mark sped south out of the parking lot, on King Kamehameha Drive toward Kealakekua Bay. They drove for about thirty minutes before Mark turned off the highway onto a dirt road that led toward the ocean. They passed a community of shanty-style homes, all one-storey, no landscaping to speak of, except bright orange and red birds-of-paradise that grew like weeds. Rusty cars and trucks sat parked on overgrown lawns. Nice neighborhood, Luana thought, as they bounced through potholes.

When the road ended, Mark stopped the truck, put the gear in neutral and shifted into four-wheel drive. He looked over to her and grinned. "Now the fun begins!"

He drove through a small stream and onto what appeared to be the outskirts of a beach. The car sank into the sand but managed to keep moving.

"Where in the world are we going?"

"You'll see. We're almost there."

They drove through a grove of palm trees, and avoided several large rocks while splashing and bouncing through more small streams. In the distance Luana saw a small, thatched roof building, which she assumed was Mark's 'restaurant.' They stopped a few feet from a building not unlike the Beach Shack, except this building was an authentic shack, the open-air structure covered by dried palm fronds. In the middle of the eating area a large tree stump held several bottles of rum, tequila, Coke, and ginger ale. A cooler filled with bottles of beer sat on the sand next to the stump.

Two men in their early twenties, wearing neither shirts nor shoes sat in the sand around a smaller stump, eating rice, beans and fish off a metal plate. Several of these smaller wooden stumps, which served as tables, were scattered around this oversized sand box, and two hibachi grills smoked away outside. The smell of the barbeque added even more of an edge to her hunger.

"Hey, dude, great to see you!"

Mark and a young man with dark brown dreadlocks gave each other a side-slap on their palms.

"Hey, Rust, you too. This is my friend Luana."

"Nice to meet you, Luana." He looked toward the tree stump/bar. "What can I get you?"

"I'd love a glass of water, thanks."

"No water here, girlfriend. How 'bout a nice, cool rum-n-coke?"

Luana looked and Mark and shrugged her shoulders. "Sure. Why not?"

"I'll have the same, Rust. But lots of ice."

"Me too," Luana said. "Lots of ice." The last thing she needed was to get drunk and end up hung-over on her second day of work.

"Be right back with those drinks," Rust said. "Why don't you two go outside and enjoy the sunset."

Mark and Luana walked outside and parked themselves on two beach chairs that sat low in the sand. Another couple in sunglasses and sun hats lolled on a blanket, drinking and smoking a joint.

"So," Mark turned to Luana, "what do you think of this place?"

"Funky, but in a fun way. How did you ever find it?"

"I've been surfing with Rust for years. Until I started working at the Kea Lani, we used to surf this beach every day, and you saw how remote it is. Surfers are notoriously hungry, but there was nothing to eat within miles. Rust's a photographer. He hasn't made a dime selling his photos so he had nothing to lose by opening up this place. I'm not even sure he has a permit, but he always has a steady flow of customers. I don't think the cops even know it exists."

She grinned as a whiff of marijuana smoke wafted past. "That's probably for the best."

Rust returned with their drinks. "Are you eating?"

"Of course," Mark said. "We're starving."

Luana noticed that he didn't ask *what* they wanted for dinner, only if they wanted to eat.

"There's only one item on the menu each day," Mark explained. "Whatever fish Rust catches in the afternoon is what he grills at night. He serves fish with red beans and rice."

Luana saw several large fish glinting silver on a tray of ice, and a pot simmering on one of the hibachi grills. "It smells delicious; I can hardly wait to try it."

Mark swirled the ice in his drink around with his finger. "So what's your story, Luana?"

"What do you mean?"

"I mean how did you end up at the Kea Lani? From my point of view, it seems a little strange. I get a call from Kirsty saying that a new girl will be starting next week. Usually there's at least an interview."

She stared at him, her mind racing as she wondered how to explain, or avoid explaining.

"C'mon, girl. Fess up. What's your story?"

Luana took a big, cold gulp of her rum-n-coke. It felt great going down. "I'm not sure you'd find my story all that interesting."

Mark finished his drink. "Try me."

Luana took a deep breath. "My goal is to eventually be a chef. I love to cook. There weren't any cooking positions available, so I was offered the chance to wait tables. I jumped at it because I thought it would at least get my foot in the door."

"That makes sense," Mark said, "but that doesn't tell me how you got the job as a waitress at the Beach Shack. I have a pile of resumes this thick." He held his hands about a foot apart. "Everyone on the island would love to work at the Kea Lani, cleaning toilets or busing tables if they had to. Not many resorts offer their employees housing with three meals a day."

Joseph must have a lot of pull, Luana thought. "Okay, if you want the whole boring story, this is how it happened." She took another sip of her drink. As predicted the ice had melted fast, and the drink was diluted. "I used to shop at the farmers market several times a week. I love all the fresh fish and produce. Every time I went, a man in a white chef's coat and those baggy black and white pants was also there. I figured he was a chef somewhere, so I finally introduced myself, hoping to get some tips from him. His name was Joseph Manley, and he works on a private estate as the head chef. We got to talking and became pretty good friends. After a few weeks of us getting to know each other, he suggested that maybe I could work with him on the estate, if his eccentric boss agreed."

"Who's that?" Mark asked.

Luana didn't really want to tell him, but if Mark looked at her file he'd find out on his own. "His name is Dr. Roland Schmidt, and believe me, the guy is weird." Luana took another sip from her drink. "Anyway, after working there for several months, I learned a ton from Joseph. I was really grateful, but I thought it was time for me to move on."

"Fair enough," Mark nodded his head. "I like that you're ambitious. I'll keep you in mind if we need a new line-chef or prep cook."

"I'd appreciate that."

"Okay, but still, I can't figure out how you circumvented the entire interview process. Usually a waitress has to go through at least three interviews."

"Joseph and Kirsty have known each other for nearly thirty years. Actually I think they might have been more than friends at one point. But that's not really my business. When I told Joseph that I'd like to explore the possibility of cooking at a restaurant, he called Kirsty. And since there weren't any cooking jobs, Kirsty pawned me off on you."

"And so she did." Mark laughed.

Luana raised her rum glass to him. "And now you're stuck with me." As the sun sank into the ocean and the breeze picked up a bit, Luana felt the chill.

Mark rubbed his finger on the gooseflesh that rose on her wrist. "How 'bout we go sit by the fire?"

Rust had built a large bonfire a bit further away from the hut, with flames soaring at least six feet into the air.

"Good idea," Luana said. "I should've brought a jacket." If she owned a jacket. She had a cotton cardigan, but she had left it at the estate during her mad rush out of there and hadn't needed one since.

She tensed when Mark put his arm around her as they walked toward the bonfire.

She liked him as a friend, but she didn't feel any chemistry with him. Also, given what she had experienced with Roland, she wasn't exactly ready for romance with anyone. She didn't want to offend him by pulling away, so instead of putting her arm around his waist, as she might have, had she felt at ease with the situation, she left her arm by her side. Mark got the hint and dropped his arm when they reached the bonfire.

The tension broke as Rust shouted out from the hut, "Do you guys want me to bring your food to the fire, or do you want to eat it back here?"

Mark waved his arm and pointed to the fire. They sat in the sand and waited for Rust to bring their meal.

"Sorry about the lack of tables out here," Rust said, as he set the plates of steaming food on the sand. "This will taste great as long as you keep the sand off the plate. Can I get you two another drink?"

"I'm fine," Luana said. She was too cold to have another rum-n-coke.

"I'm okay, too," Mark said. "But maybe after dinner, we'll have a Kahlua and cream."

"I'll check back with you in a few minutes. Enjoy your dinner." Rust hustled back to the hut.

"What's Kahlua?" Luana asked.

Mark looked at her like she was crazy. "How could you live in Hawaii and never have Kahlua?"

"I don't know," she fumbled. "I guess I've just never been in the right place at the right time."

"We'll fix that," Mark said. "You'll love it. It's like drinking a dessert."

Luana held her fork just above her plate. "Like you told me in the ocean: first things, first." She pierced the fish and took a big mouthful of fresh and delicious tuna. She couldn't detect any additional flavor besides the mesquite coals from the barbeque. So simple, yet perfect. The rice and beans were also mouth-watering, perfectly seasoned, but she couldn't pinpoint with what—possibly cayenne pepper, or maybe even Tabasco sauce.

"This is fantastic," she said to Mark. "If it weren't so difficult to get to, I'd come here every night."

"Me too," Mark said. "But I do get here once a week. You can be my standing dinner companion if you'd like."

"Sounds like you've got yourself a stand-in!"

They finished every bean and grain of rice on their plates and then walked back to the hut. The place was packed. A couple dozen people, all dressed about the same in board shorts or sarongs, shoeless and with messy hair, stood outside by the barbeques and inside by the bar. About the same number sat on the sand inside and ate off the small tree stumps.

"So—whad'ya think?" Rust asked Luana.

"It was great. You'll have to give me your secret recipe for the rice and beans."

"You'd have to shoot me first." Rust laughed, and then said, "You ready for some Kahlua?"

"Absolutely," Mark said. "We'd both love some."

Rust poured the creamy liquid into a metal coffee cup. From the cooler next to the bar, he pulled a carton of half-n-half and poured a generous amount into each cup.

"Cheers, guys—I gotta run." Rust handed them their drinks, then rushed outside to tend to the barbeque.

"How does he manage all this on his own?" Luana asked.

"Are you kidding? This guy has more energy than anyone I know. He lives for this. It's like one big party for him. He fishes and surfs all day, and then at night, all his friends show up and pay him to feed them and pour drinks."

He held his cup up to Luana. "Cheers."

Luana took a sip. "Yumm! Coffee flavored ice cream in a cup."

Twenty-One

On Luana's first Sunday off, Joseph came over to the resort to have lunch with her. He brought with him a bag of her clothes that she had left at the estate.

"I'm sure you still have some things back at the house, but this is all I could find. Most of these were left in the laundry room."

"Thanks, I've been wearing the same thing all week."

"I also brought these, your favorite." He presented a box of chocolate chip cookies.

She broke one in half and put it in her mouth. "And they're still warm—thank you, Joseph."

"What if we skip lunch for now and do a little surfing? I brought my board."

"I had no idea you surfed."

"I was quite the maverick in my day."

"Let's go then. Show me what you got."

Despite his age, and a bit of a potbelly, he impressed Luana by holding his own. After a few hours of hard surfing, they sat on the beach and shared a bottle of water.

Luana took a sip and then handed the bottle to Joseph. "What has Roland said to you?"

"I think that PI is still looking for you."

"If and when they find me, what can they do?" She shaded her eyes with her hand. "I mean, this detective can't take me against my will. That's against the law, isn't it?"

"I would think so. But I heard him say something to the PI that you're under a doctor's care, and he's your doctor."

Luana shook her head in frustration. "How could he do this to me?"

"I wouldn't be surprised if he's having me tailed." He toweled off and pushed a wide-brim hat onto his head. "I was careful to make sure no one followed me, but I think it's in your best interest if we don't see each other for a while."

"This is insane. I'm not afraid of him; this private detective would have to drag me out of here kicking and screaming."

"I wouldn't underestimate Roland. You remember what I told you about Alana? She must have been desperate to have staged such an elaborate escape."

"Maybe you're right," Luana curled her toes in the hot sand. "I'll be careful."

"Okay, kiddo," Joseph slapped her on the shoulder, "now how about some food? All that surfing has left me starving."

Luana hopped up. "I'll take you to the Beach Shack—where I work."

"You're not sick of that place? Isn't eating there like a busman's holiday?"

"I've only been there a week!"

Luana tied a sarong around her waist, Joseph threw on a big Hawaiian print shirt over his shorts and they walked back to the Beach Shack. They chose a table outside on the deck under a palm tree, where the cool breeze and shade provided welcome relief from the afternoon sun.

Joseph eyed their waitress after she took their order and walked away in her grass skirt and goofy straw crown. "Don't tell me you have to wear that?"

Luana laughed. "Hey it's not too bad—I forgot that I looked like such a fool after the first hour. This place really gets busy. No time to worry about appearances."

When they had their drinks, Joseph held up his beer bottle. "Cheers, kiddo. To your new life."

"Yup, my new life." She took a sip of the iced tea. "I just wish I knew more about my old one."

* * *

The next morning at work, one of her customers didn't seem as friendly and easy-going as the other guests. He wore dark sunglasses, which he left on when Luana approached his table to ask what he'd like to order. When he stared at her for several seconds before responding, she felt a chill go down her spine.

"I'm not too hungry," the man said. "Just a cup of coffee."

"I'll be right back." Luana felt his eyes on her as she walked away, and when she returned, her hand shook when she placed the cup on the table.

"What's your name?" he asked.

"Helen," Luana said, following her instincts. "What's yours?"

"Bob." He sipped his coffee. "Where you from?"

It wasn't unusual for customers to ask where the staff was from. After all, people from all around the world worked at the resort.

"I'm from Colorado. Denver."

"What brought you out here?"

"The surfing. What else?" She flashed a wide smile to hide her nervousness. "Anything else I can get you? I need to run to the kitchen to get an order out."

"Take your time," he folded his arms in front of his chest. "I'll be here for a while."

Luana took measured steps away from the table, though she felt like running. But instead of going to the kitchen, she went straight to Mark's office. He was on the phone, and gestured for her to come in.

He hung up and looked at Luana. "Are you okay? You don't look so well."

"I need to talk to you." She held her hands in tight fists to keep them from shaking and brought them up to her chin.

"Here." He pulled out a chair for her. "Sit down. What's going on?"

"I think I'm being followed." Luana sank into the chair, her legs shaking.

"What are you talking about?"

Luana quickly explained how she had washed ashore onto Dr. Schmidt's property nearly a year before. She told him about her rehabilitation and how Roland ended up trying to rape her.

Mark took her hand into his. "Luana, I'm so sorry. I can see why you're scared to death. But why would you be afraid to tell me? It's not like it was your fault."

"I know it wasn't my fault. It's just that it's so embarrassing to talk about."

"Listen," he said, his bright blue eyes serious. "We haven't known each other long, but I've really taken a liking to you." He tapped her knee. "You stay put and let me wait on the guy."

He grabbed a beach towel from a stack of fresh ones and draped it around her shoulders. "You're shivering. Can I get you some tea?"

"I'll be fine." She looked up at him and smiled. "But thanks. You're a good friend."

Within minutes he returned. "He split," Mark said. "But Andreas said he asked about you. He thought he was some creepy customer who had the hots for you, so he didn't say much, only that you were new."

"Smart boy. I'm glad."

"Yeah—but he'll be back. I'd better find an opening for you at one of the other restaurants."

"But I really like working here."

"And I really like having you here, but it's in your best interest to make yourself scarce. From what you've told me, this guy will be back tomorrow."

Luana brought her knees up to her chest and wrapped the towel tightly around her body. Besides the possibility that Roland was having her followed, she also remembered what Roland had told her about her father. Were the people who killed her parents now hunting her down?

"Sit tight," Mark said. "Andy can take over your tables while I make a few phone calls." He picked up the phone and punched in a number. "Let's just hope there's something else available." Mark put his finger up. "Kirsty. It's Mark at the Beach Shack." He paused. "Luana's working out great. She's a sweet girl—a real hard worker, always on time. But I have a small problem."

He told Kirsty what had just happened, and then there were a lot of 'mm-hms' and head nodding on Mark's end before he said, "Sure, we'll wait here until you give us a call back."

He hung up the phone and ran his hands though his blond hair. "Okay, here's the deal. Kirsty doesn't know of any immediate openings."

Luana frowned.

"But wait." Mark held up his hand. "Usually if an opening occurs in one of the restaurants the manager submits a form to Kirsty. I've done this several times, and I can tell you from experience that the office mail sometimes takes a few days. Don't ask me how it could take two days to get from here," he pointed to his desk, "to there." He pointed in the direction of Kirsty's office. "But Kirsty's going to walk over to each restaurant and personally talk to the managers."

"I still have a chance, then," Luana said. "Let's keep our fingers crossed."

"You're looking better. Why don't you finish your shift and check back with me at the end of the day? Maybe there'll be some news by then."

Luana handed his towel back to him. "You know where to find me if anything happens."

She finished her shift without any problems, but by 2:30 her stomach was in knots. She took off her straw hat and walked into Mark's office. "Any word?"

Mark looked up from a pile of papers and shook his head. "Not yet." He stood up from behind his desk. "Let's go surfing for a few hours. It'll clear your mind, and we can check for messages after."

"Sounds great. I'll see you down by the guard station in a few minutes."

After a quick change and a fast bite to eat, she ran down to the beach. As much as she enjoyed her afternoon surf, this could be her last day. If she had to switch jobs, she might not be so lucky the next time around.

* * *

The note taped to Mark's office door when they returned said only that the two of them should come by Kirsty's office. Without showering and barely drying the seawater and sand out of her hair, Luana wrapped a sarong around her waist and ran over to Kirsty's office with Mark. Luana knocked on the locked door, but no one answered.

She leaned her shoulder against the door. "Now what? I hope she doesn't think we blew her off."

Mark ran his fingers through his wet hair. "I'm sure she's around here somewhere."

"Do you know her home number?" Luana asked.

"Afraid not. But I once ran into her at a bar a few miles up the road. The music's great and the drinks are decent."

"Let's go!"

"This place isn't like Rust's. You need shoes and I need a shirt."

"Then I'll meet you by your car in two minutes. "Luana ran back to her room and grabbed a pair of sandals. She put on a dry pair of khaki shorts and a white linen shirt, and then tied her hair back with a leather shoestring.

Mark had the Rover running and ready by the time she stepped onto the hot black pavement. "It's not far," he said.

The air felt markedly cooler as they sped toward the windward side of the island, even more so as Mark turned off the highway to begin a winding ascent up a steep road.

Luana rubbed her arms to keep warm. "It feels like the temperature just dropped thirty degrees."

"It probably has. I should have warned you." He reached down and pushed a lever under the dashboard. A hot blast of air warmed her legs.

Out the window, Luana watched the fiery orange sun ablaze on the horizon, ready to sink into the ocean.

Mark turned down a gravel road and pointed to a group of wooden buildings clustered together. "This is Kanaka Lodge. A wealthy benefactor built it as a retreat for artists from all over the world to write, paint, sculpt or create music. The locals run the bar and restaurant and musicians staying at the retreat play free five nights a week." He pulled the Rover into the parking lot.

They walked through a courtyard where a copper sculpture of a mermaid sprayed water from her mouth, and then they entered the lodge through a thick, wooden door. When Luana stepped inside, the Pacific Ocean stretched as far as she could see behind two stories of glass windows. On the right side of the lobby a fire roared in a huge stone fireplace. The burning wood popped and a red ember bounced off the stone hearth.

Luana stopped and rubbed her hands together before Mark led her through the back door and down a crushed stone path, following the beat of soulful Samba music to another wooden structure with expansive windows. The place was packed.

They both scanned the room, but couldn't see Kirsty until Luana felt a tap on her shoulder. She whirled around. "We've found you!"

Kirsty smiled. "Mark's a clever one. I'm not surprised he tracked me down." She glanced over to him. "Let's find a place to sit."

They walked away from the band members, their steel drums, and slide guitars to a round table in the corner.

Kirsty held up her half-empty bottle of beer. "Would you like anything?"

They both shook their heads.

"Okay, Luana, I know that you eventually want to cook and not wait tables, so here's what I came up with. There's an opening in our banquet hall."

"That's fantastic."

"It's not much—just a prep cook, and the work's not all that creative, but at least it's something."

"I don't care," Luana said. "I'll take it!"

"Not so fast." Kirsty sipped her beer. "This time you'll have to interview with somebody other than me. The head chef is Jacques de Latour, and he's a real stickler. He's trained in the classic French tradition. Sauces, knife work, the whole enchilada."

"Enchilada?" Luana smiled. "I didn't know that was French."

"Very funny. Your interview's tomorrow morning."

"I'll be there." She forced a note of enthusiasm into her voice, but whom was she fooling? She had no culinary training whatsoever, and not even enough time to ask Joseph for a crash course. Sure, she was creative and knew how to cook a healthy, tasty meal, but could she reduce a sauce to perfection, bake a soufflé that wouldn't collapse on the first try or whip up a fluffy *omelette aux fine herbs*? No way. She was in way over her head.

Twenty-Two

$\mathcal{L}$uana arrived at her job interview five minutes early and walked into a clean, 1500 square foot stainless steel room. She couldn't imagine a hospital operating room any more sterile than this kitchen. The only splash of color came from copper pots that hung from a black iron bar above the countertop, secured to the bar by plastic-coated steel cords and metal locks.

At 6 a.m. on the dot, Chef Jacques de Latour pushed through the swinging doors in a starched, white chef's coat and a white toque.

"Bonjour, Mademoiselle," he said in a thick French accent. "And you are?" He raised his eyebrows.

"Luana Kramer. Nice to meet you."

Jacques skipped the formalities. "Let's get to work." He handed her a white apron that she put over her head and tied around her waist. From his pocket, Jacques pulled a key and began unlocking the steel cords wrapped around copper pans. "These pans are worth a fortune. Before bicycle locks, several went missing each month." He walked his thick fingers along the steel countertop. "Did they walk away on their own? *Non!*" His voice boomed and his face reddened. "They were stolen. I will not tolerate theft in my kitchen!"

He pulled down a saucepan, a sauté pan and a large pot.

Luana didn't know the name of the large pot, but she had used a similar one many times to boil water for pasta.

From a locked drawer Jacques removed several knives and placed them against a magnetized strip above the countertop. "All right, Miss Kramer," he boomed. "Let me see you poach an egg."

She eyed the gas stove, grateful that it was similar to the one in Roland's kitchen. Poaching an egg should be easy enough. She filled the small saucepan with cold water and placed it over the flame. She added salt to the water just as Joseph had taught her. She wanted to impress Jacques by cracking the egg with one hand as she'd seen Joseph do, but she had never really mastered that skill, so she played it safe and used both hands. She tapped the egg against the side of a small bowl and let it drop. Just as she was about to slide the egg into the boiling water, she remembered a little trick that Joseph had taught her: add a small amount of vinegar to the boiling water to keep the egg whites from running.

"Where can I find some vinegar?" she asked Jacques.

He smiled at her. "Très bien, mademoiselle." He pointed in the direction of the pantry. "You'll find all the vinegar and an assortment of oils over there."

Luana added a splash of vinegar, and then gently slid the egg into the boiling water. When the white was solid, she removed the egg with a slotted spoon and let the excess water drip back into the pot. She turned off the gas flame and placed the perfectly poached egg onto a plate.

She took a deep breath and looked up at Jacques. "What's next?"

"Next, mademoiselle, I'd like you to make the staple of all French cuisine—the *mire poix*."

Mire poix. That stumped her. *Think, think,* she silently told herself. She had in front of her several knives, a cutting board, two more pots, a pile of vegetables, several herbs, a block of butter, a chicken carcass, a slab of bacon and a bottle of olive oil.

Jacques had said that *mire poix* was the staple of French cooking, so he likely didn't want her to fry bacon. But once when she lived on the estate and a group of businessmen from New Orleans had flown in for a week of meetings with Roland, Joseph had asked her to chop an onion, celery and a green bell pepper for a jambalaya he was preparing for the evening meal. He had told her that those three ingredients, known as the 'holy trinity,' were the staple of all Cajun cooking. Cajun cooking was a spicy, loosely related cousin to French cooking, so her best guess was that she should chop some of the vegetables piled in front of her.

She had an onion, several stalks of celery but not a green bell pepper. She also saw a bunch of Italian parsley and some carrots. Her hunch was to go with the onion and celery and then choose between the parsley and carrots. She went with the carrots and hoped for the best.

She gathered her vegetables, rinsed them under cold water and patted them dry with a kitchen towel. She pulled a sturdy chopping knife from the magnetized strip above the countertop. Joseph had told her to always sharpen her knives before she started chopping, so she asked Jacques where they kept their knife sharpener. When he pointed to the metal sharpener secured to the wall, she stroked the blade against the stone a few times, making a sound like fingernails on a chalkboard, and then swiped the knife with a butcher's steel. She grabbed a big white onion, peeled its skin, and then chopped off the ends. With careful smooth strokes, she chopped the onion first horizontally and then vertically. In less than sixty seconds she had a perfectly diced onion. She moved on to the carrots and celery, and chopped each into tiny cubes until she had a colorful pile of uniformly diced vegetables.

Next she placed a sauté pan over a low flame. Now she had to choose between using olive oil or butter to sauté the vegetables. If this were an Italian restaurant, she would have chosen olive oil, but since the head chef was French, she sliced a big chunk of butter off the brick and dropped it into the pan. It melted in seconds. She slid the mound of vegetables from the cutting board with the back of her knife into the simmering butter and then gently stirred the mixture with a wooden spoon. She looked up at Jacques to see any type of reaction.

He nodded and smiled slightly. "You're doing very well, Mademoiselle."

Luana let out a huge sigh of relief. She was actually bluffing her way through this interview.

"Now," Jacques said, "I'd like you to make a clear chicken stock."

That explained the nasty looking chicken carcass sitting on the countertop.

She filled the large pot with water, salted the water, and placed the pot over a high flame. As she waited for the water to boil, she gathered the remainder of the carrots and celery that she had almost discarded after making her *mire poix*. She asked Jacques where she might find some cheesecloth to make a small *bouquet garni* with some bay leaves, thyme and parsley. He showed her the cupboard where they kept supplies like butcher string, cheesecloth and pastry bags. She ripped a small amount of cheesecloth from the roll and wrapped her herbs with it.

Into the water went the vegetables, the bundle of aromatic herbs and the chicken carcass. She added black pepper and covered the pot. Now all she had to do was wait for the water to come to a boil. While doing so, she started to tidy up her cooking surface.

Jacques, who had barely spoken to her since she began her interview, said, "I see one problem, Mademoiselle."

Luana stopped wiping the counter and looked up at him.

"You forgot to remove the giblets from the carcass. Your stock will be cloudy and useless!"

Luana slumped against the counter. "Is it too late to take them out?"

"Technically, yes," Jacques answered. "But, we can use the stock to make soup for the staff lunch, so I think it's salvageable."

So she might still be in the running. Luana lifted the top off the pot and pulled the carcass from the water with large tongs. She set it on a platter and removed the sack of giblets with her hands. She nearly burnt her fingers, but she didn't care.

"Do you want me to save the giblets for gravy?" she asked.

"Of course! We don't waste anything in my kitchen."

She placed the cleaned carcass back into the water and waited for it to boil. After a few minutes, a thick brown, bubbly liquid gathered on the top. She skimmed off the scum and dumped it down the drain. She reduced the flame, covered the pot and let the stock simmer.

"So—did I redeem myself?" she asked Jacques.

"Just barely," he said, deadpan. He paused for effect and then said, "You're hired. And you will start tomorrow."

Wow—she had pulled it off. She could hardly wait to call Joseph and Mark. "Thank you so much. I thought I blew it after that carcass fiasco."

"We all make mistakes." He held up his thick, pink index finger. "And I guarantee that you'll never make that one again."

"I am certain I won't!" She checked the stockpot, still simmering. "Now I have a question for you." She looked over to the countertop. "What's the bacon for?"

"Our breakfast, of course!" Jacques said. "I'm starving, aren't you?"

She grinned at him. "I'll fry us up some bacon and eggs. And what about toast?"

"You read my mind."

During breakfast, Luana learned that Jacques had arrived in the United States from France two years ago. He worked in New York where he met a girl who wanted to move to Los Angeles. Smitten with her, he followed her out to California. When they broke up, he kept moving west. He said his next stop would be Hong Kong.

* * *

After breakfast, Luana called Mark to tell him the good news.

"Luana—that's fantastic! I knew you could do it."

"I didn't have as much confidence in myself as you did. I almost lost my chance when I botched a chicken stock."

"What are your hours?"

"Same as before. "I'll be helping with breakfast and lunch."

"Cool—so we can still go surfing in the afternoon."

"For sure," she said. "Same place, same time. Right now I'm off to thank Kirsty."

She stopped cold as she approached Kirsty's office and saw her talking to the same man who had come to the Beach Shack. She couldn't hear what Kirsty was saying, but she saw her throw her hands up in the air and then shake her head as if frustrated. Luana stayed back, where she would not draw their attention.

Kirsty held a large key, and motioned the man to follow her down the path that led to the employee dormitories. She unlocked the front door to the dorms, and Luana's heart sank—Kirsty had led him right to her. She crouched behind a palm tree and waited until they emerged from the building and parted ways, he toward the parking lot and Kirsty back toward her office, and Luana. Unsure what to do, Luana remained motionless. She waited by the palm tree until Kirsty passed her. But then Kirsty turned around. She had spotted her.

"Luana, what are you doing?"

"I saw you walk into the dorms with that man." Luana stepped out from behind the tree.

Kirsty held out her hand to her. "Luana let me explain."

"What's going on? I'm frightened."

"As you should be," Kirsty said. "That man means business. He didn't believe one word of that 'Helen from Denver' line you fed him. He thought he could pump some information from me, so he asked to see your employment file, but I told him that was confidential. When I didn't show it to him, he actually threatened me. I told him that I was just as angry as he was. I said that you walked off the job without any notice, and left me without a waitress on a busy Friday morning. He didn't believe me, so I offered to show him. I knew that a girl left yesterday. I said I'd show him your room, but of course I showed him the other girl's."

Relief flooded through Luana. "I don't understand why you're so good to me. I barely know you and you've gone out on a limb twice for me."

Kirsty put her arm around her shoulder. "Let's grab a cup of coffee?"

"Sure." As they walked, Luana told her that she got the job as a prep cook.

"Congratulations! Jacques is a tough cookie, but if you can take the heat you'll learn a lot from him."

At the coffee bar, Kirsty ordered them each a cup.

Luana sat down on a stool. "So, seriously, Kirsty, why are you so good to me?"

"For starters, I like you. Also, it's important to Joseph. He told you that we've known each other for a long time?"

"About thirty years."

"Actually over thirty years." Their coffee arrived and Kirsty took a long sip. "We were married once. It was a long time ago, but we were very much in love."

"What happened?" Luana swallowed her surprise. "It still seems like the two of you really care about each other."

"We do. Very much. We had a child together. A beautiful baby girl." Tears welled up in her eyes. "She strangled in her crib when she was less than a year old."

"Oh my God, Kirsty. I'm so sorry. What happened?"

"The mobile above her bed must have fallen down in the night and wrapped around her neck. When we woke up in the morning, she was dead." Her voice was flat and sad.

Luana wrapped her arms around Kirsty and hugged until Kirsty pulled away. "I can't even imagine the pain you're feeling."

Kirsty shook her head. "The horrible memory never goes away. Never." She wiped her eyes with a napkin. "It's difficult for a marriage to survive a tragedy like that. We were both very young. Joseph turned to dope and I turned to booze. We didn't stand a chance."

"Yes, but I saw the way he smiled at you and the way you hugged him last week in front of your office."

"We've grown up a lot, Luana. And we've moved on." She wiped her nose with the napkin. "Anyway, he still means a lot to me and I'd do anything to help him out. So when he called me and told me your situation, I didn't hesitate for a second."

"I've been wanting to call Joseph and tell him the good news but I'm afraid to call Roland's house."

"I'll call him for you."

"But don't tell him over the phone," Luana said. "Joseph thinks the PI might tap the phone."

"Good point." Kirsty said. "I'll suggest we meet for lunch and tell him then." Luana smiled. "Even better!"

* * *

Luana did a load of laundry and cleaned her room before she met Mark at the beach. When he saw her he greeted her with a big grin. "Congratulations! Let's go out tonight to celebrate."

Luana held up her finger. "But promise me, Mark. It's my treat."

"You don't have to do that," he set his hand on her shoulder. "I know that you haven't been working long, and I know how much I pay you."

"No, seriously. It's my treat and I won't have it any other way."

"Whatever you say. For now, let's get these boards ready." While he waxed his board, Luana did the same with the Local Motion board she had been borrowing since she began surfing with Mark.

When both boards were thickly covered, Mark said, "Let's hit it!"

Over the past weeks Luana had mastered the 'drop,' a move surfers made just as the wave above them was about to crumble, so when the wave pitched above her head, she dropped her stance about a foot, until she could almost touch the board with her left hand. Mark had set her up with an ankle strap on her left foot, the 'goofy foot' in surfer's parlance. If she fell, the board wouldn't get too far away from her. She even rode the pipe. The wave wasn't like the famous Banzai pipe off Oahu, which killed several surfers each year, but it was huge enough for Luana, and it gave her the ride of her life. The feeling of her hand skimming the smooth wall of water behind her made her feel like Aphrodite, goddess of the sea.

She got barreled a few times but kept getting up for more. At one point, just as she thought she would hit the perfect wave, the front of her board submerged and she was thrown over the top of the wave. The rush felt like she could have been cascading down the Niagara Falls.

After the last of two wild waves, Luana and Mark rested on their boards between sets.

"I think you're ready for the Banyan, girl."

"What's the Banyan?"

"It's the best surfing on the Island." Mark swept his wet hair out of his eyes. "We had a great day today, but I think you're ready to move on."

"If you say so," Luana said. "I'm up to the challenge."

They ate at Rust's that night, and when the check came, Luana picked it up and gaped at it. "Twenty dollars for two great dinners, two cold beers and two Kahluas and creams for dessert? Wow."

"True, but don't forget, he catches his own fish and pays no rent."

And the place was always packed, Luana thought. *Not a bad business.*

Twenty-Three

*L*uana's first day of work was busier than she'd ever imagined. From the minute she arrived at six in the morning until the time she put her knife down at half past two in the afternoon, she remained hunched over the countertop chopping garlic, onions, celery, carrots, tomatoes and parsley. Her job was to prepare the *mis en place* for the line chef. The chef explained that this meant 'everything in place.' In other words, he needed all the vegetables to be cut and placed in bowls so that when he prepared a dish he needed only to reach for the ingredients from the bowls and throw them into the sauté pan.

She had cut so many vegetable that she had to break at least three times to sharpen her knife. For the first hour her eyes watered and stung fiercely from all the onions she sliced. Then one of her coworkers, working next to her, noticed the tears streaming down her face. He told her to place a piece of bread between her lips while cutting the onion. The bread served as a barrier that prevented the onion gas from contacting her eyes. She felt like a geek, but after wearing a straw wreath on her head and a grass skirt at her last job, she thought a piece of bread between her lips couldn't be much worse.

The other cooks told her that this pace was normal, not even a break for lunch. They also told her that although the bread between her lips deflected the odorous onion gas, no real cook would ever do that. They had played a little joke on her, an initiation that all new line chefs in their kitchen went through. The young man who had told her about the bread taught her how to really cut an onion so her eyes didn't water: use a sharp knife and leave the root of the onion in place while slicing.

As much as Luana liked her new co-workers, she missed interacting with customers. But if being cooped up in a hot kitchen all day was the sacrifice required to become a chef and open a restaurant of her own someday, she wouldn't complain.

At the end of the day, she threw her soiled white apron in the laundry basket, but couldn't throw away the smell on her hands. They reeked of garlic and onions. Soap and water wouldn't be enough to deodorize her fingers, so she cut a lemon in half and rubbed it onto her hands. It didn't eliminate the smell, but it helped.

* * *

On the drive to the Banyan, located within the White Sands Beach County Park, and some of the gnarliest surfing on the island, Mark explained that locals referred to the beach as the 'Magic Sands' or 'Disappearing Sands' because during the months of March and April rising waves swallowed the white sand beach entirely. Just north of the public beach was Banyan Bay, one of the few beaches with a lifeguard on duty. And for good reason: the surf was some of the roughest Luana had seen.

Mark noticed her playing with the leather string wrapped around her wrist. "Everyone's nervous the first time, but you gotta give it a try. It'll be the rush of your life, but if you feel like you're in over your head, don't push it."

They parked on the rocky part of the beach and unloaded their boards. Mark left the longer board in the truck and pulled out a shorter one.

"What's with that?" Luana asked.

"You can't surf these waves with the long board. Too choppy."

"But I've never even stood on a short board."

"If anyone can do it on the first try, you can." He set her board down on the rocks, and then heaved his board out from the back of the truck. "You're a natural, Luana. Your coordination and sense of balance are the best I've ever seen." He wiped some sweat off his forehead. "Are you sure you weren't a professional surfer in your previous life?"

She hadn't considered her previous life in a while. "I'm not sure what I was before my accident, but I doubt I lived any better than I am now." She looked out to the crashing waves. "A job, free room and board, and the opportunity to surf every afternoon—how much better can it get?"

Out in the ocean, she slammed against the rocks a few times. The final time she took a spill against them, she looked down at her stinging knee and saw it bleeding.

"Let's get that bandaged up and call it a day," Mark said.

"No, I'm fine, let's keep going." The saltwater stung a little, but she wasn't in pain.

"You're bleeding quite a bit. You wouldn't want to attract any sharks, would you?"

"Sharks! Let's get outta here!"

Mark carried her board out of the water, and instead of dropping her off in the parking lot, as he usually did, he helped her back to her room. "I used to live here," he said. "I know where the first aid kit is stored."

When Luana limped down the hallway, and opened the door to her room, she noticed immediately that the sliding glass door and screen were wide open. The wind had blown bits and pieces of paper off her desk and had even knocked over a lamp. She always kept the screen door closed and locked even when the glass door remained open. The hair on the back of her neck bristled.

"Mark," she said. "Someone's been in here."

"Why do you say that?" He placed the lamp upright on the desk. "The wind caused this mess."

"I know the wind did all this," she swept her arm in front of her, "but I specifically remember locking the screen door and closing the glass door. It was windy this morning and it looked like a storm was coming." She sat down on her bed and placed a washcloth over her bleeding knee. "I promise you. They were both locked when I left."

He looked around the room. "Can you tell if anything is missing?"

"Not yet. But what would someone want to steal from me? I don't own anything besides a few bathing suits and the basics in my bathroom."

"Why don't you take a look around while I get you some antibiotics and Band-Aids?"

Luana sat on her bed while Mark fetched the First Aid kit. Nothing was taken, but the intrusion meant that Roland's PI didn't believe Kirsty, and he didn't believe that she had gone to San Diego.

Mark returned and squirted Bactine on her wound. He dabbed it with gauze, and then placed a large, square Band-Aid over the cut.

"You'll be perfect in the morning."

"Thanks, but I'm pretty scared. I have a feeling that Roland's PI won't give up until he finds me."

"Well, maybe it's time for you to look for another place," he said. "We eventually all move out of these dorms. They're set up to help employees who aren't locals get established."

"You're probably right, but I sure liked the idea of not paying rent."

"Yeah we all did, but they kick you out after a year anyway."

"Kirsty didn't tell me that."

"She probably forgot to mention it. But trust me, it'll happen. The resort is constantly turning people over, and they need these rooms for the new hires."

"Where do you live?"

Mark sat down on her desk chair. "Not far from here. I can't say that it's the best neighborhood in town, and I have a slob for a roommate, but the rent's cheap and the place isn't too run down."

"I guess I'll start looking tomorrow."

"If you'd like, you can stay with me at my place tonight, and I'll show you around tomorrow. I know you're scared."

"That's sweet, but I'll be fine." She wasn't sure of that, but she didn't want to become reliant on anyone, either.

Mark left without pushing the issue, and Luana went to bed early, waking for every animal sound and gust of wind.

* * *

Instead of surfing the next afternoon, Mark and Luana toured around the island in search of 'for rent' signs. She couldn't afford much per month, so they stuck with neighborhoods in less desirable areas. She didn't want a roommate, so the only thing in her price range was a dark, musty studio apartment above a garage, down the street from a liquor store and a check cashing facility. The dreariness of the surroundings brought back unpleasant memories of living above Rick's gas station. She wanted to be reminded of the ocean and lush green foliage every day.

"That place was pretty dismal," Luana said, as they left the unit and walked down the rickety stairs. "I think I need to keep looking."

"You're right, it was depressing, but I think we've exhausted all the possibilities for tonight. I'll sleep on the floor in your room, if you're comfortable with that."

"I can't ask you to sleep on the floor. I made it through last night, and I'm sure I'll make it through another night."

"I'm sorry, Luana, but I insist. That flimsy lock on the door to the patio could be broken with a pair of tweezers."

"It could be months before I find a new place. Let's drive to the hardware store and I'll buy a deadbolt."

They pulled up to the Ace hardware store, located in an ugly strip mall. With all the natural beauty on the island, Luana couldn't understand why the shopping centers had to be paved with blacktop and devoid of vegetation. She looked for some sign of landscaping as Mark pulled into a parking space. Then she yelped and slid down in her seat.

Mark slammed on the brakes. "What's wrong?"

Luana pointed in front of her. Sitting at the coffee shop next to the hardware store, the man Luana had seen at the Beach Shack sipped a cup of coffee and talked on his cell phone.

Mark recognized him too. He threw the truck into reverse and sped away.

Twenty-Four

Luana borrowed Mark's truck every afternoon after increasingly anxious nights in the dorm, and spent the hours after work looking for a place to live. As days passed, she found nothing. The ads in the papers always over-promised and under-delivered.

One ad took her to a rundown apartment next to a Laundromat and a convenience store with bars on the windows. On the sidewalk, a group of men in dirty white tee shirts smoked and loitered. This was not the Hawaii she had grown to love. Where was the beautiful scent of plumeria that greeted her every morning when she stepped out of her dorm room? Where was the squawking sound of the black Corvid that woke her at dawn? And, where was the ocean? The only body of water in sight was a large puddle that had formed under a leaking air conditioning unit.

One afternoon she drove about a mile away toward the ocean and stopped for a cup of coffee at a local, family-run café. At the table next to her, an elderly Hawaiian woman read the paper and sipped some coffee.

She looked up from her paper at Luana. "Rough day?"

"I've had worse, but I have to say, I'm pretty demoralized."

The woman introduced herself as Mrs. Kamakea, and asked Luana to join her.

Mrs. Kamakea's deeply lined face bore the happy expression lines of a good life, rather than a hard, miserable one, so Luana shifted seats and chatted until Mrs. Kamakea brought out pictures of her children and grandchildren.

"Do you have any children?" she asked.

"Oh my goodness, no!" Luana said. "I'm too young for that!"

"Times sure have changed, haven't they? I got married at nineteen and had my first baby at twenty." She sighed and took a sip of her coffee. "My last grandchild just got married. Everyone's gone now."

"Do you mean that they all lived with you?"

"My grandchildren, no. But after college they used my little guest cottage until they found a place of their own."

"Really? Is there any chance you'd like to rent that guest cottage of yours?"

"Oh my," Mrs. Kamakea said, "I haven't even thought about it."

"I live by myself and have a good job. If you think renting may be an option for you, please let me know. I can be reached at the Kea Lani."

Mrs. Kamakea's face broke into a large smile. "My husband and I had our wedding reception there. It was such a beautiful evening. Even though it was sixty years ago, I remember it like yesterday."

"I'm a cook there. Please, come again for dinner with your husband. I guarantee the food will be better than you remembered!"

"Thank you, dear, but my husband passed away several years ago."

"I'm sorry to hear that."

"No need to be sorry. We had a wonderful life together and fifty-five years of marriage."

"Fifty-five years. That's quite an accomplishment. I hope I'm that fortunate one day."

"I don't think of it as an accomplishment, just a journey, with many ups and downs." She shook her head. "Kids these days don't have the fortitude to stick through the bad times. I wish they would."

Luana set down her coffee cup. "Where do you live, Mrs. Kamakea?"

"In Kailua Kona. Not one of those mansions on the water, but a nice house a bit inland."

Luana and Mark had driven through this ocean-side community and she had noticed the stunning homes lining the waterfront. "I'd love to see your place if you'd like to rent it."

"Oh why not? You seem like a lovely girl and the extra money couldn't hurt. The location is good, but the place needs a new coat of paint and new carpeting. Other than that it's in good condition."

Luana paid for both coffees and followed Mrs. Kamakea to a cluster of small neat bungalows a few blocks from the ocean. Mrs. Kamakea's house was painted a light yellow. Bright fuchsia bougainvillea crawled up the side of the house, and a mature palm tree shaded the lawn and front porch. On the porch, two white wicker chairs flanked a matching round table.

Luana followed Mrs. Kamakea around to the back of the house. The paint on the cottage, as Mrs. Kamakea had warned, was chipped and faded, but a gorgeous, overgrown Bella Donna plant framed the doorway. Luana felt as if she had walked into a beautiful oil painting come alive. She even smelled the sweet fragrance of a plumeria. She couldn't see the ocean, but she could hear it and smell the salt in the air; that was good enough for her.

The place was dusty, the carpeting worn, and the kitchen small, but a week of painting and cleaning would make it perfect.

"I love it," Luana said. "When can I move in?"

"As soon as I run a credit check."

Luana's heart sank. She didn't have credit—good or bad. "I'll be honest with you, Mrs. Kamakea," Luana said. "I don't have any credit. I've never had a credit card, car payments or anything."

Mrs. Kamakea didn't look pleased.

"What I do have, is a secure job and very solid references."

Mrs. Kamakea smiled. "Why don't you give me their phone numbers and I'll call them tomorrow."

"No problem." Luana ruffled through her straw bag looking for a pen and paper.

"Come back to my house and sit down," Mrs. Kamakea said. "You can give me their numbers after I make us some iced tea."

Mrs. Kamakea's home was small but tidy. Pictures of her children and grandchildren covered the walls and every available surface space. A large framed, black and white photo of her husband, dressed in a soldier's uniform, sat prominently on a small upright piano.

Mrs. Kamakea picked up the photo. "He flew during World War II and was awarded a medal of honor. We are all very proud of him." She still wore her wedding ring, a thin gold band.

Mrs. Kamakea went into the kitchen and returned with a pitcher of iced tea and small notepad and pencil. "Here, dear." She handed Luana the pad. "Write the names of your employers and their numbers in my notebook."

Luana flipped through several pages filled with notes written in Hawaiian, a written language seldom used. She wrote down the names of all her friends, employers and coworkers who had been so supportive. Then she set the pad on the table and hoped for the best.

Twenty-Five

$\mathcal{A}$ week after Luana first saw Mrs. Kamakea's charming guest cottage, she received the call saying it was hers. Luana rushed over to the Beach Shack to tell Mark.

"I found a place!"

"That's good news," Mark said. "Where is it?"

"Remember when we drove along the water through Kailua? It's a bit inland from there. I can't believe how lucky I am."

"C'mon, Luana, it wasn't luck at all. It was meant to be."

"In a few weeks, the place will be ready for guests and I'll have a party. I want you to be the guest of honor."

"What are you talking about? Why should I be the guest of honor?"

"It's the least I can do to thank you for everything that you've done for me, including letting me borrow your car."

"Luana, it was nothing."

Luana held up her hand. "I want you to bring all your surfing buddies. It would be fun to finally meet some of them."

He smiled. "If you insist."

* * *

Each day after work, Luana sanded, scoured and painted. She pulled up a corner of the ugly brown carpet, and underneath found a beautiful hardwood floor. She kept pulling at the rug until she had removed at least half of it, enough to see that the floor was in good condition. She only needed to clean it and apply a coat of varnish.

With Mark's help and the use of his truck they spent the weekend foraging local garage sales until she found a sofa, coffee table and bed, all she really needed. She could hardly wait to sleep in her new house.

Buried under a stack of boxes in the back of one of the garages, Luana uncovered some brightly colored Fiesta Ware pottery. The seller hadn't planned to sell the set, but after a few minutes of negotiation, Luana persuaded her to part with the entire set of plates and several serving platters and large bowls. Whether or not the pottery was from the original 1930s collection, Luana loved the colors, each piece cobalt blue, red-orange or yellow. She also bought a beat-up red bike to ride to and from work.

She wanted to invite Joseph to the party she had planned for Saturday night, but Kirsty warned her that it would be too risky.

"I mentioned it to him," Kirsty said, "but he was emphatic about not jeopardizing your new living arrangements."

Reluctantly Luana agreed that he was right. She had spent so much time finding her new place and fixing it up, the last thing she wanted was to get chased out of it.

On her Saturday off, she spent the day preparing for the party. She cut fresh flowers from her garden, arranged them in coffee cans and milk bottles, and placed them around the cottage. She positioned small candles, all primary colors like her Fiesta Ware, on her coffee table and on her kitchen countertop.

Mrs. Kamakea let her borrow her barbeque, and Luana grilled fish she had purchased fresh at the market that morning. She brushed the fish with olive oil and garnished it with leafy green Italian parsley and bright yellow lemons. She seasoned grilled vegetables with freshly picked rosemary and lemon thyme from the small herb garden she had planted for herself and Mrs. Kamakea. For a salad, she topped pineapple, mango and papaya with a creamy yogurt and honey sauce, and a dash of chopped mint.

Mrs. Kamakea lent her a small garden table, which Luana moved into her kitchen so she had somewhere to put all the food. She garnished her platters of cooked fish with edible flowers and vegetables, then made a big batch of fresh mango salsa and put it into a red Fiesta bowl. In a large blue bowl she emptied a bag of tortilla chips, made a pitcher of lemonade from lemons picked from a tree in the back yard, and stocked her refrigerator with a case of Primo beer.

Minutes after her shower, with her hair still soaking wet, the doorbell rang. She threw on a terry cloth bathrobe and opened the door to Mark. Next to him stood one of the most gorgeous men she had ever laid eyes on. Of mixed heritage, either Japanese or Hawaiian, his eyes and hair were jet black; his skin was smooth and the color of creamy cocoa. He stood well over six feet tall and his broad shoulders filled the doorway.

Mark kissed her cheek. "I can see you've spent all day primping for your party."

"Very funny." Luana tightened the belt around her robe. She turned to the exquisite man standing in her doorway and extended her hand. "Hi, I'm Luana."

"I'm Kahanai," he said, his grip firm and strong.

"Please," she stepped away from the entrance. "Come in and help yourself to a drink from the fridge. I'll be out in two minutes."

She closed the door to her bedroom and quickly threw on a skirt and a tank top, towel dried her hair and rubbed lotion into her skin. When she emerged from her room, Mark and Kahanai leaned against her kitchen counter drinking beer.

"We have a surprise for you Luana." Kahanai set his beer can on the counter. "I'll be right back."

Luana put her hand on her hip. "Okay, Mark, what are you up to?"

Mark gave her an evil grin. "You'll see."

Luana grabbed a beer for herself and took a sip. "The suspense is killing me."

Mark took Luana's hand and led her through the living room and out the front door into Mrs. Kamakea's backyard, where a band was setting up their equipment on Mrs. Kamakea's lawn.

Luana put her hands to her mouth. "They're from the ranch, that first night we got together with Kirsty. This is awesome! How did you get them to come?"

Mark tilted his chin in Kahanai's direction. "Kahanai knows the guy who runs the retreat, so he asked them."

"But what about Mrs. Kamakea? The poor woman, she'll have a heart attack."

"I've got it covered." Mark placed his hands on her shoulders. "When you said you wanted to have a party, I called her and asked if it would be okay to have a live band. She sounded cool when she called me asking for a reference, so I figured I wouldn't be going out on a limb by asking her. She's so excited that she invited a few of her grandkids."

Luana wrapped her arms around his neck and kissed him on the cheek. "This is the best housewarming present ever!"

When Kahanai went over to talk to the band, Luana asked, "How do you know Kahanai? Have you been friends for a long time?"

"A few years now." Mark looked her straight in the eyes. "He's my boyfriend, Luana."

"Boyfriend? As in *boyfriend*?"

"Yeah, Luana, *boyfriend*."

"I had no idea. Why didn't you tell me sooner?"

"I was going to, but no one knows—and I mean NO ONE. You know how tough the surfing crowd is." Mark shook his head. "I would've been laughed out of the water. No *mahoos* allowed. And also the Kea Lani is as squeaky clean as Disneyland. I'm not sure they would support a gay manager."

"Of course they would. It would be against the law if they didn't."

Mark shook his head. "You're right, but I have a great thing going. I don't want to jeopardize it."

Luana hugged him. "I'm so happy for you, Mark. Everyone deserves to be loved—especially by a hot guy like Kahanai!"

They both laughed and Mark held up his beer can. "I'll drink to that!"

Twenty-Six

Within the year, Jacques, impressed by Luana's work ethic and knife skills, promoted her to the position of line chef. They worked so well together that when Jacques received a promotion out of the banquet facility to become head chef at the resort's elegant, five-star restaurant, he took Luana with him. He requested a name change for the restaurant, from the Blue Marlin to La Poissoniére, and brought his French style of cuisine to the new restaurant.

The kitchen of La Poissoniére was similar to that of the banquet facility, but the dining room was as different as an army mess hall to a grand ballroom. Crystal chandeliers hung from the ceiling and gold-plated mirrors adorned the walls. Fresh flower arrangements, changed daily, were extravagant enough for the wedding of a princess. Only the finest Irish linens, the most delicate bone china and highest grade of lead crystal glasses graced the tables, along with silverware and candlesticks polished to a mirror-like finish. Luana had never seen such a grand room.

The only downside of her new job was that she worked the evening shift, starting at 4 p.m., which meant saying goodbye to afternoon surfing. Luana and Mark had become close friends over the past year, and while they still got together once a week to surf, those fun, carefree days with him came to an end once her career became her primary focus.

Now Luana rode the waves every morning by herself, on a new board of her own. The feeling of her body against the great Pacific empowered her. She made a few friends on the water, people that tended to surf when she did, but this was nothing more than friendly camaraderie, and the locals, known as the *kama'ainas*, stuck together. The indigenous Hawaiians, of Polynesian origin, often big and tough looking physically, formed even tighter groups and did not take well to outsiders—especially a woman. They protected their secret surfing spots as fiercely as they protected their waves. Luana quickly learned that if a group of indigenous surfers waited for the same wave, they would decide amongst themselves who would take it. Even if they knew that Luana had waited for several sets, they'd bully their way onto the wave and ride it home. She also learned that her choice of surfing attire didn't cut it with the indigenous crowd. The black and neon-colored Body Glove bikinis she usually wore were far too up-town for these guys, who favored board shorts and white wife-beaters.

Nevertheless, over the course of her year on the island, the *kama'ainas* befriended her, and even the indigenous Hawaiians began to block for her. If they noticed that Luana hadn't taken a big wave in a while, the guys would call out to each other to hold back and let her ride it home. After a particularly hard day of surfing, one of the men took off his muscle shirt and gave it to Luana. This symbolic gesture proved only the initial step in a partial christening that welcomed her into their group.

The final leg of the christening was a feast of freshly slaughtered octopus on the night of the full moon. As a trained chef, she assumed that the group would grill octopus steaks over an open fire on the beach. Boy, was she wrong.

After work, on the night of the full moon, Luana met her surfing buddies out on a desolate beach during low tide. By midnight several octopuses had washed ashore, and she walked with the men in search of these giant sea creatures. When she spotted one, one of the guys hovered over it and speared it nearly to death. He then picked it up and bit it between the eyes. Still alive, the octopus wrapped its slimy tentacles around the head of the tough Hawaiian and squirted black ink all over him. Luana felt as though she had stepped into a horror film.

"Now that the octopus is dead," he said, "you need to rub the tentacles in the sand to get rid of the mucus membrane."

Luana winced as she picked up a cold, slimy limb and rolled it on the beach. Then she peeled off the outer layer, surprised at how easy the membrane came off.

"Now the meat's ready to slice and eat."

"Raw?"

"Yup, raw."

She fingered the slimy bit of tentacle, looked at it for a few seconds, and then scrunched her nose and put it in her mouth. With a quick gulp she consumed it in one swallow.

The surfer held up a long tentacle. "Welcome to the club."

The raw, gelatinous octopus wasn't the worse thing she had ever tasted, but the ritual of killing and skinning it stood out as the most barbaric act she had experienced. From that moment on, she vowed to never use octopus in any of her dishes.

Twenty-Seven

As a line chef at La Poissoniére, Luana couldn't create her own recipes but had to follow instructions from Jacques or his sous-chef, creating dishes that contained enough eggs, butter and cream to fully clog a customer's arteries for life—after only one meal. Dairy products were not the only culprits. Duck liver, goose pâté, ham hocks and cow brain—euphemistically called 'sweet breads'—ended up one way or another in most entrées. When her friends asked her what she cooked, she told them her specialty was 'heart attack on a plate.'

It wasn't her place to argue with the chef, especially Jacques de Latour, known for throwing a pan at the last line chef who had questioned his menu. One time, the kitchen staff told her, he even threw a knife across the room. He didn't hurt anyone, but cooks learned the hard way that he had a temper and wasn't afraid to let it rip. His kitchen was his kingdom, the cooks his servants, and as with any serfdom, heads would roll.

Still, despite the differences in their cooking styles, Luana appreciated Jacques' attention to detail and the fact that no matter how rushed they were and how much stress they endured, he always put dishes out on time with few returns. Like a five star general, he remained calm under pressure and kept his troops in order.

As soon as she dared, Luana tested some changes. Instead of smothering a delicate piece of fish or exceptional cut of meat with a heavy sauce, she persuaded Jacques to use herb infused olive oil. Although he initially resisted, on sampling one of her sauces, he reluctantly agreed. In culinary terms, the 'proof was in the pudding.'

Diners couldn't get enough of Luana's new recipes, and as a reward, Jacques promoted her to sous-chef.

In one of the many culinary magazines that Luana scoured for ideas, she read an intriguing article about Ali Stone, one of the pioneers of the healthy California cuisine movement. On her two-week vacation Luana flew to Berkeley, California to research this movement and to dine at Ms. Stone's restaurant, Le Poppy, named for California's state flower.

On a warm evening she walked from her hotel to Le Poppy, meandering through the streets of Berkeley, and along Telegraph Avenue with its vintage clothing stores and unique shops. The sidewalks swarmed with people, most of who seemed to be students, all dressed in tee shirts, shorts and the ugliest sandals she had ever seen. She even saw some people wearing socks with them. Luana had never been particularly concerned with fashion, but wearing socks with sandals seemed just plain wrong.

If Hawaii was a laid-back place, the city of Berkeley took the art of doing nothing to a new level. Occasionally she caught a whiff of marijuana wafting from a few cafes and stores, all of them filled with people smoking, chatting and reading the paper, everyone chilled and happy, in no rush to get anywhere. Luana had never been to a big city—not even Honolulu—but she liked this one.

It seemed to offer everything: colorful characters, one-of-a-kind shops, good food, trendy restaurants and fabulous weather. At Amoeba Music she stopped and browsed a vast and varied selection of records, and then spent a half-hour at Blake's on Telegraph, a restaurant/bar/nightclub, where she enjoyed a glass of wine and listened to some great Blues music. Then, already content beyond measure, she continued walking until she recognized the white Victorian house with a red door she had seen in photos. Le Poppy. At 8 p.m., with every table booked, she arrived without a reservation.

The maitre d' suggested the bustling bar, which offered a full menu, so Luana slid onto a bar stool and ordered a glass of Pinot Noir from the bartender. In the leather-bound menu he brought with her glass of wine, a notation next to each item explained its origins— vegetables picked from their own garden, fish caught by local fishermen, and meat and chicken raised by farmers within a fifty-mile radius.

"Everything looks delicious," she said. "Do you have any daily specials?"

"Every dish is special. The menu changes daily and is based on what the local farmers deliver to us in the morning."

Twenty minutes later, along with another glass of Pinot Noir, the bartender presented Luana with a perfectly plated meal, Poulet Poppy, the house specialty.

She had never eaten chicken so flavorful and juicy. She motioned the bartender over. "Is there any way I could meet Chef Stone?"

"She'd be too busy now, but if you come back tomorrow around 11:30, you might catch her before the lunch rush."

"Maybe I should have someone ask, just to make sure it's okay?"

He flashed a grin. "I'll take care of that. Ali's my wife."

"I'll be here for sure." She extended her hand. "Luana Kramer. I'm a chef at the Kea Lani resort in Hawaii and I'd love to pick her brain."

He shook her hand. "I'm Bryan, and I'm sure she'd enjoy meeting you. She loves talking about cooking. It's her passion and her life's work."

"Mine too, but she's a master."

"That she is." Bryan glanced along the bar, packed with people drinking wine and eating olives, crostini and other nibbles off small plates. "Good luck tomorrow."

* * *

Luana woke around dawn and took a run through the leafy University of Berkeley campus. In the cool sunny air, far less humid than in Hawaii, her lungs held more air, and she felt as if she could run for miles. She also had a distinct feeling of déjà vu. The neo classical buildings had an air of familiarity, especially the obelisk clock tower that jetted high into the bright blue sky. She felt pulled toward it but could not explain why.

After her run, she showered and ran a towel through her hair and then downed a glass of orange juice. She threw on a white linen blouse and some khaki pants and walked back to the campus, where she located the registrar's office on a large campus map.

She strolled toward the office, fascinated by the crazy haircuts and colors all around her: lots of black spiky hair for the men and a preponderance of purple stripes for the women, and many more sporting the school colors of blue and yellow.

The gum-chewing young woman behind the registration desk fit right in. Her hair, bleached blonde with black streaks, didn't look out of place at all.

"Hello," Luana said, "I'm wondering if you can help me."

The young woman stopped typing on the computer, and looked up. "I'll do my best."

"I'm trying to learn if anyone by the name of Luana Kramer attended this university any time within the last decade."

Miss black-on-blonde popped a pink bubble. "Give me a half-hour and I'll see what I can find."

Luana checked her watch. Ten-thirty. She would be cutting it close to make her meeting at Le Poppy, but instinct suggested that she might be close to discovering important information about her previous life.

She went to the campus coffee shop to kill time but was too nervous to drink the coffee she had ordered. When the massive campus clock struck eleven, she paid her bill and strode back to the registrar's office.

The girl behind the desk shook her head. "Sorry, no record of a Luana Kramer anytime in the past fifteen years."

Luana frowned. "You're sure?"

The girl nodded and popped another bubble. "The computer doesn't lie. Sorry."

With no time to linger on this small defeat, she left the building, dodging hordes of students—some on bikes, some on roller blades and some just lumbering along carrying tattered canvas book bags. She rushed out to the main road and caught a taxi to Le Poppy.

Twenty-Eight

At precisely 11:30 a.m. Luana walked through the painted red door of the charming bistro, where the smell of baking bread set her stomach growling. She waited in the narrow hall for a minute or two, until a woman emerged from the back of the restaurant. Over her slim frame, the woman wore a white chef's coat with a large red poppy sewn to the lapel.

She smiled when she saw Luana. "Luana? I'm Ali Stone. Bryan said you'd be stopping by."

Judging by her unlined face, incongruous under a mass of gray hair, healthy eating agreed with her. Even so, she looked ten or fifteen years older than Bryan.

"Thank you for meeting me. I know you're busy."

"My pleasure. Bryan said you're a chef at the Kea Lani?"

"I am and I love it. It would be a great place for you and Bryan to come on vacation. We have a high standard of cooking, but I'm trying to persuade the head chef, a serious French man, to alter our menu a bit. I'd like to adopt a lighter style of cuisine at the resort."

"Let's sit down and talk," Ali said. "I was about to indulge in some fresh bread and jam. Would you like some?"

"It's all I've been thinking about since I walked in."

"We do all our baking around this time. It's impossible not to eat it warm and fresh out of the oven."

They sat at a small round table at the corner of the restaurant, next to a window that overlooked the kitchen garden, which burst with salad leaves, vines of sweet peas, rows of carrots, stalks of broccoli and bristly bushes of artichokes. A waiter brought coffee and the warm bread, which was so soft and moist it needed no butter.

Ali looked out the window. "It all starts there, Luana. Without fresh ingredients our dishes would be nothing."

"I noticed that last night. The salad—just a few leaves, some beets and a bit of goat cheese. It tasted heavenly."

"It should have. The greens and vegetables were picked fresh, and the goat cheese we get from a small farm just a few miles from here." Ali took a sip of coffee. "How can I help you Luana?"

"I'd like to study your approach to cooking. I'm trying to use more olive oil, less butter, and of course fewer fatty meats."

"How long will you be in town?" Ali asked.

"At least another week."

"What do you think about a brief apprenticeship here? My goal is to get the whole planet eating this way. I could use the help, and I see a disciple in you. We need to spread the word about the benefits of healthy eating."

"I agree. Food is like medicine. With the right ingredients and proper cooking technique, I think we'd all feel younger and live healthier and happier lives."

"Amen to that! When can you start?"

"How does tonight sound?"

"Perfect. See you at four." Then Ali hesitated. "Actually come at three so we can go into the garden and you can pick the vegetables yourself."

* * *

At 3 p.m., Ali handed Luana a white chef's coat similar to hers, with a smaller red poppy inked on, rather than embroidered.

Contained within stone walls, the garden consisted of several raised beds, also made of stone.

Ali stood between two beds. "What looks good to you?"

"I've never seen so many different varieties of lettuce and greens."

"Go ahead and pick some."

Luana put into her basket light green leaves, dark green spinach, leaves with purple stems, and even leaves entirely purple.

"That's a start," Ali said. "What else?"

"What about carrots, or fennel? Are they ready to harvest now?"

Ali directed her to a patch of fennel. Luana smelled the slight scent of liquorice even before she felt the leaves, as soft as a feather.

"If the liquorice scent is strong," Ali said, "the bulbs will be ready to pick."

Luana ripped off a few leaves and held them to her nose. "It smells like those chewy Panda sweets."

"Go ahead and pick one."

Luana bent down and removed some of the moist soil from around the bulb. When a bit of dirt was clear, she gently yanked on the stalk and pulled the bulb from the ground. She wiped away most of the dirt and turned the large white vegetable over to Ali. "What do you think?"

Ali wiped away more dirt from the bulb and patted it with her finger. She twirled it around in front of her face to have a good look and brought it to her nose. "Looks good, feels good, and smells good. Let's pick some more."

"And carrots?" Luana asked. "Are those in season?"

They walked to the carrot patch and Ali grasped a carrot top. "If you pull the leaves and the carrot comes out easily it's ready to pick. Give it a try."

Luana pulled the leaves but didn't feel the carrot releasing so she moved on to the next one. This time the carrot released without any effort, and out popped a scraggly looking carrot with long white stringy roots.

"It looks a bit bumpy but tastes delicious," Ali said. "These are special baby sweet carrots."

They picked a few and placed them in their baskets.

"Okay, enough vegetables," Ali said. "Let's see what fruit is ripe."

On the other side of the garden miniature strawberries, bright red and about half the size of traditional ones grew under a net to prevent the birds from eating them.

Luana picked one and popped it into her mouth. "As sweet as candy!"

Ali laughed. "They add great color and flavor to salads when we don't have tomatoes. We use whatever's in season. Strawberries in the spring, raspberries in the summer, pears and apples in the fall, and small tangerine slices in the winter. The only rule to healthy flavorful cooking is to keep it simple and only use fresh ingredients."

In the kitchen Luana washed everything they had picked, and then scrubbed the dirt out from under her short nails with the nail brush Ali gave her.

Next they cleaned fish and rinsed the chicken.

"So what's on the menu?" Luana asked.

"You tell me," Ali said.

"A huge salad. Grilled fennel."

Ali brought out a bottle of oil with small garlic cloves in the bottom. "Use this to grill the fennel. The oil's made from olives picked on a ranch in Sonoma county and garlic from our garden. And by the way, this isn't extra virgin olive oil. I only use that on salads, the first press doesn't stand up well to heat."

"Good tip," Luana said. "Now what about the main course?"

"We usually offer three to four dishes. Fish, chicken, beef, lamb, or wild boar. Our supplier just brought in some fabulous cuts of boar."

"Can't say that I've ever cooked boar."

"Then we'll cook some boar, as well as a fish and chicken dish. Start by cutting the tenderloin into medallions. We'll pour some olive oil into a hot skillet and sear them for a few seconds on each side. After they're seared, we'll turn the heat down and simmer them in port."

"Let me guess. The port is made next door."

Ali smiled. "Not quite. It comes from a fabulous little vineyard in Napa."

Then she stepped out of the kitchen and returned with a large box of Grass Valley cherries, which she pitted and reduced into a port sauce. Over the next few hours, all eight burners on the Wolf range were put to use grilling fish, sautéing vegetables and simmering chicken in freshly made stock.

That dinner, and dozens more made that week, formed the basis of Luana's cooking for years to come. As soon as she returned to Hawaii, she obtained approval from the management to plant a kitchen garden. Warm temperatures and consistent sun allowed most vegetables and many fruits to grow all year long, so she made a strong case for growing fresh ingredients. When she implored everyone to use only ingredients picked that morning or bought fresh from the local market where she and Joseph used to shop, her staff jokingly referred to her as the 'produce commondante.' But gradually, the dishes at La Poissoniére took on a fresher, California taste with a distinct Hawaiian twist, maintained by using the fresh mangoes, avocados and coconuts grown in abundance on the island, along with lime juice in the sauces and marinades. Traditional French-style cuisine had begun its fall from favor.

Twenty-Nine

*L*uana's first year cooking with Jacques at La Poissoniére flew by. During that year, she also persuaded the management to build a small, outside veranda for more casual dining and to take advantage of the spectacular views and favorable climate. The patio offered the same menu, with a more casual atmosphere and dress code.

She had stamped her mark on nearly every dish, but when a satisfied customer gushed and asked for the recipe, she brought Jacques out to the table to meet the guests and accept the praise.

Although never one to follow a recipe exactly, she jotted down her menu planning and the ingredients she used each day. At the end of the year she had more than enough material for a cookbook. Too busy cooking to even think about publishing, she saved her recipes in a folder for the future.

One Monday, Jacques asked her to come into work early so he could speak to her privately.

"Bonjour, Luana," he said, as she walked into the kitchen ahead of schedule. "Let's have some tea outside on your veranda."

He had prepared a pitcher of sun tea, and they sat at a white wrought iron table, beneath an awning that blocked the late afternoon sun. The tables had already been set, so Jacques poured tea into tall water glasses. He wiped condensation off his glass with his apron bottom and took a sip. "It should be no surprise that you've been a wonderful addition to my kitchen and to this restaurant."

Luana smiled. "Thank you, Jacques. I've learned a lot from you."

He took a sip of tea. "I asked you here this afternoon to discuss your future."

"My future?" Luana raised an eyebrow.

"Well, your future, and mine. I've been offered a French restaurant in Washington, D.C."

"Congratulations!"

"This California thing," he flicked his wrist, "isn't really my style. I'm a traditionalist, and I think my skills will be better appreciated on the East Coast."

"Are you taking the job?"

"Only if you accept the position as head chef here."

Luana's heart raced. "Oh my God, I had no idea." She took a deep breath. Never in a million years would she have thought that he would offer her this position. "But what about the management? This is their top restaurant. Won't they want to bring in an accredited chef?" Who would have thought that the girl who washed ashore on a beach two years ago would be appointed the head chef of one of the most prestigious restaurants in the islands?

"You've trained under Jacques de Latour! We've already had the meetings, and everyone agrees. The position is yours if you want it."

"Well then of course, Jacques. I accept. I'm honored that you considered me to follow in your footsteps."

"But listen to me, Luana," Jacques placed his thick, pink hand on the table. "I want you to create your own establishment. You have great instincts and a creative mind. The Kea Lani has been very good to me and I wouldn't want to leave this restaurant in anyone's hands except yours."

"Thank you. I wasn't expecting this." She took a sip of the tea and waited a minute to let it all sink in before speaking. "When are you moving to D.C? And when would you like me to start?"

"In three weeks."

* * *

Over the next months, Luana dove into her new job with vigor. She implemented a complete menu change, a monumental task. The kitchen staff adjusted and the restaurant flourished. In time, Luana was awarded a Michelin star, a major coup for her and for the resort. Management threw a huge party in her honor.

It had been years now since any threat from Roland had surfaced. She had begun to let her guard down, and she invited Joseph to her party. When he walked in, Kirsty on his arm, she broke down and cried. It had been so long. Too long. He looked much the same, except for an extra ten pounds and a few more gray hairs.

Mark brought Kahanai to the party, and Ali Stone flew in from California. Jacques de Latour politely declined his invitation, unable to peel himself away from his restaurant in D.C., but in lieu of his presence he sent a beautiful flower arrangement. Luana would remember the evening as one of the most satisfying of her life.

She found time to organize the cookbook she had wanted to write, and discovered that she had accumulated over 200 recipes. On each of her days off, she prepared and staged at least five dishes. She hired Rust to photograph them, and within a few months had a rough draft of her cookbook, *Light and Luscious* by Luana. She dedicated a page to Rust's red beans, rice and fish dish. With the promise of his name and photos in print, he had given up the recipe with the reluctance of a man about to miss a day surfing in twenty-foot waves. The biggest coup of all came when Ali Stone agreed to write the forward and suggested the book to HarperCollins.

They signed Luana, with a first printing of 5,000 copies. Her book—her baby, she called it—would launch in the fall.

* * *

At the Schmidt estate, Dr. Roland Schmidt sat at his desk behind a cloud of cigar

smoke. His PI sat across from him, arms folded across his chest. Roland held a copy of the local newspaper, featuring an article on Luana, and waved it in front of his PI. A picture of Luana in a white chef's apron and toque smiled back at them. "And you're sure she's not involved with anyone?" He dropped the book onto his desk. "The minute she is, I want to know!"

"No problem, sir," the PI said. "Consider it done."

Book Two:
Life Found

Thirty

"And that, Ladies and Gentlemen of the jury, is why this man," Stuart Carson pointed to his client, a distinguished, graying man in his mid-fifties, "a respectable business owner, with a thirty-year untarnished record, had nothing to do with Andrea Rockwell's accidental death."

Stuart's dark brown hair had also grayed a bit at the temples. He wore a crisp navy-blue Armani suit with a yellow tie. He nodded at his client, who looked cool and collected.

In the fifteen years since Kate's accident, Stuart had made a name for himself as a criminal defense attorney and had been promoted to partner at one of Los Angeles' most prestigious law firms. Recently he had become engaged to Vanessa Richardson, a minor L.A. celebrity.

Although he had stayed in touch with Mary, he hadn't seen her in years. Nevertheless, he wanted to tell her about his engagement in person, so he planned a business trip to Chicago and kept an extra day free so he could drive down and visit the woman with whom he shared so many memories of Kate.

His firm always provided a car and driver, but Stuart didn't want to show up in Oakdale, Illinois in a chauffeured, black Lincoln Town Car. Instead, he rented a zippy Ford Mustang convertible. The minute he left the

Loop he put the top down and cranked up the radio. With the wind blowing his hair, he could almost believe he was back in high school. How might his life have turned out differently had Kate lived? Certainly they would have married, and would have had children, probably several by now. They would have had a close circle of friends, with which they would have barbequed and perhaps even vacationed. His chest still ached to think that he would never see Kate again.

After nearly two hours of driving, rows of cornfields appeared all around him, even the nostalgic smell of manure somehow comforting. The road to Mary's farm had more potholes than he remembered, but the pastures looked the same: green and fertile. He felt lighter as he approached Mary's big white farmhouse, everything frozen in time. The house looked as if it had just been painted, and the same old swing on the front porch blew gently in the wind. When he hopped out of the car and walked up the steps, the porch creaked just as it had during his high school years. The green smell of freshly mowed grass, and the warm spring day, reminded him of when he and Kate had begun dating. Memories came flooding back. Kate taking the stairs two at a time. Lemonade on the porch, and Aunt Mary's chocolate chip cookies. How could it all have ended so abruptly?

He rang the bell, and then Mary stood at the door with open arms.

"Stuart, my dear." She hugged him and kissed his cheek. "Please come in."

The house smelled of baking, as if she had read his mind.

"My, it's been a long time," she said. "You're even more handsome than I expected." She stared at him for a few seconds and then touched his temples.

Stuart smiled, showing small creases around his eyes. "I was as surprised as you to see those hairs."

"I think that law firm is working you too hard. But it only makes you look more distinguished."

He hugged her for a few seconds. "I've missed coming down here and spending time with you on the farm."

She pulled away when a faint bell rang. "Sit down. I'll get you a cold glass of milk—fresh from our dairy cows."

Stuart sat at the same wooden kitchen table where he and Kate had shared many meals. The milk, when Aunt Mary brought it, was so sweet and cold it tasted like a vanilla milkshake. Back in L.A. he had to look hard to find milk that wasn't non-fat, everyone so preoccupied with diet and exercise that drinking soymilk was the norm, whole milk practically forbidden.

"So, how is Los Angeles treating you?" Mary asked, as she hovered over a tray of cookies, waiting for them to cool.

Stuart took another sip of milk. "I'm overloaded with work, so I don't have much time to enjoy the beaches on the weekends. And my apartment is in Westwood, which is a fun neighborhood, but again, I'm working so much that I don't get home until at least ten o'clock. I don't do much except maybe drink a beer, watch The Late Show and go to sleep."

"Stuart! That's outrageous!" She placed the spatula under the gooey cookies and transferred them to a platter. "You're telling me that dinner is a beer?"

Stuart nabbed his first cookie before Mary had a chance to put the plate onto the table. He took a bite, savoring the warmth and oozing chocolate chips. Again, he felt that he could be back in high school.

"I don't have the healthiest lifestyle, but living in L.A. does have its advantages. Primarily the weather, and my law practice is booming. But I can't remember the last time I ate a homemade cookie, let alone a homemade meal. I eat a business lunch nearly every day." He smiled. "But I try to stay away from hamburgers and fries."

Mary sat down and joined him. "No dinner? That's no way to end a hard day's work."

Stuart helped himself to another cookie. "It's a grim existence I admit, but I have so much work to crank out during the day that all I want to do is get home and sleep."

"What about all the movie premieres? And hob-nobbing with stars? Did you forget that I subscribe to *People*?"

Stuart laughed with Mary. "Not everyone in L.A. drives from beach party to movie premiere in their red Ferrari convertibles. But I've been to a few premieres, and had drinks with some B-list celebrities. That's about the extent of it."

"Maybe someday I'll come out and visit you in California."

Stuart placed his hand over Mary's. "I'd like that. I've really missed you."

"Maybe you could take me to one of those fancy movie premieres. How do you get invited?"

"I've had a few movie-star clients." Stuart paused. "And that's one of the reasons I'm here. I wanted to tell you, in person, that I've been seeing someone. She's an anchor for one of those half-hour entertainment news programs."

"What's her name?"

"Vanessa. I've asked her to marry me."

"Oh my." Mary placed her hand on her chest. "Of course, I figured this would happen someday. Especially with you being so successful and handsome. I'm sure all the girls throw themselves at you."

"It hasn't been quite like that. In fact, not even close."

"How did you meet?"

"At a house-warming party for one of my friends. Two years ago."

"Are you happy, Stuart?" Mary leaned over the table and held his hands. "Is this what you want?"

"I think so."

"You think so?" Mary leaned back from him. "You need to know so. This is a very important decision. We both know that we can never bring Kate back, but you're like a son to me. When you know deep in your heart that this is the woman for you, you'll have my blessing."

Stuart didn't want to admit that he had pushed aside his doubts. When he had first met Vanessa, she had been a features editor for the L.A. Times, a hard-working reporter with a loyal group of friends. After her promotion to the celebrity desk, her personality changed and so did her circle of friends. He had hoped that she'd tire of the celebrity scene and return to her roots, but once Vanessa moved onto television, she was sprinkled with celebrity stardust and never looked back.

"She's the only girl I've felt any attraction to since Kate. She really wants to get married, so it's the next logical step."

"Stuart, you know I want the best for you. But do you really think you should get married just because it's the next logical step?"

Thirty-One

$\mathcal{S}$ tuart left Oakdale knowing that Mary was right. He needed to be sure about Vanessa before he committed to marriage. After the Cohen case, they would take a vacation together. Maybe that would help to clarify his thoughts. The sixteen-hour workdays he had been putting in preparing his defense for the Cohen case had drained him. He needed a break. The case would finally go to trial next week; with luck, his client would be exonerated quickly.

Dr. Jonathan Cohen, a well-known and highly respected Beverly Hills plastic surgeon, had been charged with involuntary manslaughter after a middle-aged Hollywood actress died on his operating table. Everything had begun routinely. The patient's mandatory pre-op blood screen tested negative for drugs and HIV, so Dr. Cohen had performed surgery two days later. During surgery, the actress had a seizure and died. When the post-mortem showed heroin in her body, the actress's attorneys accused Dr. Cohen of negligence for performing surgery under those conditions. They also alleged that had the surgery been successful, top-bill roles would have come pouring into her agent's office, justification for the fifty million dollar suit they had filed.

Stuart would argue that she went home and shot up heroin on the day of the surgery, but after nearly a year on the case, his team still had not located her drug dealer, also wanted by the L.A.P.D. If Stuart could find him first, he would put him on the stand without police and D.A. interference. He didn't want the dealer copping a plea before he had a chance to testify.

Since the lawsuit, Dr. Cohen's practice had fallen off, so now, in addition to the defense against the manslaughter charge, Stuart had also been hired to file a countersuit against the actress's estate for slander and defamation of character. None of it left much time for Stuart's relationship with Vanessa.

* * *

Dr. Jonathan Cohen's year had not been completely grim. Just after the charges had been filed, Laurie Weston had walked into his office. A young graduate of U.C.L.A., her light brown hair framed her pretty, round face perfectly. Her smooth skin glowed, and those big brown eyes exuded so much warmth his heart melted just looking at her. He couldn't imagine for a second why this beautiful young woman would consider plastic surgery.

Laurie wanted to soften the bump on the bridge of her nose, but he had refused. "Miss Weston," Jonathan said, "your nose suits your face perfectly and I wouldn't be comfortable performing the surgery. In fact, you look a bit like Isabella Rossellini, so whichever of your parents gave you that nose, you should be very thankful."

"I'm adopted," Laurie said, "and actually not certain about my heritage, but thank you for your time." She rose from her chair and Dr. Cohen walked her out of his office.

A few weeks later, he ran into her again in the elevator, and she wore a bandage on her nose.

"Don't tell me . . ."

Laurie nodded her head. "Yup, I did it anyway. It's easy enough to find a doctor in this town to give you a rhinoplasty."

They laughed and he made a joke about drive-through nose jobs in Beverly Hills. Before they reached the lobby, Dr. Cohen asked her to dinner. By the time they exited the building, she knew him as Jonathan.

He invited her to Spago on Sunset Boulevard, where the casual atmosphere, with its white plastic garden chairs and open-air kitchen would provide a non-threatening environment for a first date. It wouldn't hurt, either, to show her that he could get a reservation and a great table in one of L.A.'s hottest restaurants. As a plastic surgeon to the stars, he was a minor celebrity himself.

Laurie lived in an apartment in Brentwood, an affluent neighborhood by anyone's standards, but her address belonged to a cluster of apartment buildings inhabited by young single professionals. On the other side of San Vincente Boulevard, mansions and palms lined the street that ran all the way to the ocean.

Jonathan parked his white Bentley outside Laurie's two-storey building on Kiowa Street. Even with the top down, the car looked ostentatious amidst all the other Volkswagen Jettas and two-door BMWs, but in his profession, he had an image to maintain, and after all, this *was* Hollywood. He noted the mountain bikes resting on every doorstep and balcony, a fact that left him feeling every day of the twenty-year age difference between himself and Laurie. He frequented the gym every morning to keep in shape, but with each year, he had more difficulty keeping his muscle-to-fat ratio in check. His receding hairline and use of reading glasses at night also proclaimed his age, but he hadn't yet gone under the knife, as so many of his colleagues had. He rationalized that it was advantageous to look a little older than his patients. They felt more comfortable with experience than with youth.

Jonathan looked in the rear view mirror and ran his hand across his hair before he walked to Laurie's front door. He had dressed in khaki pants, brown loafers and a pink button-down Polo shirt. His navy-blue blazer he had left slung over the back of the passenger seat. He didn't mind the frequent accusation that he looked like a Boston preppie. Having grown up in Greenwich, Connecticut, he'd rather look conservative than flashy.

Laurie opened the door a few seconds after he rang the doorbell. She wore a spaghetti-strap sundress, a mini that showed off her muscular tanned legs. The moment Jonathan saw her, all the emotions he had felt when she first walked into his office came rushing back.

"Would you like to come in for a minute?" she asked. "I'm almost ready."

"Take your time." He stepped over a pair of Roller Blades and wrist guards at the front door and entered her living room. Except for a stack of *In Style* magazines and a half-empty bottle of Evian that rested on a glass coffee table, everything was white. White sofa, two white chairs, and an antique white armoire, which presumably hid her television and stereo. Cher's recent single, *Believe*, blasted from the speakers. Though he was old enough to remember when *I Got You Babe* was a top hit, he liked this song and all it stood for.

"Sorry." Laurie walked to the stereo and turned the volume down.

"Don't turn it down on my account. I love this song."

She smiled and cranked it up even higher, and then bounded up the stairs to finish getting ready. As she did, another girl with blonde pigtails and obvious implants bounced down.

She blew on her nails. "I'm Jenny. I'd shake your hand but I just finished painting my nails." She yelled up the stairs, "Have fun tonight. Don't do anything I wouldn't do." Then she adjusted her pigtails and covered her eyes with designer shades. She smiled and pointed a fuchsia-tipped finger at Jonathan, "Now you better get her home in one piece, or I'm calling the police."

"Don't worry, she's in good hands." He smiled as the door slammed behind her. These girls seemed so carefree and happy. At their age he had been pulling all-nighters and working his tail off at Columbia Med School. He'd had a bit of fun, especially living in Manhattan, but he never saw the light of day and only went out on weekends, if at all.

When Laurie next appeared, she walked downstairs carrying a strappy pair of sandals and a pink cashmere pashmina. Her flawless skin struck him as fresh and beautiful, without the help of make-up. Maybe a touch of pink gloss and a hint of mascara accentuated her liquid brown eyes, but that was about it.

"I try not to walk down too many stairs in these shoes," she said, as she sat on the sofa to strap on her sandals. "I made that mistake once and ended up breaking my ankle." She secured the thin ankle straps and stood. "I'm ready. Thanks for waiting."

Jonathan opened the door for her. "My pleasure."

The sky had begun to morph from clear light blue to hazy, purplish-pink. The air had cooled and a light breeze blew Laurie's hair. The skin on her arm turned prickly from the chill, so he took her pashmina and wrapped it around her shoulders and then placed his hand gently on the small of her back as he led her to his car.

"Wow," Laurie ran her finger along the door. "I've never ridden in one of these."

Jonathan opened the door for her. "Neither had I—until last year."

When they reached Spago, red-suited valets swarmed Jonathan's car and waited for it to stop.

One of the valets opened the door for Jonathan. "Nice to see you again, Dr. Cohen."

Another held his hand out for Laurie as he opened her door. She accepted the man's hand and exited her carriage as gracefully as a Hollywood actress attending a movie premiere.

A massive, four-foot flower arrangement on a round marble table provided a dramatic focal point in the restaurant entryway. Then a hostess greeted Jonathan with an air-kiss and showed them to their table in front of the open kitchen. Several men in white hats and aprons juggled large iron fry pans and skillets over flames. A man holding a four-foot wooden spatula scooped pizzas out of a brick oven.

"Their specialty is thin-crust pizza baked in the wood-burning oven," Jonathan explained. He ordered a bottle of Laurent Perrier rosé champagne and ordered a smoked salmon, crème fraîche and caviar pizza.

When the champagne arrived, the waitress ceremoniously popped the cork and poured a generous amount into Jonathan's glass for him to taste. He took a sip and gestured for her to pour a glass for Laurie. He waited until the waitress had poured them each a full glass and had left the table, and then he raised his glass to Laurie's. "Here's to your new nose. It looks lovely."

"I know you liked the other one better, but I've wanted to change it for a while now."

Jonathan raised his hand. "Hey, if it hadn't been for your nose, we never would've met." He set his glass on the table. "I saw on your medical form that you work for an advertising agency. What do you do there?"

"I just started. I'm an assistant account executive for Ogilvy & Mather. The title sounds like I do something important, but I'm just a glorified gofer."

"How did you end up there?"

"By accident," she said. "I really wanted to be an actress. Surprise, surprise—who doesn't in this town?" She took a sip of champagne. "I had a small part in a Pizza Hut commercial that Ogilvy & Mather was shooting when I was still in school. I ended up talking to the art director, and we eventually began dating." She paused and then said, "He transferred to New York, so we're no longer seeing each other."

"That's good to hear."

"He knew I wasn't getting many acting parts so he suggested that I apply to the agency. I was shocked when they called me in for an interview."

Jonathan held up his glass. "Congratulations."

"It's long hours for not much pay, but it's paying the bills. The only negative is that I don't have time to act— let alone apply for any parts."

"Maybe later?"

Laurie sighed. "Yeah, I guess."

He reached his hand across the table to touch the tips of her fingers. "No really, Laurie. This is Hollywood, where people's dreams come true." He looked around the restaurant. "I guarantee you that every waitress and bus boy working here tonight all want the same thing you do. But you have a better personality and you're a hell of lot better looking than most of the women."

Laurie blushed. She turned her head toward the entrance of the restaurant and then touched Jonathan's arm. "Oh My God—there's Goldie Hawn. Doesn't she look great? And so does Kurt." She grinned sheepishly at Jonathan. "I'm still a little star struck. I've lived in L.A. most of my adult life, you'd think I'd get used to seeing movie stars."

"Don't apologize. It still happens to me when one of them walks into my office. I know they have an appointment so I'm not taken off-guard, but it's still a thrill to be sitting across from someone you've just seen twenty-feet tall on the movie screen the night before."

"Can you tell me who you've worked on?"

Jonathan shook his head. "Sorry."

The waitress brought their pizza to the table. Pink salmon, white crème fraîche and dark green caviar were spread over a thin, crisp crust. This somewhat resembled the red, white and green colors Laurie normally saw on pizza; but still, this wasn't *pizza*. Where was the oozing tomato sauce, spicy pepperoni and gooey cheese that always burnt the roof of her mouth?

Jonathan offered Laurie a piece and then took one for himself. He waited for her to take a bite and then bit into his own.

"Not bad," Laurie said. "I didn't expect it to be cold. I should have, with caviar and crème fraîche. The saltiness of the caviar adds an extra dimension. I'm impressed."

"I'm glad you like it. The first time I ordered this pizza, the waiter strongly suggested that the dish should be accompanied by champagne. I guess they're playing off the champagne and caviar theme."

"But of course," Laurie said, in a mock English accent. "The champagne and caviar theme. I was thinking the same thing."

"Sorry," Jonathan said, "after years of eating at these places I get a bit jaded."

"I didn't even know there was such a thing as a 'champagne and caviar' theme."

Jonathan reached across the table and touched her hand. "I'm glad you didn't."

They dined for nearly three hours before Jonathan drove Laurie home and walked her to the door. "May I call you again?"

Laurie smiled. "I'd like that."

"I have an early morning tomorrow, so I'd better leave, but I'll call you soon." He leaned over and kissed her cheek.

Thirty-Two

*J*onathan leaned back in his desk chair and looked at the only photo on his desk, a shot of his new young wife seated on a mossy knoll, her back leaning against a huge redwood. He had taken the photo himself, in black and white, on a weekend outing, and he felt a deep sense of satisfaction whenever he glanced at it. Laurie was as beautiful as any of the stars that had passed through his office, and their whirlwind courtship and recent marriage had given his entire life new purpose. He felt charmed, as if nothing could ever go wrong again.

"Dr. Cohen," his nurse beeped through on his telephone. "Mr. Carson is here."

"Send him in, Janice," Jonathan said, through the intercom.

He got up from behind his desk to greet Stuart and shook his hand firmly. "Please tell me you have some good news."

"We do, and we're going to trial next week."

"You found the drug dealer?"

"We did, and he's willing to testify that he sold Paulette an ounce of pure heroin, 'as white as snow' as he described it, a week before her surgery."

"So we're vindicated. Right?"

"We'll have to see how everything plays out in court, but his testimony should clear you."

Jonathan sat down and motioned to Stuart to do the same. "Would you like Janice to get you some coffee or something to eat?"

Stuart held up his hand. "No thanks, I just wanted to tell you the good news in person and go over some aspects of the trial. I won't put you on the stand unless they throw us a curve ball, but we have to be prepared for every possibility."

"My first patient is in an hour," Jonathan said. "Will that give us enough time?"

"It's a good start." Stuart pulled a yellow legal pad from his briefcase. "Let's get to work."

Stuart had prepared a list of questions that the prosecution would likely ask if Jonathan was put on the witness stand. During the course of the hour, they got through most of them. "That should do it," Stuart said. "If they put you on the stand, you'll be a sympathetic witness."

As he left, Jonathan called out to him. "After we win this thing, I'm taking you and your fiancée to Hawaii to celebrate."

"Let's not count our chickens before they hatch." Stuart waved a hand. "But a trip to Hawaii sounds just like what the doctor ordered. We'd enjoy a break."

* * *

The jury only deliberated for forty-five minutes before returning with a "not guilty" verdict.

The details of the countersuit would be finalized later, but it looked as if Jonathan would walk away with a substantial dollar amount in damages.

As promised, to celebrate his victory, he invited Stuart and Vanessa to join Laurie and him on a weeklong vacation at the Kea Lani, a luxury resort on the Kona Coast of Hawaii. As an extra perk, Dr. Cohen chartered a jet to fly them over to the island. Thanks to Stuart, a painful part of Jonathan's life was put behind him. Now he wanted to celebrate in style with the man who had made it happen.

Thirty-Three

The Citation X was fueled and ready to go at the Van Nuys Airport, an airfield used around-the-clock by L.A.'s jet-set. Jonathan, Laurie and Stuart sat in the executive lounge waiting for Vanessa, already a half-hour late.

Jonathan looked up from his Wall Street Journal and addressed Stuart. "What do you think is keeping her?"

"I called twice already and she said only that her appointment was running late."

"Why don't you call again?" Jonathan said, his voice clipped.

Stuart punched in the number.

Vanessa didn't even say 'hello' when she answered, but forcefully whispered into the phone. "I told you I'm almost finished."

Stuart took a few steps away for privacy. "What's taking so long? The Cohen's want to get going."

"I thought it was their plane," she shot back. "Isn't that the luxury of having one? They wait for you, not the other way around."

"No, that's not the case." Stuart looked over toward the Cohens and gave them a weak smile. "The pilot filed a flight plan and we were scheduled to take off half an hour ago. This is a very busy airport."

"Well, I'm doing my best."

In the background, Stuart heard a woman with an Asian accent say, "All dry Ms. Richards. You're safe to go."

"You're getting your nails done?" Stuart turned away so the Cohen's couldn't hear him.

"Well, yes. I wasn't about to go on vacation with chipped fingers and toes."

"Get over here as fast as you can drive." He flipped the phone shut.

He walked over to Laurie and Jonathan. "I apologize. Her appointment just wrapped up. She's on her way."

Jonathan didn't respond, just snapped his newspaper and resumed reading.

Stuart sat down next to Laurie. She had a beautiful smile and a sweet, warm face. He could see by the way her hand remained on Jonathan's knee that she was very much in love with her husband. When she got up to get herself something to drink, she brought Jonathan over a coffee before serving herself, and when they talked, she laughed a lot. She looked truly happy, and Stuart could see that she made Jonathan happy as well.

Stuart hadn't been that happy since he'd been with Kate. He had hoped to find that comforting bliss again, and once thought that this would be possible with Vanessa. The advice from his close friends was all the same: Kate was dead; he needed to move on.

So he had moved on, but onto *what*? Vanessa wasn't even in the same league as Kate.

Finally, Vanessa swept through the glass doors of the executive lounge and apologized weakly to Jonathan and Laurie for keeping them waiting, and then kissed Stuart on the cheek as if nothing had happened.

Stuart could smell the fresh nail varnish; he hoped the Cohens could not.

* * *

Jonathan had been sizing up women on a professional basis for fifteen years. Usually, when a patient entered his office, he could tell why they wanted plastic surgery. Vanessa Richards was easy to figure out. She was a woman who had probably just turned forty, but was trying too hard to look twenty-five. What most women in their forties didn't realize is that women in their twenties are not reed-thin and overtly muscular, but fit while still soft and feminine. His beautiful wife Laurie was a perfect testimonial to that theory, toned and physically fit, but not gaunt or overly muscular. Vanessa looked ten pounds underweight, which made her face look drawn and old. Her rear end had all but disappeared, and her arms and legs were so thin, they looked as if they might snap. Overall, not a good look.

Jonathan would admit that she had nearly flawless skin, likely the result of no sun and a monthly chemical peel. Raven hair fell to the middle of her back, and her blue eyes were stunning, but piercing, almost to the point of threatening. If Jonathan remembered correctly, Stuart had mentioned that she was a TV personality. She probably looked great in front of a camera, but not in the flesh. Oh well, he thought, to each his own.

On the plane, the atmosphere relaxed a bit, thanks to a magnum of Dom Perignon Stuart had brought on board.

"To your continued growth and success," Stuart said, and raised a glass.

"To a great vacation," Jonathan countered.

"To both, and to our wonderful men," Laurie added.

* * *

The first few days at the resort Stuart spent decompressing from his frantic life back in L.A. by playing golf, working out in the open-air gym and lounging under a palm tree on the beach. Vanessa spent every waking minute at the spa. She booked her appointments so tight that she seldom had more than five minutes to spare during the day, and she rarely socialized with the Cohen's.

She refused to dip one manicured toe into the ocean or pool, and only stepped out of their room with a wide-brim hat at least three feet in diameter. On the rare occasion she left the room without a hat, she wrapped her jet-black hair in a turban to avoid the risk of it lightening. She ordered hotel employees around as if they were her personal servants and demanded a larger in-room refrigerator, which she wanted stocked with gallons of sparkling water.

On their third night at the resort, Jonathan made dinner reservations at La Poissioniére. Vanessa, always on a strict diet, balked at the choice. She picked at her food, and nibbled on raw vegetables and salad without dressing.

"I read about the chef," Stuart told her. "She's renowned for her culinary talents. All of the food is supposed to be heart-healthy."

The Mahi-Mahi was light, yet full of flavor, the accompanying vegetables fresh and crisp, just barely cooked. After an exquisite sugarless cheesecake and an egg-white chocolate soufflé for dessert, Dr. Cohen asked the waiter if the chef could possibly speak with them when she had a free moment.

"Stuart, darling," Vanessa pouted, "I have to make this an early evening. I have an eight a.m. facial scheduled. The sun is wreaking havoc on my skin."

Stuart whispered in her ear: "I suggest you keep your loofahed bottom on the chair and wait for the chef to come out and speak with us." Loud enough for the others to hear, he added, "It might be in your best interest to stay. The chef is a famous author, a local celebrity."

"Really?" The word 'celebrity' caused Vanessa's eyes to light up at last.

When the chef emerged from the kitchen and approached the table, both men stood up. Her tall and willowy beauty left Stuart momentarily speechless. Thick, honey-colored hair fell to the middle of her back and round brown eyes glowed in her smooth tanned face. Jonathan pulled out a chair and invited her to sit down.

When she did, Laurie smiled warmly at her.

Vanessa only nodded and sat a little straighter.

"Hello," Luana said. She introduced herself to everyone and thanked the group for coming to her restaurant.

Stuart couldn't take his eyes off of her. She looked eerily familiar, especially her deep brown eyes.

"You look so familiar," Luana said to Stuart, returning his stare.

Before he had a chance to respond, Dr. Cohen interjected. "Stuart, my man," he patted Stuart on the back, "is a well-known lawyer in Los Angeles who just trounced our opponent in a high-profile court case."

"That must be it," Luana said. "I was just in L.A. on a book-signing tour. I must have seen your picture in the paper."

"What's the chance of me hiring you away from this resort to come and work at our estate in Malibu?" Jonathan asked.

"Thank you for the kind offer," Luana said, "but I'm not ready to leave just yet."

Dr. Cohen placed his hand on Laurie's shoulder. "Maybe you could give my wife a few pointers." He looked over at Laurie. "No offense, dear, I love your vegetarian lasagna, but a few more options on the menu would be nice."

"He's right," Laurie said, smiling. "My culinary repertoire is a bit limited."

"I'd be happy to give you one of my cookbooks," Luana said. "Just let me grab one from up front." She rose, and the men rose with her. A few moments later, she returned and handed the book to Laurie. "Forgive me, but I forgot your name. I'd like to sign it for you."

Laurie blushed. "Thank you. You're very kind." She spelled her name for Luana, who dedicated the book and passed it over to her.

"The recipes are simple and easy to follow." She smiled and gave her a little wink. "Good luck!"

Laurie took the book and brought it to her chest. "I'll do my best."

"Now I'll let you finish your dessert," Luana said. "I need to get back to the kitchen for a few minutes. It was a pleasure meeting all of you."

Stuart wondered if he had only imagined that her eyes rested on him for an extra moment when she said goodbye.

They stared after her until Vanessa broke the spell by excusing herself, reminding Stuart of her early-morning facial. "Goodnight," she said to the Cohens, and then left the restaurant alone.

Stuart waited until she was out of earshot, and then shook his head. "I apologize for her behavior. This trip has been a real eye-opener for me."

Jonathan nodded. "She's not right for you, Stuart."

"I couldn't agree more. I'm breaking off our engagement and sending her home on the first Aloha Air flight that's available. Economy class."

Laurie and Jonathan held up their water glasses to Stuart. "Well done," Jonathan said.

Thirty-Four

Their last night on the island, Stuart and the Cohen's ate dinner at La Poissoniére again. They were seated at a table on the veranda and the waitress had just served a round of Mojitos.

Dr. Cohen swirled his lime and rum drink with a plastic stick. "Why don't you stay a few extra days, Stuart? The firm will survive without you, and you've been working like a madman all year. And let's face it, your time here with Vanessa was a bit tense." He took a sip of the rum cocktail. "It would be good for you to take a few extra days for yourself."

"I don't know, I'm not used to all this rest and relaxation. What would I do with myself?"

"What about asking that lovely chef out? I noticed she wasn't wearing a wedding ring."

Stuart shook his head. "I only met her once. And besides, what's the most that could happen? We'd go on a few dates and then I'd fly back to California?"

"So you have a few fun dates," said Jonathan. "Life could be worse."

"You're right." Stuart leaned back in his chair. "After dinner tonight, I'll ask her out. Let's just hope she's single."

Before dessert, Stuart asked the waitress if the chef could come out for a moment. When Luana emerged from the kitchen in her white chef's toque and apron, Stuart pulled out a chair and invited her to sit.

"Thank you."

She held his gaze just long enough that Stuart could believe she felt the same connection he did—an indescribable chemistry that made him never want to let it go.

Luana turned to Laurie. "I'm sure you didn't do any cooking, but did you have a chance to look at any of the recipes?"

"You're right, no cooking," she said, "but I flipped through your book and I'm excited to try the grilled swordfish with the pineapple and mango salsa."

"That's one of my favorites too," Luana said. "The trick is to use the freshest and most pungent cilantro you can get your hands on, and lots of lime juice—not lemon."

"I'll remember that."

Stuart took a deep breath. "So, Luana, I've decided to stay a few extra days. Would you like to spend some time together? I read about a great place to snorkel and swim with the dolphins."

"I'd love to. I have Sundays off."

"May I pick you up, or would you rather meet me here?"

Instinctively, she had a good feeling about him. "I'll give you my address."

Stuart produced a pen and noted that Luana's hand shook a bit as she jotted down her address and quickly drew a map.

She smiled when she handed him the details. "I'm looking forward to it."

He accepted the paper and smiled back, wider than he had smiled all week. "I'll see you Sunday."

Thirty-Five

$\mathcal{S}$tuart rented a red Jeep convertible and found Luana's house without too much trouble. Luana was sitting on the porch with Mrs. Kamakea when he pulled up. He hopped out of his jeep and walked up to the porch to greet the two women.

Luana said hello and rose. "This is Mrs. Kamakea, my landlord and adopted grandmother. I moved here fourteen years ago and never left."

Stuart removed his sunglasses and extended his hand to the elderly Hawaiian. "Pleased to meet you. You have a lovely home."

"Thank you, Stuart." She stood up from her wicker chair. "Luana tells me that you're going down to Kealakekua Bay. When I was younger, my husband and I often drove down there and swam with the dolphins. It's a wonderful experience. They're so gentle."

"Have a nice afternoon with your great-grandchildren," Luana said to Mrs. Kamakea, and then she turned to Stuart. "She has four of them coming over today."

"You're a lucky woman to have such a big family," Stuart said.

"Yes, I've been very blessed."

Luana grabbed her straw bag and walked with Stuart to his car. "Cool car. Where did you rent it?"

"At the airport." Stuart backed out of the driveway and drove toward the highway that led to Kealakekua Bay. "I had one of these in high school, except it was black."

Luana looked at him and smiled. "I bet all the girls were in love with you."

"Not really. I had my share of good times, but mostly just one serious girlfriend throughout high school."

"What happened with her?" asked Luana.

"Sadly—tragically—she was killed in a plane crash."

"Oh Stuart," Luana said, "I'm so sorry."

"That's okay, you had no way of knowing." To change the subject, he said, "Luana is such a beautiful name. Does it mean anything?"

"Yes," Luana said, "it's a Hawaiian term that means to relax, be happy and enjoy pleasant surroundings. It's also the name of a rare, exotic flower found here in Hawaii."

"It suits you perfectly. Were you born here on the island?"

"No, the mainland."

Stuart glanced at her. "That's what I figured. You don't look Hawaiian, more like a born-and-bred California girl."

As he drove toward Kealakekua Bay, he glanced over at her more than once. Her smooth tan legs, lean and strong, suggested an athlete, rather than a chef at a French restaurant. Or a model. With her long blonde hair back into a thick ponytail, dressed in a sleeveless tank top and blue-jean cut-offs, she could have been on the front cover of any fitness magazine.

About twenty minutes out, he turned off the highway toward the Bay and meandered down Napoopoo Road, past a coffee plantation and another piece of property dominated by a large, gabled Victorian farmhouse. Within minutes they had reached the water. Stuart parked the Jeep on the side of the road underneath a mango tree, not far from a large monument of Captain Cook.

There wasn't much of a beach, just a large concrete pad from which kayakers and boaters launched. They rented flippers, snorkels and goggles at a nearby stand and then jumped into the warm clear water.

Below the surface a world of colorful fish and coral came to life. Stuart had never seen so many brightly colored fish in so many different shapes and sizes, some solid, some striped, all magnificent.

They snorkeled amongst the fish for a few minutes and then swam farther out into the ocean in search of dolphins. When Stuart fell behind, Luana stopped and treaded water, and when he drew closer she pointed off into the distance, where a dolphin jumped from the water and flipped onto its back.

Luana called out to Stuart. "I bet there's a whole pod out there."

"Swim out. I'll catch up."

"I'll wait for you. I think they'll be here a while."

Stuart caught up to Luana, breathing hard. He caught his breath, and they swam together toward the dolphins, until they saw several through their masks. They kicked hard and swam toward them. They were much larger than Stuart expected, and came so close he could see their eyes and open, smiling mouths. He at first held back, but Luana kicked closer until she was only inches away, and then she reached her hand out and patted one on the back. She motioned Stuart nearer. When she reached toward the dolphin again, he did, too. Its skin felt hard under his fingers, but smooth. He couldn't believe that they would stay so close, as if they had invited Luana and him into their home.

Stuart and Luana kicked to the surface for a moment and Luana said, "We touched them! I feel like Ariel, the Disney mermaid, living an underwater dream."

"Wow, you sure can swim!"

"I do a lot of surfing, so I guess swimming just comes along with the territory." She pointed her head toward the dolphins. "Let's go!"

At least thirty dolphins surrounded them. Some jumped and flipped in the air, but most swam underwater.

"Let's go under again," Luana said. "You'll see their faces. They're having so much fun playing with each other."

Stuart put his head underwater and kicked toward a group of dolphins, with Luana following him. She swam ahead and then took off her snorkel and secured it to the string of her bikini bottom. This time, instead of just petting its back, she grabbed its dorsal fin. The dolphin took off with Luana on its back. Stuart couldn't believe the speed. She looked as though she were on a jet ski. The dolphin skimmed the surface of the water, then dove, with Luana still on its back. After about a minute, she let go and swam back to where he treaded water in the middle of three dancing dolphins, their tails submerged, bodies gyrating backwards and forwards above the water.

"I've never had so much fun!" Luana said. "I thought surfing was great, but playing with the dolphins tops even that."

Then the three dolphins dove under water and swam further out into the ocean.

"I think our friends are leaving us," Luana said.

Stuart breathed heavily. "Well, I'm beat anyway. I've been pretty lax in the exercise department this past year."

"No problem. Let's call it a day." She dove under water and swam back toward shore.

At the Jeep they toweled off and agreed that the first place they saw on the roadside they'd stop and grab something to eat.

"There," Luana said. She pointed to a metal sign swinging in the wind above a wood shack that read 'Taco Hut.'

Stuart swerved into the gravel parking lot and stopped. Inside, a neon sombrero flashed above the bar and bottles of tequila lined the walls. At the bar they ordered four fish tacos, a large plate of rice and beans, and a basket of chips and salsa. They devoured the entire basket of chips before a bell rang, indicating the tacos were up. Stuart rose and brought their plates back to the table.

"Thanks," Luana said. She pushed the empty basket of chips aside. "I was a waitress once. It's hard work, but I promise to leave you a good tip!"

"You never know, I might end up doing this full-time. Practicing law is starting to get old." He placed Luana's plate in front of her and joined her. "Where were you a waitress?" He took a big bite of his taco and felt a bit of sauce dribble down his chin.

"At the Kea Lani. That's how I got my start." Luana took a paper napkin to his chin and dabbed up the sauce.

"Where did you go to a culinary school?"

"No where. I came up through the ranks, like many chefs do. I had a wonderful apprenticeship, working for a chef on a private estate, and also worked for a famous French chef, who taught me many of his techniques. I also travelled to Berkeley to work with Ali Stone, the proprietor of Le Poppy, a famous restaurant there."

Stuart looked up from his taco and stopped chewing. "Berkeley? That's where I went to law school. When I graduated my parents took me to Le Poppy to celebrate."

"I liked it there," Luana said. "Such a beautiful campus, and I love the energy of Telegraph Avenue. Crazy cast of characters, but certainly never dull."

"My parents thought the place was a freak show. I'm from a very conservative Midwestern family."

"Where in the Midwest?"

"A small town called Oakdale, in Central Illinois. I'm sure you've never heard of it."

"No, can't say that I have."

"My girlfriend—the woman I told you about—was from there too. She also went to UC Berkeley."

"What was her name?"

"Kate," Stuart said. "Her name was Kate." He took another bite and then abruptly changed the subject. "While I was nearly drowning out in the ocean, it occurred to me that I could improve my swimming skills. Would you like to join me for a swim tomorrow morning at the pool and give me a few pointers?"

"I'd love to. And maybe afterwards, we can go surfing."

"I don't know about that; remember I'm just a farm boy from the Midwest." Stuart wiped his mouth and pushed his plate away. "Have you ever been off the Island?"

"To Berkeley, and for my book tour, I traveled to Seattle, Portland, San Francisco and L.A."

"That's right, sorry; you told me that you were in L.A." He felt like he'd known her his whole life. And those brown eyes: they looked so familiar, so much like Kate's. "I meant have you been to the mainland before recently? Like, when you were a kid."

"We didn't travel much when I was younger. I'd just like to leave it at that, Stuart, if you don't mind."

"Fair enough." Stuart pushed his chair away from the table. "Give me a second to pay, and then we'll head out."

He came back from the bar and Luana reached out her hand to his. They held hands for a moment, and then Luana leaned over and kissed him on the lips. Stuart took a step forward. "Wow, I wasn't expecting that. But I must say—a most pleasant surprise."

Luana smiled. "I told you I'd give you a good tip."

Thirty-Six

The following morning Stuart went to the open-air gym a half-hour before he planned to meet Luana. The equipment and machines were state-of-the-art, and a constant sea breeze blew through the building. All the same, when Luana arrived, he was sweating on the Stairmaster. He took the white towel from behind his neck and wiped his face.

"Hey sunshine!" He slowed his pace a bit. "I have another twenty minutes on this thing, and then I thought I'd take a swim."

"I'll get changed and see you in the pool."

When Stuart finished on the Stairmaster, he took a quick shower and slipped into his swim trunks. At the pool, he stopped dead in his tracks when he saw Luana swimming laps. He felt a chill run through his body as he continued to watch her, lap after lap, flip-turn after flip-turn. He had spent enough Saturday afternoons at Kate's swim meets to know that stroke.

He jumped in the lane beside her and did a few laps himself, but he couldn't concentrate. *Could it be possible?*

Luana stopped at one end and waited for him. When he came up for air and joined her, she removed her goggles. "Okay, I was watching you underwater, and the first thing I noticed is your kick. We need to work on that first, and then we'll improve your breathing."

Stuart hardly listened. He couldn't take his eyes off her face. With her swim cap on, the long blonde hair removed from the equation, she resembled Kate even more than before. Sure, her face was thinner, her cheekbones more pronounced, but she had the same brown eyes.

"So, are you ready to improve that stroke of yours?"

"I think I've had enough exercise for the day, how about tomorrow?"

"Just let me finish my set and then I'll meet you poolside for some breakfast."

"See you in a few." Stuart pushed himself out of the pool and watched her until she joined him at the poolside café in a thick, white terry cloth robe, her hair twisted up off her neck.

"I've always wanted to wear one of these," she said. "I see the guests walk around in them all the time. Today I get to feel like one of them."

He pulled a chair for her at the table. "Anyone who sees you in it will head straight for the gift store to buy one." He had already ordered her a large glass of orange juice and a steaming latte with an extra cup of hot milk.

"Thanks, Stuart. And look at this. You read my mind."

No, he had't. *He knew her mind.* When he and Kate attended Berkeley together, she loved to drink café lattes with an extra cup of hot milk. Back then, specialty coffee shops were not as ubiquitous as they were now, but when the town of Berkeley got their first one, a Pets Coffee & Tea just off Telegraph, Kate went there nearly every day.

"I've also ordered us some fresh fruit. I figured you'd like an omelet, but I wasn't sure what you wanted in it."

Luana looked at him and smiled. "Everything. And don't forget the home fries!"

Just as he thought. Her appetite was one of the things he had loved about Kate. She wasn't one of those anorexic teenagers who only ate lettuce and drank diet Coke.

When the waitress came by, Stuart ordered an omelet with potatos for each of them, and then went silent. When he looked at Luana he found it difficult to speak.

Under the hot sun, Luana loosened the collar on her robe, and Stuart noticed a thin rectangular birthmark on the back of her neck. He looked more closely and felt a jolt of adrenaline surge through him.

He sipped some water to ease his dry mouth and then ran his finger lightly over the mark. "Is this a birthmark or a scar? I didn't notice it yesterday."

She touched the back of her neck. "I think it's a birthmark, but several years ago I was in an accident, so it could be related to that. I never really see it, so I don't think about it."

When Stuart heard the word 'accident' his heart raced. "Kay—I mean Luana, I don't mean to press, but how could you not know? Most people are aware of their birthmarks, and this looks like one."

"Oh, Stuart." Luana set down her latte. "My life is so complicated. But in a nutshell, after my accident, I lost most of my long-term memory, and I never really recovered it."

Stuart found it difficult to breathe. His brain churned so fast he couldn't process all the information swirling around in his head. He moved his chair closer to hers and held her hand.

"Do you remember anything?"

"No," she shook her head. "I don't remember anything that happened before my accident."

"What kind of accident were you in?"

"I had a swimming accident and ended up hitting my head. After that, I was in a coma for six months."

Stuart reached across the table and held Luana's other hand. "Please, Luana, tell me what you know." He stared into her big brown eyes. "It's important."

Luana ran one hand through the hair at her nape. "You're making the hair on the back of my neck stand up. All I know is what I've been told by a friend of my parents, the man who rescued me and took care of me for over a year, so I'm afraid that's all I can tell you."

"Let's start there then." He squeezed her hand tighter. "Take your time."

Luana took a deep breath and repeated what Dr. Schmidt had told her after she woke from her coma. "About fifteen years ago, I was here on vacation with my family visiting a family friend of theirs. His name is Dr. Roland Schmidt. My mom and dad had borrowed his boat for the afternoon. It was really hot that day, so I went swimming in the ocean while they lounged around on the boat deck. While I was out swimming, their boat exploded. In fact, I vividly remember the image of their boat bursting into flames.

"I swam to shore, but got slammed onto the lava rocks before I made it to the beach. Dr. Schmidt nursed me back to health and when I recovered he told me that I needed to be very careful because my father had discovered that MP Pharmaceuticals, a major drug company, was using orphaned Rwanda refugees for their Phase 1 human trials."

"I've heard of them," Stuart said. "Didn't they develop an anti-obesity drug?"

"Yes. They were using starving children to test a diet pill. Anyway, my dad found out, and the pharmaceutical company ordered a hit."

"That's outrageous." Stuart said. "And unbelievable."

Kate nodded her head in agreement. "I know, it's frightening. Dr. Schmidt told me to always watch my back and to not mention the accident to anyone." She paused and wiped tears from her eyes with the sleeve of her robe. "I was grateful to him, but then he started to get attached to me in a way that was inappropriate and extremely uncomfortable for me. He ended up trying to rape me and I've been hiding from him ever since."

Luana was trembling as Stuart moved his chair closer to hers. He held her in his arms as he had so many years ago. He understood how Luana could believe this story, however far-fetched it sounded. This Dr. Schmidt must have recovered her I.D and then done a little research. Her parents had been killed in a boating accident that she had witnessed as a child. When they were teenagers, Kate had told him that she would never forget the image of her parents' boat bursting into flames.

The doctor had deliberately lied to her, that much Stuart knew as he held Luana in his arms and whispered in her ear. "It's okay, Luana. It's okay. I'm here for you."

He continued to hold her and then gradually pulled his body away until he stared straight into her eyes. He told her what he knew about her family, and childhood. How her parents died in a boating accident when she was only four years old. How after their death, her mother's sister, Mary, became her legal guardian. Then he said, "Luana, I think Dr. Schmidt has deliberately misled you, although I'm not sure why." He thought carefully about how he would articulate his next sentence. After all, he could be way off base; but too many things were adding up. "I seriously think that you are someone I once knew."

Luanna's heart began to race.

He paused and held her tighter. "I believe you're my girlfriend from high school."

"What? How is this possible?" She could not believe what she was hearing and could not speak for a moment. "I don't understand."

"I don't understand everything either but I wouldn't have even mentioned it if I didn't strongly believe it. We'll have to do a bit of research but I know I'm right."

She began to shake so Stuart put his arms around her. "So fifteen years of my life have been a total sham? Now I'm even more afraid of Roland."

"Don't worry about him," Stuart said. "He sounds deranged, but he probably won't hurt you. It's been years since you saw him, right?"

"Yes, but he even sent a PI after me. I had to move because of him."

"Recently?"

"No." She studied his face and then her own relaxed. "You're probably right. It's true that I haven't had any trouble for all these years."

"There you go." Stuart clasped her close once again. "I'm here now. We'll find out more about him and make certain he never hurts you again."

Thirty-Seven

*I*nstead of surfing that afternoon she and Stuart flew over to Oahu, so they could do some research at the municipal library. The librarian there told them that all of the newspaper files from the last ten years had been updated onto computer discs. When she learned that they needed information about an event that had happened more than ten years back, she led them down to the dusty and dimly lit basement where the old microfiche cassettes were kept.

They searched for over an hour before Stuart found an article about a plane crash off the Kona Coast of Hawaii that would have coincided with the timing of Kate's trip to Hawaii. The article contained the same information he had read upon hearing of Kate's death, and as the facts came together, he felt as if he had awakened from a nightmare. This was unbelievable, but proved that the woman sitting next to him was Kate.

He printed the article and handed it to Luana. The headline jumped off the page: **California College Student Killed in small Plane Crash**. Luana read the article aloud, that the student's name was Katherine Kryowski. That her purse and identification was found, but not her body.

She handed the paper back to Stuart. "Did they have a funeral for me?" Her voice trembled.

"Let's go outside and talk." Stuart took her hand and they walked upstairs and outside to the courtyard behind the library, where they found an empty bench under a palm tree and sat.

Stuart put his arm around her shoulder. "Yes, we had a funeral for you, and nearly the entire town showed up. You were loved by many people." He kissed her on her head. "And still are."

"And my parents are really dead?"

"They are, Kate. May I call you Kate again? It's difficult not to."

"Yes, I understand, but please, tell me about my aunt. I grew up with her?"

"She loved you like her own child and was devastated when she thought you died. I just saw her last week. She's doing well, but she still hasn't recovered from your death."

"But I'm not dead." Kate pulled away from Stuart and looked at him. "We need to tell her right away."

"Of course we do, but let's give everything you've learned a minute to sink in."

"So who really is Dr. Schmidt? And why would he lie to me?"

"It doesn't matter now, Kate. He not only lied to you, but also slandered a perfectly decent company. The guy has major problems, but the good thing is that they are no longer yours. And don't worry. I'll get you off this island before he can find you."

Kate smiled for the first time since leaving the resort this morning. "One more question before we head out of here."

"What's that?"

"How do I pronounce my last name?"

* * *

Later that evening, Kate and Stuart finished a meal of grilled steak and vegetables, eaten by candlelight on the small deck off the back of her kitchen. Around nine o'clock they went inside and sat together on the sofa. She played Sade's most recent CD and lit more candles. In the romantic light, Stuart brought his face to hers and kissed her so passionately that she thought she must be in heaven. Already she couldn't imagine her life without him. He was warm and strong, yet sweet and gentle. She felt lost in a wonderful dream as she kissed him back, until a sound outside made her pull away. She had thought she heard the screech of tires, and now footsteps on her front porch.

"Do you hear that?"

"I heard a car pull in, but it's probably just your landlord." He tried to pull her closer.

"No, on my porch. I think someone's out there. Mrs. Kamakea rarely leaves the house in the evening and she's always in bed and asleep by nine o'clock."

Stuart sat quietly and they listened.

Kate heard the footsteps again. "Did you hear that?" she whispered.

"Yes. Stay here. Where's your phone?" He pushed himself up just as the door burst open.

Kate screamed as a man entered. "Roland? What are you doing here?"

"You think I haven't been watching you? I've been allowing you your illusions of freedom, but this

I won't tolerate." He moved toward them. "You're coming with me."

Stuart stepped in front of him. "Not so fast, gramps. She's not leaving under any circumstances."

Roland pushed Stuart in the chest. "Get out of my way unless you want to get hurt."

Stuart pushed back. "Leave before I call the police."

Roland tried to punch Stuart in the face, but Stuart blocked the punch and threw him to the floor. Roland remained still for a few seconds, but when he turned over he held a gun. "Luana, if you don't come with me, I'm shooting your lover boy."

"My name is Kate, and I'd never go anywhere with you. You're despicable. You deceived me and then tried to rape me. You should be in jail!"

Without thinking of the consequences, she threw herself on him. Stuart grabbed Roland's wrist and slammed it into the floor. As soon as he had the gun, he shouted at Kate to call the police.

Kate's fingers shook so badly that she could hardly punch in the emergency number. When she reached the police she gave them her address and stayed on the phone with them until she heard sirens in the distance.

Stuart held Roland at gunpoint until the police arrived a few minutes later. Within seconds they had him in handcuffs and had escorted him from Kate's house.

Two officers stayed for nearly an hour as Kate and Stuart provided statements and told the police what they knew about Schmidt's cover up. Then they stood together in the middle of the room, alone at last. Kate reached for Stuart.

Without missing a beat, he embraced her. "Now where were we?"

* * *

Kate emerged from her shower fresh and energized. She still couldn't believe all that had happened in the previous twenty-four hours. Despite her buoyant feeling that she had met her soul mate, her brain was on overload trying to process everything and she needed to focus on what to do next. She found Stuart in the kitchen, leaning against the counter drinking a cup of coffee. When he saw her, he handed her a steaming hot mug.

"We need to call your aunt."

"I was thinking the same thing. But how can we make that call without sending her into a state of shock? And what will I say? I honestly don't remember her."

"I'll talk to her first, but give me a minute to think about what I'll say."

She took a sip of her coffee. "While you're doing that, I'll call the resort and tell them that I need to take an emergency leave of absence. I want to go back to Illinois and see Aunt Mary in person." She set her coffee down and moved closer to Stuart and wrapped her arms around his shoulders. "Will you come with me?"

"Of course. I wouldn't have it any other way."

"I also need to go back to Roland's estate to say goodbye to Joseph—he was my ally and friend while I was living there. I imagine Roland's still in jail."

"Even so, I'm going with you."

She rested her head on his chest. "I don't know what I would've done if I hadn't met you."

He cupped her face and held it up to his. "We're meant to be together, Kate. When we return to Illinois I want us to get married."

"Married? Are you sure?" She wanted to say, 'but we barely know each other,' but that wasn't true. They were like twins separated at birth.

"Of course I'm sure, aren't you?"

"I've never been so sure about anything!"

Thirty-Eight

$\mathcal{I}$n Kate's bedroom, Stuart held Kate's hand as he listened to the phone ringing through. Then he said, "Mary, hello, it's me, Stuart. Yes, I'm still in Hawaii. I had the most amazing vacation ever. I'll tell you more later; but what I'm really calling you about is to tell you that I will indeed be getting married when I return home."

He listened for several seconds and then said, "Oh yes, I'm certain she's the woman for me." Stuart winked at Kate and squeezed her hand. "But I think you'd better sit down before I tell you the rest."

Kate also sat on the bed, her knees wobbly, her heart pounding.

Stuart joined her. "This may be impossible to believe, but Kate's alive. I'm sitting right next to her."

Kate heard her aunt's voice rise on the other end of the line, the words inaudible but agitated. "Stuart," Kate said. "Hand me the phone."

Her hand shook as she held the receiver, and she suddenly felt very cold. "Aunt Mary, it's me, Kate. I'm alive and I'm okay. Stuart found me."

"Oh dear God," Mary said. "I can't believe what I'm hearing."

"We have so much to tell you."

"Oh, Katie, my dear. God has answered my prayers. I always felt you were still with me. What happened?"

"It's too complicated to tell you everything over the phone, but we're flying home tomorrow so we can talk in person."

"This news – it's wonderful. I can barely speak and honestly think I'm about to faint."

"Can you call a friend to come stay with you? We'll be there in less than twenty-four hours."

"I won't sleep a wink until you get here."

"I'll see you tomorrow." Kate hung up, and then she sat a moment and let an avalanche of mixed emotions roll over her—elation, sadness, fear. When the trembling in her hands eased, she called ahead to make sure Joseph would be at the estate when she arrived.

"Roland spent the night in jail," he said, "but his lawyer will have him out on bail by noon. You'd better get out here as soon as possible."

Kate assured him she would and replaced the receiver. "Stuart, let's go. I want to see Joseph before Roland gets home."

Stuart threw her the keys to the Jeep. "You drive. You know the way."

Kate adjusted the seat, steering wheel and mirror and then pulled onto the street. The thought of returning to the estate filled her with dread, but she couldn't leave without saying goodbye to Joseph in person.

From the circular drive, everything looked exactly as it had when she had run away. Sprinklers had left light dew on the manicured lawn and the flowers were in full bloom. She slowed the Jeep to a roll and pulled in behind the kitchen.

Joseph greeted her with a tight bear hug.

Kate introduced Stuart and then grasped Joseph's arm. "Oh my God, Joseph, can you believe it? Roland burst in on us. I would've thought that he had given up on me."

"Not on your life," Joseph said. He wiped his hand on the towel that hung from his waist and extended it to Stuart. "Excuse my manners. Did you two have breakfast yet?"

"There's no time," Kate said. "I only came by to say goodbye. I'm leaving the island tomorrow and I may not be back for a while."

"I hope Roland didn't run you out of here?" Joseph asked. "He's facing jail time. I'm sure he won't bother you again."

"It's not that." Kate took a deep breath and gave him the Reader's Digest version of what had transpired.

"What a story, Luana—I mean Kate." Joseph whistled. "I think your next book should be about that, not another cookbook."

Kate shook her head and laughed. "No thanks. I know how much work it is to publish a book, and for now I just want my old life back so I can begin to enjoy my new one."

Joseph turned to Stuart. "For most men, a woman like this doesn't come along once, let alone twice." He pointed a finger at him. "Now don't go losing her again."

Stuart held up his hands. "No chance of that."

"You should follow Stuart's example, Joseph," Kate said. "There's a beautiful woman back at the Kea Lani who told me that she has loved you for thirty years."

Joseph looked into his coffee cup. "You're right. It's probably time we stop letting the past come between us. Does Kirsty know you're leaving?"

"I spoke to her this morning. My sous-chef, Raphael, will be taking over indefinitely."

"He won't be you, but the restaurant will survive."

"I was hoping that while I'm here, I could get the recipes I scribbled on scraps of paper while I was working with you. They're a great memory of you and our time together."

"I have no idea where they would have gone. They're not here in the kitchen."

"Do you think Roland took them?"

"Why don't we check his office?" Joseph took off his hat and apron and looked up at the clock. "We'd better make it fast, though. He could be home any minute."

In Roland's study, the pungent smell of stale cigar smoke nearly knocked Kate over. She repressed a wave of nausea as the smell of whisky and cigar smoke brought back the memory of Roland trying to force himself on her.

She looked on his bookshelves, but found nothing of a personal nature there.

Joseph lifted the lid of Roland's wooden cigar box and felt under the cigars. With a flourish, he produced a small, gold key. "I was in here once and saw him do this. Check his desk drawers."

Kate took the key and unlocked the drawer. She fingered through several manila folders, and let out a small cry when she saw one marked, Kryowski, K. Her hand shook as she opened the folder. Yellowed newspaper clippings of a plane accident stared back at her. They contained the same information she and Stuart had discovered at the library. Roland had known all along about her identity, and he had withheld it from her to steal nearly fifteen years of her life.

She pushed the folder over for Stuart to see. "Let's get out of here. I can't spend another minute in this house."

Thirty-Nine

When Kate and Stuart entered the terminal at Chicago's O'Hare airport, Stuart waved to Mary in the crowd of people waiting for friends and family to deplane. Mary's face was flushed but creased with a huge smile. Stuart ushered Kate over to her.

"My God, Katie, it's really you." Mary hugged Kate and touched her face tenderly before her hands began to shake. "I'd recognize those big brown eyes anywhere!" She burst into tears.

"Hey—what kind of homecoming is this?" Kate asked. "I thought you'd be happy to see me."

Mary wiped her eyes and laughed. "Oh, Katie, you really haven't changed have you?"

They drove back to the farmhouse without talking too much at first but then Kate started firing off questions about her childhood, her friends, her hobbies and anything else that she thought may help her regain her memory.

"I can't tell you how happy I am to hear all these questions. I was afraid I might overwhelm you," Mary said.

"Are you kidding?" Kate said. "I'm starting from scratch here. I need to learn as much as possible—as soon as possible."

Mary didn't stop talking the entire way home, nor did she stop while she was cooking dinner or while she and Kate washed and dried the dishes.

"I love your stories," Kate said, "but I honestly don't feel any familiarity. It's like hearing about the life of a neighbor or friend."

Mary, elbow deep in sudsy water, scrubbed a large iron pan. "Just give it some time, and speaking of friends, my dear, your best friend from high school, Cindy, can hardly wait to see you."

"I'd like to meet her, but I'm too exhausted to think right now." Kate finished drying the last dinner plate. "I'll give her a call in the morning."

She kissed Mary and Stuart goodnight, and then went to her room and closed the door.

Mary and Stuart looked at each other and smiled. Stuart had taken their luggage upstairs earlier, but neither of them had told Kate which of the many rooms upstairs was hers.

Forty

$\mathcal{K}$ate opened the door to a woman wearing tortoise shell glasses, her strawberry blonde hair pulled back in a ponytail. Her aunt had told her that Cindy, her best friend from high school, married a boy she met at the state university and was eight months pregnant with her third child.

"Well hello!" she said, glancing at her friend's large belly. "I've been hearing a lot about you, and apparently some of it is true."

Cindy threw her arms around Kate. "Oh My God! I can't believe what I'm seeing. Is it really you?"

"In the flesh. Please come in and let's sit down. Would you like some water? Or milk?"

"I'm fine," Cindy said. "I just want to talk with you. I can't believe I'm not dreaming."

Kate invited Cindy into the sitting room. "So we were best friends in high school?"

"We did *everything* together." Cindy pulled a large photo album from her bag. "I know this might be hard for you, not remembering anything, so I brought this. Maybe it will help."

They flipped through the album for the next hour. Cindy explained every picture. She showed her pictures of their swim meets, school dances, riding bikes, and swimming at Mirror Lake. When Kate saw pictures of the lake she paused.

"This looks familiar." Kate pointed at the group of pictures taken at the lake.

"It was a special place for all of us. Every spring, when the weather warmed up, we would pile into Stuart's Jeep and stay until the sun went down. And in the fall, if we had a hot Indian summer, we'd spend afternoons there and burn a huge bonfire at night."

Cindy smiled and lowered her voice: "It was a special place for you and Stuart also."

"Why's that?" asked Kate.

"It was where you and Stuart first," Cindy paused, "how should I say this, *got together*."

Kate looked at her like a child caught out by her parents. "You mean?"

"Yes, that's exactly what I mean."

"It's a shame I don't remember. It must have been wonderful."

Cindy hesitated. "Maybe we shouldn't talk about that night."

"Please, Cindy, I need to know as much about my past as possible."

Cindy touched her stomach. "I don't want to overload you—especially not the first day."

Kate placed her hand on Cindy's knee. "I'm okay. I need to know."

"You got pregnant that night."

Kate gaped at her, stunned. "What? Are you serious? What happened?"

Cindy explained how they had driven to Chicago to have an abortion without anyone's knowledge. She had kept Kate's secret and had never told Stuart, or Aunt Mary.

"Cindy, this can't be true." Kate found it impossible to believe what she had just heard. "I would never have aborted Stuart's baby. I love him, and I want nothing more than to have a baby with him."

"Trust me, it was awful, but remember this was more than twenty years ago. You were adamant about the abortion. You bounced back physically, but emotionally you never fully recuperated. I honestly thought that after the procedure you'd never be the same." Now Cindy buried her face in her hands. "I shouldn't have told you. At least your amnesia allowed you to forget all the guilt and anguish you put yourself through.

Kate gave Cindy a soft hug. "It's okay. As painful as these memories are, I need to know about them." She pulled away from Cindy and looked in her eyes. "Are you sure Stuart never knew?"

"He never knew."

Kate closed Cindy's photo album. "I think we both could use a break from our walk down memory lane."

"I agree." Cindy held her stomach. "This pregnancy has really wiped me out, and I'm sure you're exhausted too.

"Can you join my aunt and her friend Claire for lunch tomorrow?" Kate asked. "I could use the moral support."

After Cindy left, Kate searched her bedroom at her Aunt Mary's house for her old yearbooks from high school and her books from Berkeley. She flipped to the pictures taken from Stuart's senior prom and jotted down the date. Next, she found one of her biology books that discussed fetal development. What she feared came to life on the page. The textbook showed a picture of a sixteen-week fetus, six inches long. It had a beating heart and developing bones. She crawled into her bed, covered herself in a quilt and cried herself to sleep.

Forty-One

The customers at the coffee shop in downtown Oakdale all stopped talking when she and Mary walked through the door. Several people got up to shake hands with Kate or to give her a hug. Most of the residents of Oakdale had lived in the small town for generations. Both Mary and Stuart had told Kate how supportive everyone had been after her disappearance, and Kate wanted to be as polite as possible, but she did not feel up to explaining everything that had happened over the past fifteen years.

When Cindy walked in just a few minutes after they arrived, Kate shot her a look that screamed, 'get me out of here.'

Cindy took Kate by the elbow. "I'm going to walk Kate around the town. We're hoping something will jog her memory."

"I'll be having a small party for Kate's homecoming next week," Mary added, to a group of people sitting at one of the booths. "I'll make sure you're all invited. Who knows, maybe by then, Kate's memory will have come back."

While they walked along the river that ran through town, Mary and Cindy pointed out various landmarks to Kate—the library and bank, the grocery store that had been there for 100 years.

But nothing clicked. Kate shook her head. "I'm sorry."

Mary glanced at her watch. "Oh goodness, it's nearly noon. Let's make our way over to Claire's office."

"You'll need to fill me in again on what Claire does."

"Claire's the manager of an adoption agency in town," Mary said. "She's been there for thirty years and is basically married to her job."

"Does she have children?" Kate asked.

"No, none." Mary kept up a brisk walking pace. "She never married and never had any children of her own, but she feels that all the babies she places with loving families are her children. I rarely get to see her on weekends because she's so busy attending birthday parties and weddings of *her children*, as she calls them."

When they arrived at Claire's office, a plump redhead wiggled out from behind her desk and ran across the reception room to greet them. She squeezed Kate so hard Kate could barely breathe.

"My heavens! Look at you! What a gorgeous young woman you've become."

Kate glanced around the reception room. Most of every wall was covered with snapshots of babies and happy parents. Then she noticed Cindy, holding a brochure that explained the services of Claire's agency.

"Cindy, what's wrong?" Kate asked. "May I see that?" Kate took the brochure from Cindy's hand, looked at it and then gave it back, no wiser.

Cindy placed the brochure in her handbag. "Nothing, my hormones are in overdrive, and I'm feeling a bit dizzy."

Claire overheard Cindy and said, "I think it's time we all have lunch. I prepared everything this morning. I live only three blocks away, so we can walk."

Claire's cozy bungalow had a stone pathway, lined with bright flowers that led to her front door. She had decorated with simple good taste. As at her office, photographs hung and rested everywhere.

As she approached a baby grand piano covered with framed photos, Kate's gaze swept over children's birthday parties, weddings and professional portraits that covered the surface of the piano. One photo in particular caught her eye. She picked it up and stared.

"I know these people."

Cindy rushed over to Kate. "You remember something?"

"Not from my past," Kate said. "I met this couple last week in Hawaii. This man," she pointed to the photo, "he's a client of Stuart's."

Kate showed Cindy the wedding picture of Dr. and Mrs. Cohen and explained their relationship to Stuart. She then took the picture over to Claire.

"Claire, how do you know these people?" Kate asked.

Claire looked at the picture. "Oh yes, what a beautiful young girl. That's Laurie Weston. Of course she's Laurie Cohen now. She married that lovely plastic surgeon last year."

"I've met them," Kate said. "I know it's hard to believe, but Stuart introduced me to them while I was in Hawaii."

"Who is this?" Cindy pointed to a man in one of the photos.

"That's Dr. Franke. He's the man that founded our adoption agency, but he only comes to the office with new babies." She squared her shoulders. "I run the day-to-day operations."

"I've seen him before," Cindy said, "but where?"

"You know how small this town is," Mary said.

Claire shook her head. "I doubt Cindy would've seen him here in Oakdale. His medical practice is in Chicago."

Cindy put her hands under her protruding belly and sat on Claire's sofa, looking fatigued. "I'm sorry, it doesn't matter. We have so much else to talk about, namely Kate."

* * *

After lunch, Mary drove Cindy and Kate to their old high school, where she kissed them both goodbye and left them to wander around the campus together.

"Okay, Cindy," Kate said, as they sat on a park bench under a huge oak tree by the front door to the school. "Spill it. What's bothering you?"

"Nothing really, but did you notice all the photos on the wall at the agency?"

"Of adorable, drooling babies and their happy parents?"

"Right. But what else?"

"I don't know what you mean."

"They were all Caucasian. I didn't notice one Asian or African American baby."

"Why is that so unusual?"

"It's extremely difficult to adopt a Caucasian baby, unless couples spend years on a waiting list. I have several friends who adopted an African American baby or a baby girl from China or Korea because they got tired of waiting."

Kate swooped her hand in front of her. "We're right in the middle of Wonderbread America. It doesn't seem unusual that there would be a lot of young white mothers giving their babies up for adoption."

"I'm not convinced, but 'ya know what?" Cindy patted her stomach. "It's not my problem as I get my babies the old-fashioned way."

"Exactly." Kate got up from the bench, and offered a hand to help Cindy stand. "Let's go take a look around the school."

Cindy showed Kate their old lockers, the swimming pool and the gymnasium. Kate and Cindy sat down on the bleachers in the natatorium.

"Wow—this place sure has changed," Cindy said. She stared at the soaring ceiling, where light flooded in from huge windows. "It used to be dark and dingy with a low, flat roof and no windows."

"I still don't remember a thing," Kate said. "I think my memory is a lost cause."

"Even if it is, you have your whole life ahead of you. Stuart's a great guy and you're lucky to have found each other again."

"I know, it really is a miracle. I can't believe that I actually get to spend the rest of my life with a man I'm crazy about. I want you to be my matron of honor."

"I'm honored. Let's just hope I don't go into premature labor on your wedding day!"

Forty-Two

Stuart and Kate held their wedding at Mary's farmhouse in late summer. Rosebushes grew in abundance around the white picket fence that surrounded the house and created a wall of red, white and pink blossoms. Mary attached huge round pink peonies, like fluffy pom poms, to a wicker arch under which Kate and Stuart stood when the priest married them. Joseph, Kirsty, Mark and Kahanai flew in for the wedding, and Joseph walked Kate down the aisle. When Kate threw her bouquet, made from daisies picked from the garden, Kirsty caught it and then handed it to Joseph. He took the bouquet from Kirsty and then kissed her tenderly, to the delight of the other guests, who clapped as they would at the end of a Broadway performance.

* * *

Stuart and Kate moved to an old brick house in Hinsdale, a western suburb of Chicago known for its family atmosphere, with good schools, a charming downtown and low crime.

Kate and Cindy now lived three hours apart but still spoke daily on the phone.

"Everything is perfect with us, except that I can't get pregnant," Kate confided to Cindy, as Cindy's newborn cried and then quieted in the background.

"We know that you *can* get pregnant, but now that you're older maybe it's not as easy."

"I'm forty, not exactly ancient! Do you think there was a complication during my abortion?"

"Jeez, Kate, that was so long ago. I don't remember anything, but you could always call the clinic and ask."

"I'd feel better asking them in person. Maybe one of the nurses still works there."

"I'll go with you," Cindy said.

* * *

"Does any of this look familiar?" Kate asked Cindy as they waited in the reception room of the Life Institute near Chicago.

"Yes, if you can believe it, the furniture is exactly the same, and so is the rug." She pointed to the red and blue Persian carpet. "But I don't recognize any of the people."

"Maybe the receptionist can help." Kate approached the front desk and waited until the woman acknowledged her. "Good morning," she said, "I had a procedure here almost twenty-four years ago. Would it be possible access my records?"

The woman shook her head. "After twenty years all our medical records are incinerated, and it's unlikely the doctor would remember anything without them."

Kate perked up. "He's still here? May I speak with him?"

"Let me check for you." The receptionist got up from her desk and walked into a corridor that led to the doctor's office.

When she returned to the reception area with the doctor, Cindy gripped Kate's hand. They both stared at Dr. Franke, the man from the brochure and the man who founded Claire's adoption agency.

Forty-Three

"Since it's been such a long time," Dr. Franke said, "we'll have no way of knowing whether there were any complications without a full gynecological exam. I'm fully booked today, but speak to Helen, our receptionist, on your way out. I or one of the other doctors should have some space next week."

Kate thanked him, and then she and Cindy bolted. Outside, they spoke in unison. "Holy shit!"

When they got in the car, Kate turned to Cindy. "Maybe it's just a coincidence?"

"That an abortion doctor also heads an adoption agency? That's just weird."

Kate strapped on her seat belt. "Doctors these days don't make much money working through HMOs. Maybe the adoption clinic is just another business venture."

Cindy didn't look convinced.

"You're right," Kate said. "That doesn't make sense. Laurie Cohen is in her mid-twenties. That means the adoption clinic has been in existence that long. I'll ask Claire. I think she's been working there for at least thirty years."

Cindy started the car. "I think we have enough to worry about, Kate. It's none of our business what this doctor does in his spare time."

"Shoot!" Kate said. "I forgot to make the appointment."

"I'm not surprised—we both ran out of there like the place was haunted. Phone when you get home."

* * *

The next time Kate drove herself to the clinic. She fidgeted in the waiting room until the nurse ushered her into the exam room and asked her to undress and put on a hospital gown.

Nearly fifteen minutes later, a young female doctor entered and introduced herself. With cold hands, she tapped the inside of Kate's elbow and took a blood sample. Then she gave her a full gynecological exam and told her that the blood work would be ready in a few days.

Kate dressed and exited the exam room; not realizing that she had turned right, instead of left toward the reception area, until she found herself lost in a maze of hallways and additional rooms. All the doors looked the same, until she reached a large metal door marked *Do Not Enter*. In an attempt to find a nurse to direct her back to reception, she pushed the door open and walked into a cold, steel-gray laboratory.

At first she noticed only the metal walls and metal floors, and a strong antiseptic smell. Then she heard the sound of classical music—a beautiful Mozart concerto. Curiosity gripped her, and she crept along until sheer horror stopped her. Glass ovals hung from the ceiling, containing what appeared to be human embryos floating in fluid. Thick glass tubes fed the containers with bubbling liquid.

She turned and fled, backtracking until she found the original long corridor and made her way back to the waiting room.

"You look pale," the receptionist said. "Would you like to sit?"

"I'm fine," Kate said. "Visits to the doctor always make me nervous."

She paid her bill and ran to her car. Her hands shook so much she could barely insert the key into the ignition. She had to get to Cindy's fast to tell her what she had just seen!

* * *

Nearly hyperventilating, she rapped on Cindy's door so hard her knuckles turned red.

"Calm down," Cindy said. "What happened?"

Kate fell onto the sofa in the living room and explained to Cindy what she had seen. "Don't you get it? They're growing babies from aborted fetuses."

"That's crazy. I'm sure that's against the law."

"Of course it's against the law, but think about it. Stuart and I may have a baby—an adult child—out there somewhere!"

Cindy only shook her head in astonishment.

But Kate felt sick to her stomach. "I have to go. I can't lie to Stuart any longer."

* * *

Kate sat in her living room and waited for Stuart to return home from work, unable to watch TV or even read a magazine. When Stuart walked in, she remained motionless on the sofa, waiting in the dark.

Stuart turned on a floor lamp. "Kate, what's wrong?"

"I think you may want to sit down."

"What's wrong?"

"Remember the first time we made love, on your prom night?"

"Of course."

"I got pregnant that night."

Stuart finally sat. "And you never told me? Did you miscarry?"

"I had an abortion."

He abruptly stood again. "You what?"

Kate had never seen him look so hard and angry. "I must have thought it was the best thing to do at the time. Cindy said I was frightened, worried about your parents, your career . . ."

"But how could you have not even asked me? You . . . you killed our child."

Kate broke into tears. "I know I did, and I feel awful. I'm so sorry."

"Sorry isn't good enough, Kate. That child was as much mine as it was yours. I had a right to know. That decision should have been ours—not yours alone."

"I wish I could explain—"

"But let me guess. You can't remember." He turned and stormed out of the house. The door slammed behind him.

* * *

Four agonizing hours later Stuart returned home, subdued but still distant.

"Let me tell you what I know," Kate said.

"I'm listening."

"We were teenagers, Stuart. Both you and your parents had such high hopes for your career. Who knows if you would've accomplished all you have achieved if you'd had a child at such a young age."

"You could've at least asked me. *Told me.* Something." Stuart buried his head in his hands. "I had no idea."

"Well now I'm asking for your forgiveness. There's nothing we can do to change what happened . . ."

He held out his arms and pulled her to his chest.

When she had the courage to speak again she lifted her head away from him. "There's something else."

His face froze. He dropped his hands and pulled away. "What?"

Kate attempted to explain what she and Cindy discovered about the abortion clinic and its connection to the adoption agency where Claire works.

"That can't be possible."

"I know it sounds crazy, but I also know what I saw in his lab. And nothing will ever make me forget it." She held Stuart's hands. "I need to know if we have a child out there somewhere."

Stuart got up from the sofa and shook his head. "Don't even think of going there, Kate. We need to start building our future, not stir up the past. If you do, I won't have any part of it."

* * *

As much as she loved Stuart and wanted to respect him, Kate couldn't let it go. When Stuart left for work the next morning, she drove to Claire's agency.

Claire came out from behind her desk to hug Kate. They talked about Cindy's new baby, and then Kate tried to steer the conversation toward the agency.

"Claire, I need to talk to you about the possibility of adopting." Kate sat at Claire's desk. "Stuart and I are having trouble conceiving."

"Oh sweetheart," Claire said, "I'm so sorry."

She held up her hand. "It's okay. It happens to many couples, especially older women." She inwardly cringed at her deception, but she needed to learn more about how the agency operated. "What's the procedure for adopting a baby through this agency?"

"Well, this sure is exciting." Claire straightened some papers on her desk and sat behind it again. "First we'll need to schedule a meeting with Dr. Franke."

Kate's chest tightened. "Couldn't we arrange everything through you? After all, you've been here half your life. You probably know more than he does about how this place runs."

Claire's face flushed. "It's true, I'm the only one who handles the database, and that's how we'd find a match for you."

"What do you mean by 'a match?'"

"We ask you to fill out a questionnaire. Things like: do you want a boy or girl? What color hair, what color eyes? That sort of thing."

"And everyone gets what they want?"

"Yes, they do."

"How is that possible?" Kate asked, even though she knew that Franke would simply choose a baby from his lab.

"To be honest, I'm not quite sure. Dr. Franke makes all the arrangements."

"Here." Claire booted up her computer. "I'll get you the form."

Kate watched over Claire's shoulder as she typed her password.

She hated herself for planning her next move: breaking, entering and stealing information from the computer; but she had to know.

Claire printed out the form and handed it to Kate.

"Thank you." Kate stood and kissed Claire on her cheek. "After Stuart and I review all these papers I'll give you a call."

Before she left, she stopped in the washroom and used tape to prevent the back door from locking. The door appeared locked, but she had depressed the bolt with tape.

That evening, while Stuart was still at work, Kate returned to Claire's office, and entered through the back door as she had planned. She typed Claire's password and pulled up Date-of-Birth information from twenty-four years ago. Based on when she had conceived, the baby would have matured around the middle of March. She scrolled down until the birth of a baby girl appeared. But as she scanned the screen, a chair scraped in the front office. Her heart jumped to her throat. She pressed the print button and looked up just as Claire appeared in the doorway.

"Kate!" Claire gasped and brought her hand to her mouth. "How did you get in here? What are you doing?"

Kate struggled to remain composed. "Claire," she said. "Please calm down. I can explain."

As Claire listened, Kate revealed all that she had discovered about the connection between the abortion clinic and the adoption agency. "I can't emphasize enough how sorry I am for not being honest with you this morning when I asked all those questions about how we'd go about adopting. I wanted to make sure my instincts were legit before I got you involved."

"What makes you so sure that you're right?" Claire asked.

"What clinched it for me is when you said that all we have to do is request the sex and ethnicity of the baby, and we will get the child we want. I know that isn't normal. It's too good to be true."

"I've been working here for so long," Claire said, "I'm afraid I've begun to believe it's the norm."

"I don't want to jeopardize your job situation. But if you'd like to help me, I'll tell you why I'm personally so concerned."

"Of course I want to help you, Kate. You and Mary are like family to me."

"But you need to promise me, and I mean *promise* me that you won't tell Aunt Mary. She could never handle another shock like this."

"You have my word."

Kate explained about her abortion at Dr. Franke's clinic, twenty-four years previously, when the procedure was considered illegal. She also explained what she had seen in his laboratory the previous week.

Claire put her hand to her chest. "Oh Lord. I had no idea."

Kate let Claire grasp the severity of what was happening within the world of Dr. Franke. "Okay, are you ready for more?" She handed her the page she had just printed. "I think this baby is mine. Can you help me find out who she is?"

Without hesitation, Claire took the paper. "Move over, honey," she said, kicking her out of her chair. "I have work to do. You do know this is illegal, don't you?

Kate nodded.

"Well never mind. If what you're saying is true, this is the least of my problems."

An hour and a pot of coffee later, Claire discovered that a couple, Fred and Nancy Hunt, had adopted the baby that Kate thought might be hers and Stuart's.

Kate didn't want to disrupt the Hunts life; she only wanted to know how her baby girl was doing. She envisioned a beautiful brunette, athletic and smart, with Stuart's bright blue eyes.

Claire unlocked a filing cabinet. When she found what she wanted, she handed a copy of the adoption certificate to Kate.

Kate took the piece of paper and held it like lost treasure. "Thank you for this. I know you're putting your job on the line."

"Don't worry about me, sweetheart. I'm just as curious about all this as you are."

Kate had so many questions about the Hunts: Did they live in a fashionable suburb of Chicago? Were they highly educated? Were they philanthropists or patrons of the arts?

To Claire she said, "Can you tell me anything about the Hunts?"

Claire frowned. "This is unusual, but I don't know anything about them. Normally I keep in touch with the babies and their parents, but not this particular family."

"I'll do a bit of research myself," Kate said. "It's better if I don't involve you anymore. You really went out on a limb for me tonight."

"Dr. Franke spends most of his time at his clinic in Chicago. He'll never know what we've been up to."

Kate folded the birth certificate and put in into her purse, uncertain as to how or if she would break the news to Stuart.

But when Kate let herself into their house, Stuart was still not home from his meeting. She fell asleep, hoping that after a good night's rest, she'd have more clarity.

Forty-Four

Kate drove to the address she had for the Hunts, in a small town outside Chicago. After several days of searching, she knew where her daughter had lived and gone to elementary school, but she had learned no more—nothing about high school or college, let alone graduate school. Now she guessed why.

Most of the homes in the area resembled unkempt shacks with peeling paint and untidy lawns, and the Hunt's house was the worst on the block, with a rusty car parked on the dry brown grass. Weeds grew over a foot tall in the front yard. A twenty-year-old pickup truck was parked on the gravel driveway.

She couldn't summon the courage to go to the front door. What would she say? *Hello, I'm your mother. If I had been thinking clearly twenty-four years ago, things would be different. But because I was a stupid teenager you ended up here.*

Kate drove to the local diner. Pick-up trucks similar to the one she had seen at the house were parked out front. She ordered a cup of coffee from a server who could have been in her seventies.

"You're not from these parts, are you, doll?"

"No, 'fraid not." Kate focused on her coffee, in no mood to chat.

"Just passing through?"

"Not really." Then realizing that the woman might know something, Kate made eye contact. "I'm looking for someone."

"Who's that?" The woman smoothed out the skirt of her pink and white uniform. "I've been working here for twenty-five years. Nothing gets past me."

"I'm looking for a friend of my mine. Fred and Nancy Hunt's girl."

"Oh my." She whistled. "You sure have been out of touch. Her husband shot her five years ago. Killed her and her unborn baby, too."

Kate couldn't hear anymore. How could this have happened? Now she was responsible for two deaths. She pushed her coffee cup away, threw five dollars on the counter and ran out the door.

She felt as if she were in the middle of a terrible nightmare. But when she tripped on the doorsill and fell onto the searing-hot blacktop in the parking lot, she knew that this was not a dream. She pulled herself up from the ground and for a minute wished that she could return to Hawaii and forget that she had ever tried to learn the truth about her past. She couldn't tell anyone what she had discovered about her daughter, not even Stuart, and would keep this tragic secret if it haunted her for the rest of her life, ruined her sleep and made it impossible to look herself in the mirror.

She drove home on autopilot, and when she pulled into her garage she could not remember the drive. In her miserable trance she didn't notice the blood that had trickled down her legs from the scrapes on her knees until Stuart walked her into their kitchen.

"What happened to you?"

"Just a bad fall."

Stuart helped Kate sit. He went to the sink and soaked a paper towel in water and dabbed her knees. "Did you learn anything?"

Kate looked at him and her eyes filled with tears. Still, she said nothing. She wanted to keep what she saw and learned today a secret, but she would hate herself even more for lying again to Stuart. But how could she tell him that their daughter and grandchild were murdered?

"Don't look so surprised," he said. "I knew you couldn't let it go. Do you want to tell me what happened?"

"After all the time I wasted today," Kate said, "I think it's probably best if we just concentrate on our future. We have so much to look forward to and I don't want to be trapped in the past."

"I couldn't agree more."

"I also want to start cooking again, Stuart."

"Great, I'm starving."

Kate smiled. "I mean on a professional level." She washed her knees and threw the bloody paper towel in the garbage can. "But I'm hungry too. If you fire up the barbeque I'll grill some steaks."

Over dinner they split a bottle of 1989 Chateau Margaux, and after the wine kicked in Kate began to relax. "You've become quite the connoisseur," she said. "You always choose great wines."

"I think we both could use a vacation," Stuart said. "The Anderson trial should wrap up next week. What do you think?"

Kate sipped her wine, and held the smooth liquid in her mouth while she considered Stuart's suggestion. "I think you're right."

"Any ideas where you'd like to go?" Stuart asked.

"Surprise me."

"How about California? The Cohens have a home in Malibu and for years they've been inviting me to spend a week with them on the coast. I never wanted to subject them to Vanessa for any length of time. But they adore you. What do you think?"

"I think a little California sunshine is just what I need."

Forty-Five

The Cohen's home in the north end of Malibu up by Zuma Beach was as spacious as it was stunning. Luigi Vietti, an Italian architect best known as the master architect for the Costa Esmeralda in Sardinia, had designed it. Also known for designing the Aga Khan's personal residence, he had created not only a home but an environment. Kate's jaw dropped when she walked into the open foyer and looked through the arched corridors with views out to the crashing waves of the Pacific Ocean.

"I've never, ever, seen a house like this. Not even in magazines," Kate said.

Laurie smiled. "Trust me, I hadn't either. It turned out better than we both could have imagined."

"Thank you so much for inviting us, Laurie," Kate said.

"It's our pleasure," Laurie said. "We're isolated up here, so it's great to have friends enjoy all this with us."

"As my hostess gift to you I'd like to do the cooking this week," Kate said.

"You don't have to do that. I have a full-time cook."

"Well, give her the week off. Seriously, it's my treat."

"Well—if you insist." Laurie lowered her voice, "Her food doesn't even come close to the meals we ate at your restaurant in Hawaii."

"Thank you," Kate said. "Now that's settled, let's hit the beach!"

"I heard from Stuart that you're a good surfer. Would you mind giving me a few pointers? I tried to get up on my own last summer, but I was hopeless."

"Absolutely! A friend of mine in Hawaii taught me. And believe, me, I knew nothing."

Laurie took a few spills and then got the hang of being on the water. They both surfed until the sun went down and then returned to the house. Laurie asked her chef to do the shopping for the week and then gave her the next five days off. She and Kate could shop for vegetables on a daily basis at Trancas, her favorite market on Pacific Coast Highway.

After a quick shower, Kate was in the kitchen ready to get to work. Although designed as a working kitchen with state-of-the-art appliances, the finishes were exquisite, everything from the granite countertops to the marble pastry-making station. "We'll have fun here," she said.

"Let me show you where everything is," Laurie said. "But I have to say, I'm not all that sure myself. I really only prepare a few things on the weekends, and even then Jonathan likes to go out a lot."

Over the next half-hour they opened doors and drawers and inspected the pantry, both of them getting to know the kitchen.

"Do you mind if I play sous-chef?" Laurie asked. "I'd love to surprise Jonathan with a delicious five-course meal one day."

"Of course. It's wonderful to share the gift of cooking good food with friends."

An hour later Kate and Laurie had poached a salmon with vegetables in parchment paper, made shrimp risotto and an endive and green apple salad garnished with crumbled goat cheese.

As they cooked, they shared a bottle of wine. Laurie told Kate that she had fulfilled her dream and had started a career as an actress. She had recently finished filming a car commercial and had just tried out for a part on a soap opera.

"That's fantastic," Kate said. "In a couple of years we'll be seeing you in major motion pictures."

"I'm not so sure about that, but I'm happy to have the parts that have come my way so far."

Over the week, they realized that they had more in common than surfing and cooking. They took long walks on the beach together, watched the same sappy *Lifetime* movies at night and swapped paperback books. When Kate and Stuart left at the end of the week, Kate and Laurie vowed to stay in touch.

They talked on the phone for hours each week, Kate from her little study off her kitchen as she looked at her giant oak tree out the window, while Laurie spoke from the sitting room off her bedroom, where she watched the swells of the Pacific Ocean.

Kate's experience teaching Laurie to cook made her realize that she'd rather teach cooking than open a restaurant, as she had originally planned. She would start a business called Kate's Kitchen. There she would teach group cooking classes and each class would share a fabulous meal at the end of the instruction. It would be almost like entertaining. And in the store space, she'd sell everything one would need to outfit a kitchen. She'd also include wine pairing as part of the curriculum, an idea Stuart loved.

While Kate was out with a realtor researching available space, she received a call from Laurie on her cell phone.

"You're not going to believe this, but I just found out we're pregnant. We've been trying for a while now."

Kate nearly dropped the phone. "Laurie, that's fantastic!"

"I can't tell you how thrilled we are. Jonathan and I want to invite you and Stuart out to celebrate. Also, Jonathan mentioned he has some business to discuss with Stuart. Wills and trusts—that sort of thing."

"I'm sure Stuart will clear his schedule as soon as he hears the good news. I'll call the airlines and book a flight for this weekend."

Stuart and Kate flew back out to California to celebrate and at this time the Cohen's asked Stuart and Laurie to become their baby's legal and financial custodian.

* * *

Sharing the joy of Laurie's pregnancy, and the birth of nine-pound baby Nathan had made Kate feel even more broody; she desperately wanted a baby with Stuart, but as much as they enjoyed trying to conceive, nothing happened, even after several sessions of in-vitro.

One night, when Stuart returned home from work, he found Kate on the sofa asleep. She awoke, her eyes red from crying.

He held her hand. "Don't beat yourself up about this. Many couples aren't able to get pregnant. I'm not sure why we can't, but don't worry, we will."

Kate felt certain that the real reason for their infertility had something to do with her abortion. But after what she had seen in Dr. Franke's lab, she never followed up with her appointment, even when the clinic sent her a letter saying that more tests were necessary to determine why she couldn't get pregnant.

"You need to stop worrying so much." Stuart smiled at her. "This doesn't mean we'll quit trying, of course, but let's lighten up on ourselves. You've been planning your cooking school long enough. Why don't you focus on getting that up and running? All that time and effort will keep your mind on something other than trying to get pregnant."

Kate sat up and hugged him. "What have I ever done to deserve you? Thank you, Stuart."

Kate selected a space for her store and within six months opened her business, incorporating the Luana flower into her company's logo. For her, the flower symbolized Hawaii and the memory of everything she had learned there. And of course her cookbook was written under the name Luana Kramer.

Most nights she worked until nine o'clock, and in many ways her business became her baby. She often wondered how she would cope with a new business and a new baby. She and Stuart still saw the Cohen's every few months, and over Christmas they all met in Aspen for a week of skiing. The Cohen's brought along Laurie's mom, Stella Weston, to watch Nathan while the adults skied.

They ended the last day with a challenging run down the black diamond Gentleman's Ridge, followed by a round of drinks at the Caribou Club, where they toasted to a fantastic ski week, and promised to do it again the same time next year.

* * *

When Kate's office phone rang, she let it go to voice mail. "Continue beating the egg whites until firm peaks form, like mountains."

Ten students, each wearing aprons with the Kate's Kitchen logo, watched Kate demonstrate how to make meringue using a whisk and copper bowl.

Then her cell phone rang.

"Now fold the meringue into the egg yolk." She demonstrated with her spatula. "Excuse me," she told her students. "I'll be right back."

She pressed the message button and heard Laurie's raspy whisper, barely audible. "Jonathan's had a heart attack. The doctor doesn't think he'll make it."

Forty-Six

Kate didn't listen to the rest of the message but immediately called Laurie's cell. When she didn't answer, she replayed the message and learned that they were at Cedar Sinai hospital in L.A.

Kate called Stuart at home and told him the news. "I need to be there for Laurie. She wouldn't have called me if she didn't want me there."

"Of course," Stuart said. "I'm just as upset as you are. We'll take the first plane tomorrow."

"No, we need to go tonight. I've wrapped up my class and I'm driving straight to the airport. Last time we flew out to see them we took the quarter to seven flight. Traffic is horrible this time of day, but I should be there by six."

"Okay, I'll give United a call and see if they have two seats. If they don't I'll try American."

"Thanks, Stuart. I'll see you soon."

When Kate arrived at the airport, Stuart was already there on his cell phone.

He held up his hand. When he finished talking, he folded Kate into a comforting hug. "Jonathan's secretary told me he just went into surgery. He should be out by the time we get to the hospital."

* * *

They found Laurie in the waiting room in the cardiology wing, her face ashen. She looked as if she had aged a decade. Stella cradled little Nate, whose second birthday had just passed.

Kate held Laurie's trembling body for several seconds. Laurie didn't say anything and Kate didn't ask any questions. They could do little but wait for the doctor.

After an hour, the surgeon emerged from the operating room, his light green cap and shirt soaked through with sweat. The women stared, waiting for him to speak. He shook his head. Laurie screamed and sobbed, thrusting her face into Kate's shoulder.

"I'm very sorry, Mrs. Cohen," the doctor said. "We did everything we could."

Laurie couldn't speak and only continued to sob while Kate held her.

"I won't leave you, Laurie." Laurie had no immediate family, aside from Stella, who was in her seventies and lacked the energy to look after a rambunctious two-year old. "I'll stay as long as you need me."

Kate and Stuart moved into the Cohen's Malibu home to help Laurie, and Stuart worked from his firm's LA office while he sorted out Jonathan's estate. After a week he flew back to Chicago, but Kate stayed to help Laurie regain her strength, so that at a bare minimum she would be well enough to comfort her baby boy.

Laurie could barely get out of bed, let alone care for her son, so Kate fed Nathan, bathed him, and played with him. Soon she dreaded returning to Chicago because she had grown so close to the little guy, but she also missed Stuart, and her business could not run without her indefinitely.

Almost a month after Jonathan's death, Laurie and Kate stood in the foyer of the Cohen mansion. Kate looked out at the vast blue ocean one last time and gave Laurie a hug goodbye.

"I can't thank you enough, Kate. I don't know how I would've survived without you and Stuart."

"Please don't even give it a second thought. You've suffered a terrible loss. Now focus on that adorable baby boy of yours." Tears welled in her eyes at the thought of leaving them.

"Don't you start crying, too. I've cried enough for both of us this past month. Nate and I promise to come out to Chicago and visit soon. I still can't believe I haven't seen your cooking school."

"I'll hold you to that promise. Maybe we could plan on a traditional Christmas together. If it snows, Chicago's beautiful that time of year."

* * *

Kate was just throwing a load of laundry in before she headed to work when she heard her cell ring. "Hi Laurie," she said. "You're calling early. How's sunny California?"

"I had to call. I think I know why I've been so sick lately."

"Of course, you're still grieving."

"That, and I'm two months pregnant."

"Oh my God, Laurie. That's wonderful news."

Laurie's voice broke. "I know it is, but I'm just so sad that Jonathan isn't here with me. He wanted a big family."

"Try not to think about it that way, although I know it's difficult not to. Think of it as a blessing from God, and as a very special gift."

"I'll try, but I've been so sick lately it's been hard to think about anything. I can barely get out of bed."

"I'm so sorry. How's little Nate?"

"We're managing okay. Rachel, our cook, is coming in early to drive him to playschool. I'm sure I'll be better in a week when she leaves for her holiday."

"You said you were two months pregnant. Right?"

"Right, eight weeks, according to my doctor."

"Didn't you tell me that last time you were sick all through the first semester?"

"For a solid twelve weeks."

"That's what I thought," Kate said. "Now hear me out. I've hired a great assistant who managed to keep Kate's Kitchen going while I was gone last month. I'll ask her to do the same while I come out to help you with Nate."

"Thank you, Kate, but we'll be fine."

"I'm not taking no for an answer. Stuart knows how close we've become. He'd insist that I help you." She waited for a response but heard only sobs. Her grip tightened on the phone. "Laurie, what's wrong? Did something happen?"

"No, I'm just overly emotional and touched by your kindness and generosity. No one except Jonathan has ever done so much for me."

"I'm happy to help. And besides, it will give Stuart a good reason to come out to visit. We both love it out there."

* * *

257

During Kate's time in Malibu, Laurie was too sick to surf, but she and Kate took long walks on the beach every morning and then again with Nate, to let him play. One afternoon they buried Laurie under buckets of sand. Still not even three months pregnant, she wasn't showing yet, but Nate convulsed with laughter as they built a bump as big as a mountain on her stomach. Kate also ran with him into the water, so cold that they mostly ran from the waves, only wetting their feet.

Rachel, Laurie's cook, went on vacation as planned, so Kate took over most of the cooking, with Laurie and Nate in the kitchen watching.

"I gotta tell you, Kate," Laurie said while sitting on one of the bar stools in her kitchen. "With all the dishes I've learned to cook from you, I could write a cookbook too."

"You should. You've been so diligent about writing everything down. It would be fun to pass these recipes we've created together down to Nate and the new little Cohen when they're older."

"Maybe I'll call it Laurie's Little Helpers." She tickled Nate and grinned at Kate.

On Kate's last night in Malibu they made a variation on Nate's favorite meal: pasta. Kate spiced it up with roasted tomatoes, fresh basil and buffalo mozzarella bocconcini balls, which melted on contact with the warm spaghetti. Laurie wasn't drinking, so they toasted with their water glasses to Kate's last night.

"I can't believe I've been here a month." Kate pulled Nate onto her lap. "Can I take him home with me?" She had gotten so attached to him that she couldn't imagine not seeing him every day.

"Maybe after I have the baby." Laurie looked down at Nate. "What do you think?"

"For real?" Nate asked. "Can I, Mommy?"

* * *

In Chicago, the autumn leaves had turned brilliant colors of orange, yellow and red. Stuart and Kate woke late Sunday morning, and had a huge breakfast of home fried potatoes, Canadian bacon and eggs. Kate put on a thick, cream-colored fisherman's wool sweater and worn, brown walking boots and handed Stuart his navy-blue wool coat.

"It's such a gorgeous morning. Want to take a walk with me?"

"Love to," Stuart said.

They walked arm in arm through the forest preserve behind their house and kicked through piles of dry brown leaves, crunching with each step. The earthy, dusty-smelling air felt crisp and cool, the sky a cloudless blue.

"I love this time of year," Stuart said. "It brings me back to some great times we had together."

Kate wrapped her arm around Stuart's waist. "I wish I could remember those days."

Stuart kissed her on the head. The cool air had turned her cheeks pink and her hair smelled like the fresh, crisp air. "You will, sweetheart. It will gradually come back to you."

"I'm not so sure about that," Kate said. "The doctors said I may never remember what happened before the accident."

"Well let me help you try to remember some of the fun times." Stuart stopped and pulled Kate over to a large maple tree that had a pile of raked leaves next to it. "When we were in high school one of the things you had to do was rake the entire front yard. Of course, being the gentleman I was and am, I offered to help. The two of us could rake all the leaves in about three hours. We gathered the leaves into about twenty piles each, probably five feet high. At the end of the day, we were both exhausted, but not too exhausted to have a little fun."

Kate looked up at him and smiled coquettishly. "What kind of fun?"

A leaf fell from the oak tree above onto Kate's head. Stuart brushed it off her face. "We buried ourselves into a pile of leaves and made love for an hour. It made those previous three hours of breaking our back worth it."

"I wish I could remember, but since I can't . . ." Kate pulled Stuart down into the pile of leaves, crawled on top of him and kissed him.

"Hey, Kate, I'm all for some R-rated fun, but this is a public forest. We wouldn't want to get caught by a family out on a Sunday walk."

"Okay, let's find somewhere more private." She pulled him up from the leaves and led him to a more secluded part of the woods behind an old oak tree. She gathered a pile of leaves with her hands, kicked more onto the pile and then pulled Stuart down to her.

After, Kate and Stuart lay together—her head snug between his shoulder and neck. The sky had turned a deep purple. The sun had dipped behind the hill and the air had become much colder, but Stuart's strong arm wrapped around her body kept her warm.

"I want to have a baby, Stuart. We're in our forties. We can't wait forever. If I don't get pregnant this month, I want to adopt."

Stuart took a deep breath. "Okay—let's see if this afternoon results in what we both want, but if not, I'll speak to some of my partners to see if they know of a legitimate agency."

Kate knew what Stuart was thinking. "You're right. We shouldn't even consider Claire's agency. What I saw there gives me the creeps."

Forty-Seven

The first snow of the season had fallen as Kate drove down to Oakdale to visit her Aunt Mary. As much as she had prayed she was pregnant, her period had arrived on time the previous day. With a layer of snow over the brown grass and treeless leaves, the farmhouse looked cold and desolate as she drove up. But a plume of smoke floated from the chimney and she could smell logs burning. Now, despite her mood, as gray as the November skies, the thought of seeing her aunt made the day more promising. A car she didn't recognize was parked in the driveway.

When Kate walked into the house, the smell of baking cookies enveloped her. She had learned that although visual memories may never return, memories of smell cling strongest. She'd never forget the comforting aroma of freshly baked cookies.

She found Claire and her aunt in the sitting room, a porcelain tea service on a wooden tray beside them.

"Kate, my dear." Mary stood up. "I worried about you with all this snow. Here, let me take your coat."

Kate hugged both women and sank into a chair. She helped herself to a warm chocolate chip cookie. "This is a nice surprise, Claire. I wasn't expecting to see you."

"I've been so busy at work lately that Mary and I haven't had a chance to visit in months."

"I'll let you two catch up while I start dinner," Mary said. "We're having roast beef and my special mashed potatoes, your favorite, Kate."

Kate didn't remember this being her favorite dish, but it was a cold night and comfort food would do her good. When Mary was out of earshot she whispered to Claire. "I can't believe that Dr. Franke's still in business. What I saw at the Life Institute really scared me."

"It scared me too, but when I started asking questions Dr. Franke explicitly told me that I'd better worry about the book keeping and office management and leave the rest to him. I'm so close to retiring. After working there thirty years, I don't want to lose my pension."

"I agree. It's better to not ask any more questions. But the minute your time's up, run away from there as fast as possible."

Claire sipped her tea, leaving a red lipstick mark on the cup. "But, Katie, how can I just sit there and not want to know more? If what you saw is even halfway true," she shuddered, "I can't even imagine . . ."

"Neither can I, but you shouldn't get involved any further."

"You're right. I've worked so hard—" She stopped as Mary returned to the sitting room wearing her apron.

"Dinner's ready ladies."

* * *

Despite her conversation with Kate the night before, Claire spent the next day on the computer investigating and discovered some astonishing news: the baby girl that Kate thought was hers, Fred and Nancy Hunt's daughter, could not be the biological daughter of Kate and Stuart.

Her date-of-birth put her birth at only thirty-six weeks. All of Dr. Franke's babies were born at full term, forty weeks. Kate must have calculated her due date based on nine months, a calculation most people place at thirty-six weeks.

Her inquisitiveness piqued, she began a more thorough investigation. Based on what Kate had told her, Kate's due date would have been around the middle of April, and only one baby had been brought to the clinic at that time.

She printed the information and immediately called Kate's house, leaving a message asking her to call as soon as possible. Hours later, when she still had not heard from Kate, she called Mary.

"She flew to Los Angeles this morning," Mary said. "Laurie was hemorrhaging and had to be rushed to the hospital."

"Oh that poor girl." Claire asked for Stuart's number and was dialing his office when Dr. Franke stormed into the room. She replaced the receiver and jumped up.

Dr. Franke came close and grabbed Claire's arm. "Why are you searching my records from twenty-five years ago?"

"I wasn't," Claire lied.

Dr. Franke pushed Claire back onto her chair. "You stupid woman! My computer in Chicago is linked to the ones here at the agency. You've been messing around with those records for weeks."

"I'm sorry, I was just trying to clean up some old files."

"As of this minute," Dr. Franke said, "you are officially retired. I'll pay out your pension, but you are no longer welcome in this office. And if you ever, and I mean *ever*, disclose what you've learned, you won't see a penny of your pension."

Forty-Eight

In California, Kate waited in the emergency room for news of Laurie's condition. The doctor had mandated an emergency cesarean to deliver the baby.

When he emerged, he looked exhausted. "Laurie knows you're here," he said. "She'd like to speak with you." He put his hand on Kate's shoulder, his voice low and grave. "She may not make it. She lost a lot of blood and her internal organs were severely traumatized."

"Oh my God. What about the baby?"

"The baby is alive, but his breathing is compromised. He's in an incubator and we're doing everything to keep them both alive."

The doctor handed Kate a mask and she rushed into the post operating room, where Laurie breathed through a ventilator and was hooked to a myriad of tubes, conscious, but weak. Kate gripped Laurie's hand.

Laurie squeezed back. "Please take care of my children," she whispered.

"I promise," Kate said, "but you're strong. You'll make it." She squeezed her hand harder. "Fight for your life. For Nate's. And for your beautiful, newborn baby boy."

Laurie managed a smile. "I will."

Kate drove to Nate's pre-school to pick him up. She arrived a few minutes late and her heart sank when she saw the little guy sitting on the steps all alone.

She rushed over to him and enveloped him in a hug.

"Where's my mommy?" he asked.

"Honey, your mom's in the hospital but she'll be fine."

"God's not going to take her, is he? Like he took my daddy?"

Kate took his hand. "The doctors are working very hard to make her better. But you know what? You have a new baby brother. Your mom named him Jonathan after your daddy. You can call him JJ for short."

A bright smile lit up Nate's face and he clapped his hands together. "Let's go see him!"

Kate returned to the hospital with Nate, and as they entered the waiting room, he called out to an elderly woman. "Grandma!" he said.

Without Nate, Kate would not have recognized Stella. They had met only once in Aspen, and now, with shoulder length gray hair and sallow skin, she looked years older than she had the previous Christmas.

"Come here my big guy." Stella took Nate onto her lap. "You're mom is getting healthier by the minute." She turned to Kate and whispered. "She's going to make it."

Kate broke into tears and wrapped her arms around them both.

* * *

Laurie had been home less than a week when Claire called, asking if she could drop by to see JJ.

"What a lovely surprise," Laurie said, welcoming her inside. "I'm so pleased to see you."

"I'm visiting friends in L.A.," Claire said, "and I just had to come. I'll never forget the day I met you. You were one week old. Your mom was the happiest woman on the planet the day we placed you in her arms."

Stella entered the foyer holding a dishtowel. "And I still am." She dried her hands and took Claire's jacket. "But if you can imagine, even happier now that I have two adorable grandsons."

Claire, Stella, Kate and Laurie took shelter under an umbrella on the terrace. The ocean lay calm and sparkling under the bright sun, and in contrast both Laurie and Stella looked like anemic versions of themselves. Laurie had lost thirty pounds since the birth of JJ and had not regained her strength. And to make matters worse Stella, Laurie had confided to Kate, had recently been diagnosed with Alzheimer's disease.

After lunch, Kate urged her to lie down. "I'll take care of the dishes."

"I think I'll take a little nap, as well," Stella said. "Thank you, dear."

Left alone on the terrace with Kate, Claire leaned toward her. "I have a small confession. I'm not here visiting friends. Dr. Franke caught me searching his personal computer files late one night, and I've been fired."

Kate put her hand over her mouth.

"But don't worry. I'll keep my pension as long as you don't go to the authorities." Claire extracted an envelope from her handbag and gave it to Kate.

"You need to read this in private. The contents will change your life."

"What do you mean?"

"You'll understand after you read it." She leaned over and kissed Kate on the cheek. "I'll leave you alone now."

Kate saw Claire out, and too curious to wait, she left the cleaning up and walked to the ocean to read what Claire had given her. She sat on the sand and let the waves gently break at her feet. Then she opened the envelope and read.

Forty-Nine

Kate read and re-read the words on the birth certificate several times, unable to believe that Laurie Weston Cohen was her daughter. Immobilized by the contents of the envelope that Claire had given her, the lapping waves lulled her into a hypnotic state.

Her whole life had just been turned upside down. She felt paralyzed with fear and confusion. She had already grown to love her friend Laurie like a daughter, but telling her that she had planned to abort her all those years ago could destroy their relationship forever. For a split second she thought she might dilute the truth and say that she had put her up for adoption, but what child wanted to hear that from her birthmother?

The clouds rolled in, and still Kate sat, until the clouds obscured the glow of the setting sun and turned the blue sky gray. Kate shivered, but the prickling of her skin brought some feeling back to her limbs. With stiff cold muscles she lifted herself from the sand and walked to the house. The warm lights illuminating the windows provided a false sense of welcome. If Laurie knew the truth, she'd throw her out in a second.

"Hey," Laurie greeted Kate with a huge smile. "We were beginning to worry about you."

Kate nodded and did her best to appear normal, but she lacked her usual cheerfulness.

"Is everything okay?" Laurie's smile faded. "Did Claire give you some bad news?" And then with a concerned voice she asked: "Did something happen to Mary?"

"Mary's fine," Kate said. "I'm afraid I fell asleep on the beach."

"You're shivering." Laurie picked up her fleece running jacket from the kitchen chair and handed it to Kate. "Put this on. I'll make some tea."

Kate put on the fleece and rubbed her arms. "I think I'll pass on the tea and go straight to bed."

"Are you sure? I was going to attempt some homemade pizza. We have that beautiful wood burning oven that I never use."

"No thank you, sweetheart. I think I just need to sleep." She bit her tongue after calling Laurie "sweetheart," not something two friends would call each other, but she let her slip pass, hoping Laurie didn't notice. "I'd like to give Nate and Jonathan a kiss good night though."

"Of course."

Kate followed Laurie back to the playroom adjacent to the kitchen. Little Jonathan was on his back, lying on a blanket under a fabric bar from which hung mirrors and toys. Nate crashed two plastic trucks into each other. Tears came to her eyes as she realized she was watching her two grandsons play. She wiped her eyes with her sleeve. "I think allergy season has gotten the best of me." She leaned down to kiss Nate, and squeezed him extra hard, and then whispered, "I love you" in his ear. Nate looked up at Kate and said, "I wuv you too, Aunt Katie." She then got down on her knees and scooped Jonathan into her arms. She cradled him until her eyes began to water again.

"I might have some Claritin in the medicine cabinet," Laurie offered. "Can I get you some?"

Kate lay Jonathan back down on his blanket. "I'll be fine. I just need a good night's sleep."

But thoughts of aborting Laurie prevented her from sleeping. All through the night she considered her options. Finally, knowing she could not hide her emotions, she packed her suitcases. As the morning sun brightened her room, she wrote Laurie a note. She would call when she got back to Illinois.

Fifty

"*P*lease Stuart," Kate begged. "Say something. We have to deal with this. *Together.* Don't shut me out."

Stuart shook his head. He could not speak; even if he had tried no words would explain his emotions.

"I know this is a huge shock for you," Kate said. "I still can't believe it. But we need to decide how we'll tell Laurie."

After several minutes Stuart spoke, his voice slow and steady: "We are not going to tell Laurie."

"But we can't lie to her. She's our daughter."

"Listen, Kate, she's been through enough. She nearly lost her life delivering JJ, and she's still grieving Jonathan's death. Her mother is ill. Why shock her with something that we can barely understand ourselves?"

Kate covered her face with her hands and sobbed into them.

"Kate, listen. She's just getting her feet on the ground. And remember: she and Jonathan respected us enough to ask us to be her son's godparents. They'll be in our lives forever."

"But how can we keep this terrible lie from her?"

"We have to," Stuart said, "for *her* sake, not ours."

"I'm not sure I can do this."

Stuart wrapped his arms around her. "You can, and you will."

Kate looked up at him through teary eyes. "You've been through so much with me Stuart. Are you sure you're happy you found me again?"

"Kate you know how much I love you." He took her by the hand. "Now let me show you."

* * *

Forty weeks later, at the age of forty-three, Kate gave birth to a healthy seven-pound baby girl, named Ashleigh, after the mother Kate barely knew.

Kate and Stuart arranged to save Ashleigh's umbilical cord and store it indefinitely, a practice offered to all pregnant women. Should Ashleigh someday need her own stem cells to fight off a terrible disease, they would be available.

Six weeks later, Kate sat at her kitchen table, her hands wrapped around a large coffee mug.

Stuart entered the kitchen looking as handsome as ever in a dark blue suit and yellow tie. He leaned down and kissed Kate on the cheek. "Running late, sweetheart. Due in court in a half-hour."

"Just quickly, honey. I thought we could go to California for the weekend. The weather is terrible here and I could use a change of pace."

"Can Ashleigh travel this young?"

"Of course! And I really want Laurie to meet Ashleigh when she's still a baby."

"Okay, you're the boss. When are we leaving?"

"Tomorrow morning. Ten o'clock. I already bought the tickets."

* * *

When Laurie greeted Stuart and Kate at the door of her Malibu mansion, she looked thin and pale. Stella also looked frail and remained sitting in a soft chair in the living room as they entered.

"My mom's not doing well," Laurie said. "She's really gone downhill these past three months. Most of the time she can't even remember the boys' names."

"I'm so sorry, Laurie," Kate said. "I had no idea it had gotten this bad."

"She still has some good days. She loves living here with me, but I've had to hire a nurse to look after her."

Stella's face lit up when she saw Kate and Stuart enter the room with Ashleigh.

Laurie's expression brightened as well. "Looks like she remembers you."

Stella extended her arms and asked to hold the baby. "May I?"

Kate gave Ashleigh to Stella and Stella rocked the baby in her arms. "Oh, Laurie, my baby, you're so beautiful."

Laurie touched her mother's shoulder. "This is Kate and Stuart's baby, Mom. Her name is Ashleigh."

"Noooooo," Stella began to cry. "This is my baby, *my* baby."

Stuart and Kate both tensed up, realizing that Ashleigh must look identical to Laurie when she was born. The nurse entered the room and gently asked Stella to hand Ashleigh back to her parents.

"Nooooo," she screamed. "This is my baby! I had to wait so long . . ."

Laurie intervened: "Mom—let me take the baby. You need to get some rest."

Stella jumped up from her chair and stumbled, nearly dropping Ashleigh. But Stuart was there to catch her while Kate helped steady Stella.

"I'm really sorry for this," Laurie said. "We can't blame her. This horrible disease has ruined her mind."

"Please, Laurie," Kate said. "There's no need to apologize. You're right, it's not her fault. It's mine. Let me explain."

"Kate," Stuart interrupted, "Ashleigh looks like she's due for another feed. Let's take her out to the terrace for a few minutes. I'll sit with you."

Kate glanced at Laurie and then at Stuart. She had fed Ashleigh in the car on the ride up, and she would not be hungry. But Stuart looked at her with desperation. She didn't want to betray Stuart, the love of her life, the father of her child—her *children* for God's sake—but she couldn't live this lie.

"We have all weekend to chat," Laurie said. "Go ahead and feed Ashleigh."

Kate took Ashleigh from Stuart. "We'll be right back."

Stuart shut the door behind them. The ocean looked as smooth as a pond. A woman with a long blonde ponytail jogged along the beach in front of them. A few kids threw a Frisbee while their Golden Retriever jumped to intercept it. How could the world appear so normal?

"What were you thinking?" Stuart asked.

"It's killing me seeing how this has affected Stella." Kate wrapped Ashleigh in her blanket. "That poor woman. It's not fair for us to betray her too."

"Let's sit down." They sat on a bench facing the ocean. "You're feeling incredibly guilty, and let's face it so am I. But we can't think of ourselves right now. What good would it do to throw another curve ball at Laurie? Would it help her ailing mother? No. Would it change your relationship with her? Yes, and for the worse. You two have a wonderful bond and friendship. Something any mother/daughter would love to have. Why don't you just keep it that way?"

Kate looked down at her beautiful daughter who had now fallen asleep in her arms. She was so lucky to be given this second chance at motherhood.

"Because it makes me so sad to know that I wasn't there for Laurie when she was this age."

"We can't change what happened, Kate. We need to count our blessings and move on with our life, for the sake of everything. Trust me, Laurie can't handle any more trauma right now."

"You're right, Stuart. We can't change the past. We all deserve this chance at happiness. And we're going to be wonderful parents."

Stuart breathed a great sigh of relief.

Kate rested her head on his shoulder and then turned her face to his and smiled. "Did anyone ever tell you that you'd make a great lawyer?"

They returned inside to find Laurie wiping tears from her face.

Kate handed Ashleigh to Stuart and went to Laurie. "What's wrong?"

"I'm so worried about my mom. She's really deteriorated."

"Can the doctors do anything?"

Laurie shook her head. "No, not at this point."

Kate tried to comfort her. "Alzheimer's is a cruel disease. It destroys families and robs people of their precious memories. The only bright side is that the patient is much better off than their loved ones are. The one afflicted with the disease is left in a cocoon. Apparently they don't realize what an awful state they're in."

Laurie nodded her head. "I've heard that too, but it's still horrible to see."

"Of course it is. And dangerous, too; she might leave the oven on, or light candles and forget to blow them out, but I know you're vigilant and with the help of her nurse, she'll be fine."

"Yes, I'm lucky to have a lot of help, but it's still hard." Laurie wiped her eyes and changed the subject. "So how long can you stay?"

"I'm afraid only a couple of days. I was lucky to pull Stuart away for a long weekend."

Laurie managed a smile. "How about we make some lunch and head down to the beach? It's such a beautiful day. We should enjoy it while you can!"

Fifty-One

After three nights in Malibu, the Carsons flew back to Chicago. Kate unpacked her suitcase while Ashleigh slept in her crib. Stuart entered their bedroom and put his hands on Kate's shoulder. He leaned over and kissed her neck. "I know this wasn't easy for you, Kate, but we did the right thing."

Kate turned around and snuggled into his chest. "I've heard that people who continue to lie eventually begin to believe their own story."

Stuart kissed the top of her head. "Maybe, but the difference with us is that we never fabricated anything. We just haven't told her the macabre details of her birth. Really, Kate, who would want to hear something like that?"

Their tender moment ended with the ringing of the telephone. Kate flinched.

"Let it ring." Stuart whispered in her ear. He pulled her down onto their bed and kissed between her breasts as he undid the top button of her blouse. By the time he reached her waist, he had left a trail of kisses and had pushed her open blouse aside.

"I love you," Kate said. "You're my best friend, my rock, and the love of my life. Some women never experience true love at all. For me to have found it twice is a miracle."

* * *

When Kate awoke in the morning, she listened to her messages. Two missed calls from Laurie, the second telling them that Stella had died, passing peacefully in her sleep.

She sat on the edge of the bed and called Laurie. "I just picked up your message. How are you doing?"

Laurie sounded as if she'd been up all night. "I knew this would happen eventually, but it's still hard to accept." Her voice cracked and she paused. "I guess I should count my blessings. At least she died in her sleep and her health didn't degenerate any further."

"Would you like me to come out and help with your children? It won't upset Ashleigh's schedule. She's such an angel, and so easy to care for."

"That's what my mom used to say about me, that I was such an easy baby. I'll be fine. But thank you. Rachel, our cook, and mom's nurse are helping me make the arrangements. We'll probably have the service next week."

"I'll be there for sure. How are the boys doing?"

"JJ's too young to understand, but Nate's really upset."

"After the service, what if I bring Nate back to Chicago with me? He's been begging to come visit, and I'd love to spend some time with him."

"That would be good for him. Thank you, Kate."

* * *

Their two weeks with Nate flew by. Kate took him to one amusement park after another, indoor ice rinks, and every kid's favorite—but every parent's nightmare— Chucky Cheese. This one was as loud as all the others, with bad food, and as always, situated in a strip mall in a dodgy part of town. Exhausted, Kate even hooked Nate up with some little boys in the neighborhood for afternoon play dates, so she could catch up on her work.

Before bedtime, on Nate's last night in Chicago, he looked up at Kate with his big brown eyes and said, "Do I really have to leave tomorrow, Aunt Katie?"

Kate closed the book from which she had been reading aloud. "Your mom really misses you, sweetheart. You've been here nearly two weeks."

The ringing of the telephone interrupted them, and Kate answered it. She listened and then felt the blood drain from her face. "How is that possible?"

Fifty-Two

Kate arrived at Cedar Sinai Hospital in Los Angeles by nine p.m. A nurse showed her to a room down the hall. When Kate opened the door to see Laurie lying in bed asleep, she held back a scream when she saw that half of Laurie's face had dropped.

Kate spoke to the nurse through her tears. "How can such a young, healthy woman have a stroke?"

"I'm very sorry, but I can't answer that. You'll need to speak with Dr. Becker." She squeezed Kate's arm in a comforting gesture and left the room.

Kate sat next to Laurie's bed and held her hand. Her beautiful, sweet daughter. Aloud, she said, "I promise you, Laurie, I will do everything I can to make you well again. And I know you're a fighter. You'll get through this."

So focused on Laurie, she jumped when someone tapped her on the shoulder.

"Mrs. Carson," the doctor whispered. "Hello, I'm Dr. Becker."

"What happened?"

"We're not sure. Mrs. Cohen's house cleaner found her collapsed in the bathroom."

"How bad is it?"

"She has suffered brain damage and has minor paralysis on her left side."

"But I thought that nowadays stroke victims are given TPA. It's supposed to prevent paralysis and brain damage."

"That only works if the patient gets to the hospital within two hours of having a stroke."

"So this is permanent?"

"I'm afraid it is." The doctor spoke in a grave voice. "Of course, she'll have rehabilitation, but there'll be permanent damage. She'll have to relearn even the most basic tasks, such as how to brush her teeth, how to spell and read and write."

"Can she walk?"

"That will take time, but she will walk again."

"How could this have happened?"

"This is something we'll never know. Most likely she's had a blood clot for years, and it finally burst."

"Could it have been prevented?"

The doctor shook his head. "No."

"I'm sure I've heard about some clinical trials that refer to this exact problem. I remember hearing Stuart talking on the phone about this. At least he was talking about some company that had something to do with stem cells."

"As far as I know there's only one company, based in Southern California that is experimenting with this type of technology. The company is called Stemedics, but I believe they're only in early stage clinical trials."

"Is it possible we could get Laurie involved in the trials?"

"I can't answer that, but I'll look into it for you."

While Laurie slept, Kate logged onto a computer and researched everything she could find on stem cell research and the company Stemedics. She wanted to be prepared when she spoke again to Dr. Becker and to Stuart.

She printed what she had discovered and searched for Dr. Becker. For Laurie to participate in human trials, they only needed to find someone with an exact blood and tissue match.

The doctor, when she found him, looked dubious. "It's not as easy as you think to find a match, Mrs. Carson, but we'll try."

"What about myself or Stuart?"

"We'll test you both, but usually parents are not an exact match."

He was right. Both Stuart and Kate came up negative. A five-day extensive worldwide computer search also failed to find a match. Kate refused to give up. She left the hospital and drove straight to Stuart's office.

Stuart was on the phone when she arrived. He took one look at her and said, "Sorry, Rick, I have to call you back."

Nearly hyperventilating, Kate managed to speak: "We couldn't find a match, but, Stuart, both you and I know Laurie has an exact match."

"Ashleigh."

"Yes Ashleigh. It's possible that the stem cells from her umbilical cord will help reverse the damage. But how can we use Ashleigh's stem cells and not tell Laurie?"

Stuart reached for the phone. "We'll figure that out later. We need to get this process started and we need to do it now."

"Put the phone down for a minute, Stuart," Kate said. "What if they don't let us participate in the trial? Remember it's only Phase 1 now. They haven't experimented on a human yet. We need to have a back-up plan."

Stuart picked up the phone. "There is no back-up plan."

When someone answered on the other end of the line, Stuart shot a look of relief at Kate. "Bryan. Stuart here. I need a favor."

Kate strained to understand the conversation and wished he had put the receiver on speakerphone. Stuart had a long list of influential acquaintances. If anyone could get to the right person he would. She assumed that he had called Bryan Fleming, Stuart's law partner and the head of the securities practice. Stuart's law firm had several biotech clients; Bryan had taken one public on the stock exchange last year that had made them all a fortune.

Stuart continued speaking: "Who do you know at Stemedics?"

She saw him write down a name. "Thanks, Bryan," Stuart said. "I'll explain everything later."

Stuart hung up the phone and began dialing again. "Bryan knows the CEO of Stemedics. He did the legal work for the biotech fund that financed the company."

He watched Kate as he listened and then left a message. When he hung up, he reached across the desk and took her hand, "Don't worry, honey, he'll call me back."

* * *

Dr. Becker's office was void of color and had few personal items. It seemed like a bleak place to work, but Kate thought that it must be difficult in general to work in a hospital. They may be safe havens for some, but she had experienced only grief and misery since Laurie's admittance. She once got excited when she saw the bed next to Laurie's made up fresh, thinking that Laurie's roommate had gone home, but the poor woman had died.

Now Kate sat on an uncomfortable chair on the other side of Dr. Becker's desk and opened the conversation. "Laurie doesn't know that she's my daughter."

"What do you mean, she doesn't know?"

"I gave her up for adoption when she was born and have regretted it ever since."

"I see."

"I saved Ashleigh's umbilical cord, which should be an exact match for a blood transfusion."

"Ashleigh?" Dr. Becker asked.

"Our other daughter. She's still a baby."

"That's good news. It could possibly be just what we're looking for, but Stemedics is years away from helping humans."

"I'm not so sure. My husband's talking with the CEO today to see what can be done."

"I need to tell you, Mrs. Carson, Laurie's condition has gotten worse. She's no longer conscious. The stroke was more extensive than we initially thought—"

Before he finished, Kate jumped up from the chair and ran down the hallway to Laurie's room. She put her hand over her mouth when she saw her daughter hooked up to a breathing tube, her eyes closed. The right side of her face, which had been drooping since the stroke, was now fully collapsed. Kate fell to her knees beside Laurie's bed, sobbing. Laurie was a fighter. She had recovered from Jonathan's death, had nearly died after giving birth to Jonathan Jr., and had survived her mother's death. But this would be the biggest battle of her life.

Kate continued kneeling at Laurie's bedside, willing every cell in her body to give her daughter strength, until her cell phone rang. Stuart. Her eyes so filled with tears that she could hardly see the numbers on her phone.

"Honey, we have some good news," Stuart said, when she picked up. "Dr. Shesnovich, from Moscow, the doctor who pioneered this stem cell technology, has agreed to see Laurie. Human trials are scheduled to start at the end of the month, and Laurie will be his first patient."

"That's wonderful." Kate collapsed onto one of the chairs in the hallway. "What are the risks?"

"There are many. The first is that the stem cells won't take and then she'll need brain surgery, and we've already discussed the risks with that."

"We have no choice. She's too young and vital to be left a vegetable for the rest of her life."

Fifty-Three

With both Stuart and Kate in agreement, Laurie was airlifted to the University of California at San Diego hospital, where Dr. Shesnovich stood by ready to perform the procedure. With stem cells already harvested from Ashleigh's umbilical cord, he injected them directly into Laurie's brain, using Mannitol as the delivery mechanism to help the stem cells break the blood-brain barrier. The entire procedure took less than an hour.

For two weeks, Kate and Stuart alternated at Laurie's bedside, hoping for a sign of recovery that never came. Then Dr. Shesnovich called them both into his office. He removed his black-framed glasses and smoothed wiry gray eyebrows.

"I am sorry to report, Mr. and Mrs. Carson," he said in his heavy Russian accent, "but Laurie's condition has worsened. Her brain activity has slowed to the point that she is barely keeping herself alive. Brain surgery is the only option."

"We are prepared to go ahead with that. Will you perform the surgery?" Stuart asked.

"No. Dr. Keith O'Neill is the best neurosurgeon on the West Coast. He's on standby to fly down from San Francisco and will operate this evening."

* * *

Kate and Stuart watched on a video monitor as Laurie's head was placed in a metal horseshoe and shaved on the right side. Nurses isolated her scalp with surgical drapes and prepared it with antiseptic.

With the surface area ready, Dr. O'Neill cut through the scalp and pulled back a flap of skin. He cauterized the exposed area and attached several scalp clips to prevent further bleeding. With the bone exposed, he drilled into the skull in four places.

Although the monitor had no sound, and Dr. O'Neill had briefed them on what to expect, Kate clenched Stuart's hand as the doctor cut from one hole to the next and lifted the bone away from the dura, the toughest of three meningeal layers.

Given the severity of Laurie's stroke, Dr. O'Neill had explained, he would have to find and remove the dead brain matter. Stuart and Kate watched as he used a fine tipped ultrasonic aspirating device to remove the pale, swollen tissue. He irrigated the surgical bed, and they saw Laurie's brain pulsate gently, which meant that it was adequately decompressed and ready for the next and most important step, when Dr. O'Neill placed the stem cell solution directly into the stroke lesion within the brain cavity.

He did this, and the brain remained relaxed and continued to pulsate with no evidence of an adverse reaction. He glanced up at the camera and nodded, then sutured the membrane back in its original position, applied a sealant to keep the area watertight, and covered the area with a tissue patch. He replaced the bit of skull he had removed earlier and clamped it into place with titanium rivets.

After nearly two hours of delicate work, he left the operating room looking as calm as when he had entered it. Everything had gone exactly as he had said it would.

Fifty-Four

Kate collapsed onto her bed in Laurie's guest room. In the seven days since Laurie's brain surgery, she hadn't left the hospital until now.

Stuart took her shoes off and poured her a glass of water. "Why don't you take these clothes off? You'll be more comfortable."

Kate didn't respond. She was already asleep.

Nearly twenty-four hours later, she awoke to a dark room and held her wrist close to her eyes. Seven o'clock, but whether a.m. or p.m., she had no clue. She eased herself out of bed and shuffled into the bathroom. Even turning the taps on in the shower felt like a major effort and taking off her clothes proved even more of a struggle.

Stuart handed her a thick white towel as she emerged from the shower. "You must be starving."

"I am. Anything you find would be better than the vending machine food I've been eating at the hospital."

"Sit tight, I'll be right back."

Kate dropped her towel and put on a pair of clean jeans, so loose at the waist she must have lost at least ten pounds. She found a belt and cinched it to the last hole.

Stuart arrived with a cup of tea and some toast on a tray. The fresh butter on the toast tasted heavenly—something so simple but so delicious. She reached for another piece and slathered it with strawberry jam. "This is the perfect breakfast."

"It's actually dinner time but I guessed that since you haven't eaten in a while, breakfast would be a good start."

Kate took a sip of tea. "I think that I need to be with Laurie full-time. *We* need to be with Laurie. Her rehab will be tough and I want to be there for her."

"I was thinking the same thing. The office in LA would be happy to have me back there. Are you prepared to leave Chicago and move to California?"

Kate reached for his hand. "If I could, I'd move tomorrow."

"I'll speak to my partners today."

"And I'll talk to the girls at Kate's Kitchen. They've been running the place on their own for the past three months. I'd love to expand the business out west."

* * *

Kate cooked for the staff of nurses that lived around-the-clock at the Malibu mansion for six months during Laurie's arduous recovery, until she could tend to basic functions on her own. In addition to the daily physical rehab, the music therapy recommended by Dr. O'Neill had helped her the most. Instead of re-learning to read, write and speak the traditional way, the doctors had set up a program that allowed Laurie to sing songs and learn melodies.

The morning before Kate left, she found Laurie in the bathroom brushing her teeth.

Laurie saw Kate in the mirror and put down her toothbrush. "I never thought I would be so happy to brush my own teeth!"

"And to think that just a few months ago you didn't even know what a toothbrush was. But now look at you. And the way you ate your dinner tonight was nothing short of amazing."

Kate leaned against the vanity in the bathroom. "I'd like to discuss something with you. Why don't you finish getting ready and we can sit and talk. I'll be in my room packing my things."

Minutes later, when Laurie joined Kate, she had brushed her hair and had even applied some makeup, something she hadn't done in nearly a year. "I wish you didn't have to leave already," she said.

"I know, the time has flown by. But you've made such tremendous progress."

"I'm going to miss you, Kate."

Kate blinked back her tears. "I'll miss you too." Her voice cracked. "And the boys." She sat and motioned Laurie to do the same. "Stuart and I have been thinking . . . we'd like to move to California to be closer to all of you. Stuart enjoys working out of the Century City office and I could easily open a Kate's Kitchen here in Malibu or in Pacific Palisades. What do you think?"

"Are you kidding? I'd love it. And so would the boys."

Kate grinned at her. "Then it's all settled. I'll come out next month and start house hunting."

"I could help with that. I'm dying to get out of the house and do something productive."

"And you have fabulous taste!"

Kate walked over to her bed which was piled high with clothes and suitcases. From the outside pocket of her handbag she removed a file folder. "While I'm packing I'd like you to read something."

Fifty-Five

Any color that Laurie had accumulated on her face since her return from the hospital washed away in an instant as she read the contents of the file folder. Her lower lip trembled as she spoke: "What do you mean, 'Ashleigh is my sister?'" Laurie asked.

"And Stuart is your father," Kate said.

"What are you saying? And *who* is my mother?"

Kate felt as though she were trying to speak through a mouthful of sand. She willed the words to come out. "I am your mother, Laurie."

Laurie sank onto the bed, her expression one of shock and confusion. "*You* are my mother? How can that be?"

"I got pregnant when I was in high school."

Laurie stared at her mother, speechless. "With Stuart?"

"He never knew I was pregnant. I was young, and I believed that I had no choice but to give you up for adoption. Claire never knew it was I who put you up for adoption. Only when Stuart and I asked about adopting a baby of our own did she figure it out."

"How?"

"It's really too much to get into now, but I promise I will tell you later. Stuart wasn't certain I should tell you this much, given all the trauma you've experienced recently."

"So when we met in Hawaii you had no idea?"

"Not at all. I didn't even know who I was. All I knew is that I had just met a very handsome young man and a newly-married and very happy couple."

Laurie shook her head. "I don't know whether to scream or to cry."

"I've done both. Many times. It's a lot to take in. But Laurie, please believe me when I tell you that I've loved you like a friend, a sister and now a mother. This is why Stuart and I plan to move to California. You're our daughter. We want to look after you and be close to our grandsons."

Laurie nodded her head and then started to cry. Through muffled tears she spoke: "I wish Jonathan was here with me. He'd help me figure this out."

Kate stroked Laurie's hair. "I wish he were here too, honey."

Laurie pulled away. "Jonathan never knew about this?"

"No, he never did. In fact, Stuart didn't know for a very long time either. It killed me to tell him."

Laurie looked at Kate with red eyes. "That must have been really tough for you."

"You have no idea. All I can say is that what happened is in the past. But luckily Stella adopted you. She was a wonderful woman and mother. And then you met Jonathan, the love of your life. I'm sure that if I had raised you when I was only seventeen you would not have turned into the beautiful woman you are now. Things would have been tough for us—really tough. And you most certainly would not have met Jonathan and had those two adorable boys."

Laurie dabbed her eyes with a tissue and nodded her head.

Kate also reached for a tissue and wiped her eyes. "If you agree, let's mark today as the first day of the rest of our lives. You and those two little boys mean everything to me. And believe me, I'm going to make up for lost time."

Laurie's expression brightened. "You'll have your hands full with this group: an adult daughter with years of physical therapy ahead of her, and two rambunctious toddlers."

Kate smiled at her. "I wouldn't have it any other way."

Laurie reached out and embraced her. "Okay, Kate. Or should I say Mom? Let's try it, shall we?"

Kate hugged her back. "Nothing would make me happier."

The End

About the Author

$\mathcal{J}$ill $\mathcal{S}$t. $\mathcal{A}$nne is the pen name for Jill Zajicek Wickersham. She was an award-winning investigative journalist in college. After her undergraduate work, she received an MBA in International Business. Her most recent job in the corporate world was with Chase Manhattan (now JP Morgan Chase) where she worked in the Private Client Services department, helping the bank meet the financial needs of high-net worth individuals in Silicon Valley. She currently lives with her teenage daughter in South Kensington, London, San Francisco and British Columbia, Canada. Each country and city mean something special to Jill: London is where she enjoys entertaining a revolving door of friends and business associates from all over the world; San Francisco is where she works closely with her Silicon Valley associates developing and raising funds for two high tech companies she created; and in British Columbia she finally gets a chance to breathe, sleep, swim, kayak and WRITE.